Hustler's Dreams, Federal Nightmares

Hustler's Dreams, Federal Nightmares

Amir Sanchez

www.urbanbooks.net

Urban Books, LLC
97 N18th Street
Wyandanch, NY 11798

Hustler's Dreams, Federal Nightmares Copyright © 2013
Amir Sanchez

ISBN 13: 978-1-60162-575-5
ISBN 10: 1-60162-575-8

First Printing October 2013
Printed in the United States of America

10 9 8 7 6 5 4 3 2 1

Distributed by Kensington Publishing Corp.
Submit Wholesale Orders to:
Kensington Publishing Corp.
C/O Penguin Group (USA) Inc.
Attention: Order Processing
405 Murray Hill Parkway
East Rutherford, NJ 07073-2316
Phone: 1-800-526-0275
Fax: 1-800-227-9604

Hustler's Dreams, Federal Nightmares

by

Amir Sanchez

Prologue

Coming up on the cold streets of Kill Adelphia, murder mania, a nigga had to learn the ropes real quick in order to survive under those fierce conditions. Living in a city that held the crown for being the murder capital of the United States, bodies were dropping all over the place. Guns were as common as colds, and easily available for those seeking to purchase them illegally. Shootouts was a everyday occurrence, keeping the morgue and the ER busy, leaving the police staggering to keep up with their overload of investigations.

To make matters worse, the killers, drug dealers, and the goons were also the snakes, rats, and gorillas. They could easily have a nigga robbed, killed, or set up with those folks, FBI! Forced to maneuver around these shiesty niggas, one could easily become a victim or an inmate!

Fortunately for me, I came up under my old head, Shake. An original gangster by nature, he was certified and official in all aspects of the game, as well as with life in general. On the mean streets of Philly, he was indeed a treacherous dictator worthy of all the praise and respect the streets gave him, either willingly or by force. Over the years, his guidance and influence gave me the structure and mindset that I needed to be a winner and reach the top. The most valuable piece of advice that he ever gave me will go on to live with me forever.

He told me, "Never make friends with those who have the traits and characteristics of your enemies, and never make enemies with those who have the potential to be controllable associates. It's a thin line between death and dishonor, love and hate, and real and fake. Best to keep everyone in arm's reach, eye's view, and close range of your pistol."

Ever since being schooled with those wise words, I've incorporated it into my heart, mind, and everyday hustle. Where I'm from, a true boss is acknowledged and recognized by his leadership, courage, and commitment to get the job done regardless of the setbacks and obstacles that may appear. He brings ease to difficulty, and makes the impossible possible!

When this is done on a regular basis, and is constantly marked by success and accomplishments, one acquires status and attributes that are descriptive and representative of his conduct and performance.

Although my government name is Amin Hassan, the streets dubbed me Boss. By all means, niggas respect my name and my G to the fullest degree. It's who I am and what I do.

Step into the life of a true boss, and witness the extravagant lifestyles, luxurious living, and expensive taste that only a nigga who lived it could understand and explain.

Chapter 1

By summertime 2010, a nigga was well established and sitting on something nice. Shaking paper, fucking bitches, and stuntin' was an everyday occurrence, more so a way of living. The fruits of my labor kept me laced in the finest linen, jewelry, and vehicles money could buy. "Money over everything" was my motto and killing and robbing everything over money was a routine practiced all year long.

Stuntin' was a habit, a concept that I swore to participate in every day of my life. From the flyest designer clothes money could buy to the VVS diamonds that flooded my wrist and neck. Waking up one sunny Friday morning I couldn't help but to notice the intense itch I felt in the palms of my hands. That meant two things if you was a nigga coming up in the neighborhoods that I came up in: either you had some ashy-ass dry hands or money was sending you an invitation to come and get it. In my case it was money calling me. Not wanting to delay my calling, I got up out the bed, took a shower, and threw on a pair of True Religion cargos, with a purple-label Polo shirt. Nike Air Max sneakers, a fitted hat, and Gucci shades completed my dress.

Stepping outside was like walking into an open oven. Fortunately for me, my car was equipped with the automatic start, allowing the car to be chilled and cooled before I got inside. My all-white Porsche Panamera easily separated the boys from the men. As I drove slowly through the streets of West Philadelphia, Jay-Z's classic hood anthem, "Streets Is Watching," cranked loudly through the custom state-of-the-art Bose system. The music played so crisp and clear, one would have thought the rapper was having a live concert from inside my trunk.

As I pulled up to the light on Fifty-fourth and Berks Street, all traffic on the busy strip came to a halt. All attention was focused on me. The haters did what they did best and stared at the whip like they were choking on chicken bones. But the bitches? Dressed in next to nothing, my presence, car, and choice of music seemed to inspire an all-out dance competition. They began shaking ass and popping pussy like they were vixens in a Luke video. Through their seductive dance moves, they telegraphed loud and clear how they would fuck me if I gave them a day in my life and a night in my bed. Bitches! Laughter overwhelmed me as I pulled off, killing their lifelong dreams and fantasies in the process.

My laughter was cut short by the sight of White Mike's Range Rover parked outside the Dominican store. There was no need to do a double take. I was sure it was his. Triple black with the twenty-four-inch rims and air holes on the front side panels made it one of a kind. Funny how the sunny weather always seemed to lure the hustlers and gangsters outdoors in the open. That is, until you put the heat on high on they ass and have them running for cover like roaches when the lights come on. After months of homework and anticipation, White Mike finally surfaced. The type of paper he was sitting on, the nigga was a robbery waiting to happen. In fact, beyond waiting!

My two young niggas Buddha and Ryddah had been robbing niggas with me for years. This was their line of work and I knew they would be delighted to hear the good news. Removing my chirp phone off my waste, I sent him an alert.

Buddha responded immediately. "Old head! What it do?" he rejoiced upon connection. "What you know, no good?"

"You ain't going to believe this. The nigga White Mike is out in the open like it's sweet. Let's stop fucking around with this nigga and line him up right now."

"Now, that's what I'm talking about! Me and Ryddah together right now, and we got the chopper on deck. It's whatever with us." He spoke with real hunger in his voice.

"Meet me over the whop in five minutes, and hurry up!" I commanded before closing the chirp and heading over to the location myself.

By the time I arrived over at the whop, Buddha's all-black, tinted-out Caprice was already there, parked up with the engine running. Quickly parking and securing the Porsche, I walked over to join them. As soon as I opened the back door, thick clouds of smoke escaped into the atmosphere. I let as much of the weed smoke out as I could before getting in the car.

Buddha and Ryddah were two black spooky-looking motherfuckas with long, thick beards like Muslims. Since robbery was their only form of steady income, they robbed everything moving as if there were no tomorrow. They had no picks! If they caught wind that a nigga was holding, they were coming for it. When niggas saw their signature long, thick beards, and cok-fitted hats, they knew some shit was about to go down. Their presence alone brought those types of vibes.

"Y'all niggas with all this fucking weed smoke is killing me!" I complained while fanning the smoke away. "Y'all lucky I fucks wit y'all and respect the work y'all put in." Getting down to the business at hand, I told them, "Anyway, listen, the nigga White Mike's Range is parked up on the strip right now. I think he inside the Dominican store. Nigga has to be up there either serving them, or copping up. Either way we running down on him today. I'm tired of this nigga ducking and skating on us. Let's snatch this bitch-ass nigga up right now."

With the mere mention that the time had come to put in some work, the robbers put the weed out, lit up their cigarettes, and headed over to the strip on Fifty-fourth Street. That's what I loved about these niggas—their hunger eliminated all opposition and put them straight in move-out mode.

Upon driving down the strip, relief shot through the car when we rode past White Mike's Range Rover still parked there. Just as I said it would be. Buddha quickly circled around the block and found a perfect parking spot where we were able to blend in with the other cars parked on the street. More importantly, it gave us a clear view to our main objective. At that point, it was all a waiting game. To pass time and prepare for the move, Buddha put on Meek Mill's underground CD and cranked it up. Him and Ryddah sang along to every lyric while smoking back-to-back Newports. They were killing me!

About forty-five minutes and ten cigarettes later, White Mike finally emerged from the store. I wasn't a jeweler, but the canary yellow diamonds that flooded his neck and wrist appeared to be easily worth a few hundred grand. He had our undivided attention. Since he was accompanied by one of the Dominicans from the store, we ain't hop out on the nigga right there and then. Instead we waited on the perfect moment.

Suddenly White Mike began to look around nervously. In the blink of an eye he quickly shook hands with the Dominican man, jumped in his Range, and pulled off. He moved so fast, we ain't know if he spotted us or what. There was no telling because he was one scary-ass nigga. My blood started to boil at the thought of this nigga skating on us again. As if reading my mind, Buddha reacted just as I was hoping he would.

"Man! Fuck all this! This bitch-ass nigga ain't about to duck today. Pass that chopper under your seat up here. This won't be the first nigga we robbed in broad daylight. Let's run down on his bitch ass!" he announced before bringing the Caprice's V8 engine to life and gunning in the direction the Range Rover traveled.

Placing gloves on my hands and a bandana over my face, I passed Ryddah the AR-15 and pulled out my chrome .44 Bulldog. None of us were wearing seatbelts but everybody in the car was strapped up and ready to ride out.

It wasn't but a few blocks away before we caught up with him. Here the nigga was pulled over on the side of the road conversing with a sexy little redbone who was walking a small poodle. The nigga was so caught up stuntin' and talking his shit, he never noticed us pulling alongside his car until it was too late.

Before we even came to a full stop, Ryddah was hanging out of the passenger-side window, busting the chopper off. His shots were aimed at the Range Rover's tires. The powerful force behind the assault rifle's firepower shredded the driver-side wheels and snapped the front axle, making the car inoperable. At full speed, I hopped out of the Caprice, reached into the driver-side window, grabbed him by the shirt, and pulled his ass straight out. A quick pat down for a weapon came up negative. I forcefully pushed him into the back seat, keeping the .44 trained on him the entire time.

The redbone screamed in panic before picking up her dog and running for her life. Immediately, I advised him of his two non-negotiable options as soon as I got in the car. "You know what this is, nigga! Either take us to the money or we sending you to your grave."

"What? What the fuck? Y'all niggas crazy? Y'all know who I am?" he asked with arrogance as if knowing who he was was supposed to deter us. "Y'all niggas gots to kill me. I ain't giving up shit!"

If he was fucking with an amateur, he may have been able to get away with that weak shit he was talking. But not with me. To show him how serious things were, I aimed the gun at his foot and fired a shot.

"*Bloaka!*" His agonizing screams nearly deafened us as fire and fear shot though his body.

"Pussy! I ain't gonna ask you again. The next bullet is going into your fucking forehead!" With that final warning, I raised the .44 to his head.

"No, no . . . no! All right! Please don't kill me!" He was quickly coming to his senses and showing the first signs of cooperating.

Although it was a struggle for him to speak, I clearly understood the submission in his tone and expression.

"Everything . . . is at the Mont Visa on Sixty-third Street. Let's get this over with as fast as possible. Please! I need to go to the hospital before I bleed to death . . . Awww shit!" he groaned after staring down at his bloody sneaker.

Upon arriving at the location, White Mike gave up his house keys, and the apartment number, including where the money and dope was hidden. I decided I'd babysit him at gunpoint while the young niggas went inside to retrieve the goods.

Before exiting the vehicle, Buddha had one request. "If we don't chirp you within five minutes, kill this nigga! Better yet, you should put one in his bitch ass right now," he suggested. And he was dead serious.

"Naw, little nigga. Stick to the script. If the nigga play it right, we going to cut him loose. But if not, you already know what's going to happen to him." *I* dictated what was and what wasn't going to happen. "Now stop wasting time and bullshitting! Little nigga, this is a kidnapping."

Realizing that my patience was growing short, Buddha knew better than to continue procrastinating. Emerging from the car, the two robbers walked to the front entrance of the building and disappeared inside.

A few seconds afterward, White Mike let out a laugh that was somewhat in between demented and hysterical. At first I thought the nigga was crying due to the pain of his injury, but when he raised his head up, and the sound got louder, there was no mistaking it—the nigga was laughing!

"What the fuck is you laughing at nigga? You think this shit is funny?" I asked before pressing the .44 on the side of his head and cocking the hammer back.

What the nigga said and did next will forever haunt my nightmares.

Lifting his shirt up, he revealed a thin wire taped to his chest, connected to a small microphone. "I told you stupid motherfuckas that y'all ain't know who you was fucking with! Didn't I? But you ain't listen. I'm going to make sure that you motherfuckas get put *underneath* the jail!"

Before I could react or warn Buddha and Ryddah, a swarm of Dodge Chargers and Pontiac Grand Prix came approaching and surrounded the building from front to back. For a second I froze up as my senses seemed to go dead.

In that split second, White Mike opened the door and jumped out the car. As he limped away, he waved his hands in the air screaming out for help and pointing at the Caprice.

That was more than enough to snap me out of the trance I was in. Following my first instinct, I climbed into the driver seat, threw that bitch in drive, and recklessly sped away. From the rearview mirror I witnessed several men and women wearing navy blue jackets that bore FBI in bright yellow letters. Half of them stormed the apartment building while a few others ran to White Mike's aid.

Just when I thought I'd made a smooth getaway, a black Dodge Charger pulled behind me with sirens blaring from the lights in the center of the windshield. Putting the pedal to the floor, I pushed the Caprice to its full performance. In a desperate attempt to shake the *federales,* I ran through red lights, weaved in and out of traffic, and cut corners like Dale Earnhardt in the Daytona 500.

Thanks to my superb driving skills, I managed to get ahead a nice distance on them. That is, until I approached an intersection where a funeral chain was passing through. As the hearse approached, I could see there was a nice amount of space between it and the other cars that followed. That was my only chance to get away. Slamming the gear down to drive two, I floored the gas, and sent the Caprice accelerating at full speed.

Shooting out in front of the hearse, the sounds of brakes screeching, horns blowing, and sirens wailing was all I heard as I slid past, barely making it. Had I been one inch off or one second too early, the hearse would have probably had another dead body in the driver seat and in need of another one to come pick up my dead ass.

Glancing in the rearview mirror, I saw that those cocksucking *federales* didn't dare to pull the same stunt. Hell, I barely escaped. I drove straight back to the whop, grabbed the chopper, and left that Caprice running in the middle of the street. Once in the comfort of my own car, I felt a little relief. That is, until I heard helicopters hovering above. They were close, but they weren't on me. They were heading in the direction of the Mont Visa Apartments. Police sirens echoed through the hood nonstop.

What the fuck went down back there? I wondered. I damn sure wasn't waiting around to find out. I took my ass straight home until shit cooled off and I figured out my next move. . . .

Chapter 2

For the remainder of the day, I stayed indoors looking out of the front window with one eye while watching the news with the other. Ever since White Mike lifted his shirt and showed me that wire, I'd been living federal nightmares, even though I was awake. It wasn't until the eleven o'clock news came on that I got a detailed version of all that had transpired inside the apartment complex.

I wasn't surprised in the least to learn that Buddha and Ryddah went out in a blaze of glory while shooting it out with the feds. During the gun battle that cost both of them their lives, they managed to hit two of the federal agents, critically injuring both of them. Knowing how them young niggas moved, I knew that jail wasn't an option for them. I ain't blame them. They did it how the gangsters do it. I had to tip my hat to the young niggas.

To keep it a hundred, learning that Buddha and Ryddah hadn't made it out of that predicament alive gave me two less worries and a sense of relief. Not to say that they would have ratted on me, but nowadays you couldn't be too sure of anybody. The two little niggas went out doing what they did best and loved doing. They were indeed true soldiers, but just like the rest of my soldiers, they were all expendable. They would be missed, but easily replaced.

It may sound heartless, but in my line of work, I never allowed myself to get mentally or emotionally attached to any of these niggas out here on the streets. I learned a long time ago that this game was filled with risk, dangers, failures, and plenty of disappointments. If a nigga came up on anything around this motherfucka, he better count his blessings and consider it a temporary luxury. Because it was only a matter of time before the police, haters, or jack boys was coming to take your life, and everything you own! That's what it all comes down to. But this was the life I chose, or better yet, the life that chose me. Therefore I took the bad with the good, and the bitter with the sweet, and kept it moving.

After the drama-filled day that I'd been through, a nigga needed therapy in the worst way. And there was no therapy in this world that had the ability to soothe my nerves and clear my mind like a shot of good pussy, a dutch, and a few ounces of syrup. I already had everything I needed on reserve, except a bitch. The mood I was in, I wanted some of that wet, wild, thug pussy.

Feisty Felicia was the first to come to mind. She was far from a dime piece, but her fat ass, small waist, and attitude made up for any shortcomings within her beauty. Not to say that she was ugly, but shorty definitely had a rough look to her. I guess after spending seven years in state prison for an armed robbery, she was justified in looking and acting the way she did. I decided to give her a call.

Seeing my number come across her caller ID must have made her night because she answered on the first ring with a hint of happiness in her voice. Even though she tried to appear all nonchalant about it, I knew better. I read these bitches like books.

"What up, Boss? You must be horny and in the house by yourself because that's the only time a bitch get a call from your little yellow ass." She spoke the truth.

"Bitch! Who the fuck you think you fooling? You know our arrangement, so don't get on no new shit. I've always had and always will have rights to that pussy. Now bring your black ass over here and hurry the fuck up," I barked at her. I usually wasn't that disrespectful to the ladies, but that was the only language Felicia seemed to understand. Not to mention the fact that any physical and verbal aggressiveness was a major turn-on for her.

After lining up some pussy for the night, I went into my bedroom and rolled up a dutch of that purple haze. Between each pull of the dutch, I took slow sips of the yellow syrup straight out of the eight-ounce bottle. Afterward, I headed to the bathroom for a hot shower.

I wasn't in the water but for ten minutes before the doorbell began ringing nonstop. I figured Felicia's little pussy was growing impatient. Hopping out the shower I went downstairs to answer the door, dick and balls swinging freely all over the place. As I walked through the living room, I stopped briefly to glance at the flat-screen surveillance monitor hanging from the wall that showed live footage of the entire perimeter of my house. From there I observed Felicia standing there, still ringing my doorbell like she had lost her fucking mind.

In my mind the doorbell was the bell indicating the beginning of the first round. Snatching the front door open, I pulled her straight inside and threw my tongue down her throat while grabbing a handful of that fat, soft ass. After a few seconds of tongue swapping and lip locking, she stepped back and placed her hands on her hips, looking all ghetto fabulous.

"Damn, nigga! I done got all pretty for you and your ungrateful ass can't even give a bitch a compliment?" She began posing seductively like a prostitute trying to lure a trick.

The bitch wore one of those Beyoncé weaves, and was dressed in a red mini skirt with the matching thigh-high leather boots. I was willing to bet the house that she ain't have no panties on. Before I could compliment her on her looks, she turned her back on me and walked toward the door, as if she was ready to leave.

"I'm out, Amin! You be playing too many fucking games," she complained, snapping her neck as she spoke. "You ain't ready for a real bitch like me."

Before she could open the door, I had her gripped up by the back of her hair, escorting her toward the stairs. With each step she climbed, her mini skirt rose up a little higher. Just as I suspected, her nasty ass wasn't wearing no panties. I couldn't resist giving that fat ass a nice hard smack. The way it bounced and jiggled as a result made me walk a little faster and push her up the stairs a little harder.

As soon as we entered my room, I pushed her down onto the bed. The look on her face reflected that she was loving how rough I was handling her. As I slowly approached the bed, she suddenly reached in her boot and pulled out a small Peggy Sue (.22 revolver). That shit there took me by complete surprise. If this was any other bitch, I wouldn't have been scared out of my mind, but this was a woman who'd been known and convicted for putting in work with those pistols.

Where I'm from, when a motherfucka points a gun in somebody's face, one of three things is sure to follow: a shooting, a murder, or a robbery. I ain't know which scenario shorty had in store for me, but I was hoping it was the least of the three.

"Put your motherfucking hands in the air, and don't move unless I tell you to," she commanded aggressively.

Because she had the drop on me, I had no choice but to comply with her demands. In a matter of a few minutes, my mood went from wanting to fuck to wanting to kill. But for now, she had the upper hand. "I knew you was a shiesty skeezer. If it's money you want, let's get it over with. Bitch, but you won't live to spend a penny of it. I promise you that, bitch!"

"Didn't I tell your ass not to move? That goes for those big, sexy-ass lips of yours, too. But since you can't seem to stop running your mouth, come over here and run those juicy motherfuckas over this pussy," she ordered.

At first I was a little hesitant. It was apparent to me that this was all some sort of freak game she was playing. But when she cocked the hammer on her gun back, I decided not to take no chances. At that point, she knew she had me. With a smile on her face, she lay back, spread her legs open, and began massaging her insides with the fingers on her free hand.

Wasting no time with the foreplay I went straight to work. As if the pussy was hot soup, I blew on it, licked, sucked, and slurped up all the juices that came out. She moaned lightly while her eyes rolled in and out of the back of her head. Turning things up just another notch, I spread the lips of her vagina apart until her clit became fully visible. Up, down, and side to side, I licked it slowly while my middle finger went in and out of her insides at full speed.

After she came once, I switched the method up and licked it fast and fingered it slow. The technique kept her off balance and drove her crazy. My tongue game gave her more pleasure than her body could take. As if the Holy Ghost inside her was being rejoiced by the good Word, she began shaking, hollering, and rocking as a full-body orgasm violently erupted. The force behind the orgasm that shot through Felicia's body caused her to lose the grip she held on the pistol, sending it falling to the floor! The moment I was waiting on. It was time to teach this bitch a lesson about playing with guns.

As she lay there still going through the motions, I climbed on top of her and rubbed the head of my dick on the insides of her vagina teasingly. In all actuality, I was just lubricating it enough to discipline her for her actions.

Just as she was starting to enjoy the pleasure of me being inside her, I pulled out and drove into her asshole without mercy or warning. She screamed, scratched, bit, and fought hard in an attempt to get me up off her. All of her efforts were useless. I was stronger and on a mission to set an example.

All the long, hard, deep strokes had her screaming in agonizing pain. Still I showed no sympathy. After a while it must have started feeling good to her. First her tensed muscles relaxed, then her screams turned into loud, passionate moans. It wasn't much longer before she started fucking back, and accepting my long, lengthy thrusts with submission and satisfaction. She begged me to continue fucking her in the ass, but from the back, so I flipped her ass over and gave it to her doggie style. Gave it to *her?* Shit! I mean she gave it to *me!*

The ass was super tight and the way she was throwing it back made it impossible for me to hang too long. As her moaning intensified, I know that she was on the verge of coming. My timing couldn't have been more perfect. The second she began to climax, I drove my dick deep down inside her and exploded. What started out as an exercise in discipline turned out to be some of the best sex I ever had.

For her amazing performance, not only did she get a hot five, I also let her share my bed with me for the night. After smoking another dutch of purple haze, we put on one of those body-and-soul CDs, fucked again, and went to sleep cuddled up as if we were a couple.

The following morning, I was awakened by the delightful aroma of fried turkey bacon, cheese eggs, and home fries cooked with onions and green peppers. After last night's heavy fucking and weed smoking, a nigga definitely built up a fierce appetite. Quickly throwing on some sweatpants and my Hush Puppies house slippers, I went down to the kitchen to get me a plate.

When I entered the kitchen, Felicia was standing over the stove, tossing it up like a gourmet chef. Wearing nothing but one of my old football jerseys, her ass was still visibly wide and fat. As I stood there eye-fucking her from the bottom to the top, my cataract erection went soft when I noticed how discombobulated her hair looked. It was intact last night when she arrived, but now it was all over the place. When she noticed the look of disgust on my face, she knew exactly why.

"Don't be looking at me with your face balled all up, nigga! My hair look the way it do because of your freak ass wanting to go anal last night. I could hardly walk down the damn steps this morning. Motherfucka," she voiced before playfully punching me on the arm.

I just laughed at her.

"It ain't funny, Amin." She referred to me by my government name, knowing that it would get under my skin.

Unless it was used by someone I truly loved and respected, I never responded to or even acknowledged my real name. If we were on the streets somewhere and she or anyone else called me anything but Boss, it would have been a problem. As crazy as she may seem, she wasn't stupid. I knew she was just trying to get a reaction out of me. I just looked at her with the look of death, prompting her to move on with the conversation.

"Anyway! Back to my hair. This weave cost me almost two hundred dollars for the hair, and damn near another two hundred to get it done. You fucked it up, so I know you're gonna pay to get it redone, right?" She kept her hopes high while desperately trying to comb her hair back into place with her fingers.

The game she spat let me know I was fucking with a true ho and not a whore. What nigga wouldn't pay to keep a fine piece of ass like hers on standby?

While eating breakfast, we viewed the morning news broadcast on channel six. As expected, the top story revolved around yesterday's drama. After giving a full, detailed version of the incident, they reported on the condition of the wounded federal agents. One of them was expected to survive, while the other was still fighting for his life. What got my full and undivided attention was when they mentioned that a $15,000 reward was being offered for information leading to the arrest of the getaway driver who eluded authorities.

I couldn't stand it when the media used its broadcast to encourage snitching, promising money and anonymity to those who came forward. Snatching the remote from the table, I shut the power off and continued eating. Complete silence overcame the dining room until Felicia opened her big mouth. She just had to add her two cents concerning the news segment we just saw.

"Shit! Fifteen thousand dollars! Somebody gonna turn that nigga in before the day is over," she suggested.

"Bitch! What the fuck is you saying? If you knew who it was you would turn them in for the money?" I was two seconds from losing my temper and grabbing the bitch by her neck.

"Hell no! You know me better than that, Boss. I'm a real bitch, but there is a lot of niggas running around on these streets faking it," she said, desperately trying to clear up the comment she made. "These niggas out here will turn their mothers in for the right amount."

"Yeah? Well, it sounded to me like you was condoning that snitching shit. When they mentioned that reward money, you seemed to be rejoicing. I seen that shiesty-ass look on your face," I exposed while staring at her in disgust. "Bitch, if I ever find out you snitched on any motherfucking body, I'll personally see to it that you get a bullet in your forehead. Now hurry up and finish eating, then get your musky ass up outta my house!"

"Damn, nigga! My bad. I was just trying to make conversation," she pleaded. "If I ain't know any better, I would think that you . . ."

The look I gave her discouraged her from saying another word. She didn't even finish her breakfast. Her nasty ass put on the same clothes she wore last night. No shower, brushing her teeth, or face washing. She stomped out of the house broke and humiliated. Fuck her and her hair. I wasn't giving her a coin. In my book, a free fuck was as good as a free lunch.

Chapter 3

Nobody had ever gotten Felicia as mad as Boss did that morning. It took all restraint for her not to pull out her gun and shoot his ass, fo'real. The way he reacted to her comment was unnecessary. But, because of that reaction, she was not suspicious that he was somehow involved with the incident. If that was the case, then she should have been the last bitch he disrespected and treated like shit.

The little bit of love and feelings that she used to have for him were now replaced with hatred and vengeance. Once Felicia stopped dealing with a nigga on bad terms, they became subject for robbery, burglary, or some other form of a setup. In this particular situation, $15,000 for a hairdo, a mean fucking, and a disrespectful nigga's actions just might settle the score. In desperate need of a new car and a shopping spree, turning his ass in was extremely tempting.

Far from a snitch, she considered it more so being an opportunist. That is, if she even decided to do it. By all means, she wasn't 100 percent sure that he was the person they were looking for, but she damn sure was going to do everything in her power to find out. And once she did, she was strongly considering turning his ass over for the dough.

Chapter 4

On these mean streets of Philly, everybody had a spot in the food chain. In this instance, it was the stick-up boys sticking up the stick-up boys. For some reason, niggas seemed to be under the impression that because they earned their pay through robbing, killing, or selling dope, they were exempt from falling victim to the same sword they lived by.

Boss was a perfect example of this misconception. He ran the streets robbing, hustling, and causing massive havoc to a degree that he must have honestly believed he was the only one doing it and the best to do it. Had he not been so set in his ways, he may have discovered that he himself was the center focus of a vicious plot constructed by two dangerous robbers from the streets of North Philadelphia.

Rudd and Bey had been crime partners for over ten years. They'd been robbing and stealing together since they were twelve years old. Starting out snatching pocketbooks, earrings, and gold chains, they eventually graduated to armed robberies, kidnappings, and home invasions. Like true robbers, they lived for the day and treated every hour as if it was their last. It was common to see them stunting in the clubs, flaunting other niggas' jewelry, and flashing their stolen cash.

Over the past two weeks, the crime partners had been keeping close tabs on the nigga Boss from West Philly. His lavish habits and extravagant stunting landed him on their radar a few months back. Through their intense homework, they knew where he lived, what he drove, and his hustle. From what they observed, they figured he was easily holding a few keys and maybe a million dollars or better. With that type of money on the line, this was more than just a robbery in the making; it was the heist of their lifetime.

The day they went to make their move on Boss, they got a hell of a surprise instead. After following his Porsche all morning, they observed him meeting up with two young niggas driving a tinted-up Caprice. Believing that some sort of drug transaction was about to take place, they stayed close behind and patiently waited.

It wasn't long after that they witnessed Boss and his affiliates put some work in on some nigga who was pushing a Range Rover. The fact that they were bold enough to commit a shooting and kidnapping in broad daylight, on a busy street, let them know that they weren't fucking with the average nigga. Certainly, he was more than just a common drug dealer. This nigga was involved in the same shit that they were.

Even after what they witnessed, they still decided to stick around and see what the trio was up to. At a safe distance, they maintained close visual on their every move. Through their robbery career, they'd pulled off several similar capers. Realizing what was occurring before their eyes, they decided to allow the trio to finish up their business and, at the end, they would rob them for everything they acquired and whatever they had back at their homes.

Shortly after two of the kidnappers entered the apartment building, flocks of federal agents came out of nowhere and surrounded the complex from every direction. Just then the kidnapped victim jumped from the car and the Caprice quickly sped away. Several agents pursued the vehicle, while a dozen other agents stormed the building.

The heavy presence of police and feds in the immediate radius had the streets of West Philly on fire, while police and news helicopters hovered overhead, lighting up the night sky. Under those circumstances, Rudd and Bey knew that it wouldn't be a smart move to be driving around with the arsenal of weapons they always traveled with. Instead, they emerged from the car and blended in with the crowd of nosy neighbors, all curious to learn what could have possibly transpired that was severe enough to draw federal agents, police, and news reporters.

Chapter 5

"'I'm the realest nigga in here, you already know, got Trapper of the Year three times in a row. What they give you? A lifetime supply of baking soda clientele, a Roley watch, three pots and two scales.'"

Whenever I was in hustle mode, I let that classic Young Jeezy shit crank. *Thug Motivation* was one of the most inspiring, influential albums of all time! The lyrics seemed to represent my everyday life.

Here I was, without a care in the world, driving through traffic with a half of key underneath the passenger seat and a Glock .40 with an extended clip sitting on my lap. Not the feds or anybody else was going to get in the way of me getting this money, whether it was drug money, taking money, or however else I decided to earn mine.

Being as how I was still sitting on a few of them things from a previous home invasion, I was hitting niggas around the city with work on a daily basis. Shortly after Felicia's stinking ass left, I got a call from one of my customers looking to score a half of joint. The little nigga still owed me money from an earlier arrangement, but since he assured me everything was correct on his end, I promised to deliver it to him before noon.

Nothing had the ability to move my spirits like that almighty dollar. Too bad my good mood was short-lived. The second I turned down Fifty-third and Arlington Street, I spotted this clown-ass nigga, Tamir, posted up on the steps of the crack house where he hustled at with this dusty young girl with him holding a duffle bag. I couldn't believe this nigga was stupid enough to telegraph that some sort of transaction was ready to take place. Never did he draw this sort of attention on me during our previous business dealings, nor did he ever bring anyone else along. This was some new shit, and I needed to know why.

It didn't take me long to figure the shit out. As soon as he got inside the car and started talking that heavy Tony Montana shit, I knew he was trying to impress the little bitch who was with him.

"What's up, Boss? Eh, look, this my fiancée, Geraldine. Baby, this my mans I been telling you about," he introduced.

Through the rearview mirror, I noticed that his "fiancée" couldn't seem to stop blushing and smiling from ear to ear. No doubt she was starstruck.

Immediately after introducing us, Tamir started dick eating worse than a groupie. "Anyway, I'm trying to get money like you, nigga. You out here pushing the Porsche Panamera and looking like a million dollars. It's on now! I got the block pumping like a shotgun, so I'm going to start copping at least two bricks a week—"

"All right, nigga, won't you shut the fuck up! You talking real stupid and reckless!" I cut him off in mid-sentence. Fear and surprise consumed his face as I continued putting him in his place. "Furthermore, you wouldn't know what a million dollars looked like if it smacked you upside your head. I'm going to tell you this one time and one time only: don't you *ever* bring no bitch or anybody else with you in an event that we do business in the future. Now get that bag from that bitch and conduct business like you got some motherfucking sense!"

There was no further protest. Instead he did what he was instructed to do. After all the money was counted, and the work was exchanged, I gave him one last piece of advice and a reminder before dismissing him.

"Remember what I said, because I hate to have to repeat myself. You say that you out here trying to get money like me, but that will never happen until you change your habits and keep these little smut bitches out of your business. If you think shorty going to take a case for you, then you got the game all fucked up. I tell you what you can expect when you deal with these hood bitches on a personal level—bad blood! She gonna end up either telling your business to the police, the jack boys, or anybody else who will listen. And you know what that's gonna bring. Now go ahead about your business," I warned him.

With his pride damaged, Tamir exited the car without saying another word. I'd be damned if his "fiancée" didn't remain seated in the back. Instead she sat there blushing and smiling. When I turned around to confront her, she slowly licked her lips and spoke before I could say a word.

"I know this may sound odd, but I never been in the presence of anyone as powerful as you in my life. When you speak, my heartbeat speeds up and the juices down low start to flow like never before. I probably done soaked your seats. Umm, umm, ummm." She shook her head and bit down on her lip. "Anyhow, it's obvious I'm fucking with the wrong nigga. I should be fucking with a real boss such as yourself. So what's up?"

"Is you serious?" I asked in a state of disbelief. "Didn't you just hear what the fuck I told your man? Shorty, you far from the level of bitches I fuck with. Furthermore, I don't fuck with the help or the helpers of the help. I mean, look at you! What could you possibly give to me other than some dirty, beat-up pussy and some head? Why don't you do us both a favor and get the fuck out my car? Your *fiancé* is waiting for you."

I couldn't believe the boldness of the little smut. She had the audacity to flirt and offer me some pussy while her man stood just outside the car. I just shook my head and drove away laughing as I watched Tamir through the rearview mirror grabbing and smacking her up. As far as he was concerned, I wasn't trying to play him, but every now and then, I had to remind these niggas of their positions and where they stood in this world. I was always taught to kill bad habits before they grew to be big problems. There was no telling what these stupid, reckless niggas would do or say if they felt they were at liberty to do as they pleased.

Chapter 6

Later that evening, I received a phone call from my old head, Shake. Somehow he seemed to always sense when I had been involved in some bullshit or needed his guidance through a rough situation. The telephone never really been his style, so he invited me down to the shop to holler at him face to face.

The "shop," as we called it, was half beauty salon, half barber shop. It was one of the many ventures Shake owned throughout Philly. When hair wasn't getting done up or cut, Shake used the place to conduct drug deals, discuss hits, robberies, et cetera.

Shake was more than just my old head; he was really like a father to me. As a youngster running the streets, I was into everything from robberies to boosting to selling drugs. When the older drug dealers refused to give me packs or front me weight, I sold soap. It was either that or starve. With a crackhead mother who basically ran the streets day and night, most of the time I had to fend for myself.

Once Shake caught wind that I was pushing fake product in the hood, he sent a few of his men to snatch me up off the streets and bring me to his presence. Upon meeting me and learning my story, he took an instant liking to me and took me into his home, accepting and loving me as if I was his very own. Ever since then I been on, and never looked back.

Coming up under Shake came with a lot of benefits and advantages. I was able to witness firsthand how he operated and conducted business on the streets. I observed the many manipulative tactics he used to control others while he stayed in the background and got rich and powerful. Still, he kept everybody in his circle paid and in position. He fed the goons, wolves, and hustlers from the palm of his very hand. In return, they were at his disposal, willing to die and kill on his behalf.

When I asked Shake how and why he was so influential over the others he responded, "True leaders are born to be followed, as kings are in a position to dictate and rule. The streets recognize those who possess those characteristics and qualities and automatically fall in line."

Shake was one crafty, slick-talking nigga. He possessed a humble demeanor, but a violent nature. Dangerous enough to have a nigga touched, killed, or kidnapped, but smart enough to have a fifteen-year-old run without any run-ins with the law. On top of that, he was rich, successful, and an entrepreneur at heart. The game I inherited from him is the sole source of my existence, accomplishments, and success.

When I entered the shop, Shake was there alone, sitting in one of the barber chairs, eating a soul food platter. He stopped momentarily to acknowledge me.

"My little nigga, Boss! Look at you, son," he spoke with admiration while looking me up and down. "Whenever I see you, I'm always reminded of a younger version of myself. Anyway, what's good with you? I could hear the worry in your voice during our conversation earlier."

"Damn, Shake! If I ain't know any better, I would think you was psychic or some shit!" I shook my head with amazement before continuing. "Nevertheless, I definitely needed to holla at you about this situation that I was involved in yesterday."

After giving him a detailed version of everything that had happened, his entire attitude changed toward me, and for the first time ever, I witnessed a side of him that I had never seen. Slamming his platter to the floor, he jumped out of the chair and gripped me up by the collar. "What the fuck is wrong with you nigga? How in the fuck is you supposed to be my son but pulling amateur moves like that?" He stared into my eyes with anger and rage. "I can't believe your stupid ass is out here doing serious crimes with some petty-ass street thugs! After everything I taught you! What a motherfucking waste!" He spoke with disappointment.

Once he let my collar go, I attempted to make things right between us before shit got blown out of proportion. "Hold up, Shake, you ain't got shit to worry about and neither do I. Nobody seen my face, and don't nobody know who I am. With all due respect, I ain't just start robbing niggas and getting money. I know everything that come along with this shit." I held down my ground.

If the things he said wasn't hurtful enough, this man whom I loved as a father turned his back and spoke to me as if I meant nothing to him. "You fucked up big time with this one, Amin. I only pray that the situation dies down and doesn't come back to bite you in the ass. I personally won't allow you or anyone else to bring that kind of heat around me, my people, or anything else associated with me. I got too much to lose, and if the feds come for you, they gonna snatch you and everything and everybody around you. Until this shit passes by, don't come around me or call any of my phones. If I need to reach you, I know where and how to find you. Now go ahead and bounce," he shot coldly over his shoulder with dismissal.

Never in a million years did I think that Shake would turn his back on me. This was my father and the only family I had. Instead of questioning his decision or

Chapter 7

Since it was basically me against the world, then fuck the world! The way Shake treated and spoke to me had put an ice box where my heart used to be. But as I said before, life is full of heartaches, headaches, and disappointments. That night, I realized that in all actuality the only nigga I needed was the one in the mirror. What didn't kill me would make me stronger in the long run. If Shake thought that I couldn't make moves without his blessings, he had me fucked up. I'm a boss by blood, not relation.

In hopes of clearing my head I decided to pack up a few things and shoot over to Atlantic City for a few nights. Sometimes a nigga had to go away just so he can make a comeback. Besides, I was well due for some vacation and relaxation. Before driving across the Ben Franklin Bridge, I copped an ounce of purple haze and an eighth of yellow cough syrup.

During the hour-long drive, I smoked a dutch stuffed with that good exotic, while sipping syrup straight from the bottle in between each puff. The heartfelt lyrics of Tupac Shakur in "Me Against the World" pumped as loud as the volume permitted. The things he was rapping nearly fifteen years ago made sense way back then, but even more so now since I was actually living proof of it.

By the time I arrived in Atlantic City, I was as high as a giraffe's ass! The colorful bright lights reflecting off the dozen or so casino buildings was alluring in itself.

There were hundreds of billboards advertising events, contests, tournaments, jackpots, et cetera. People came from all over hoping to win some easy money. Although the odds and chances of winning were low, people tricked themselves into believing that they were among that small percentage who would actually win.

Bally's Hotel and Casino was my casino of choice. I frequented the place enough to be a regular and a black comp card holder. Whenever I walked through the door, I was immediately acknowledged and accommodated with the top-of-the-line treatment and VIP status, including high-roller suites, a credit line, bottles, five-star dinners, et cetera. It was the life of a boss, and it was all mine.

After being situated inside the fully furnished deluxe suite, I lit up another dutch, took a shower, and got dressed. Out of the $50,000 I brought along for the trip, I secured twenty of it inside the digital safe before heading downstairs. While on the elevator, I happened to glance in the mirror and get a look at my reflection. I must say, my appearance and wardrobe was on another level. Grown-man status.

The all-white Gucci sweat suit I wore had the red and green stripes coming down the side. I rocked a plain Breitling timepiece and a diamond-studded necklace with an emblem spelling out my name in canary yellow diamonds. That alone gave me rights to stunt with the best of them.

Stepping out onto the casino floor, I'd clearly become the center of attention. All eyes were on me. From the dealers to the regulars and anybody who was somebody recognized that a true boss was in the building. They all greeted me with the utmost respect as I passed through. The bitches in attendance was giving seductive looks, lip-licking and smiling, praying for my attention or some sort of acknowledgement. Even those who were accompanied by a man reacted similarly. Knowing that I could probably fuck any and every last one of them had I wanted to only boosted my arrogance and self-esteem. It showed in my demeanor as I strolled over to the craps table with confidence in every step I took.

After cashing in $20,000 in chips, I began placing my usual bets around the table. I put thousand-dollar bets on the four, six, nine, and ten, plus a hard six, eight, and twelve. With dice in hand and feet planted firmly, I began shaking them up before releasing them with a casual flick of the wrist then concluding with the finger snap. The well-calculated form made me a winner on that roll and many more to follow.

For the next ten minutes or so I was on a roll, literally! That was, until the baddest bitch I ever laid eyes on approached me and asked if I minded her joining me at my side. Her presence alone was so captivating that the entire table of rowdy gamblers including myself got quiet, humbled by the beauty she possessed. Instead of responding to her request, I lifted the Gucci frames from my eyes and stared into the face that went with the body of sheer beauty—from head to toe.

Her hair was long, jet black, bone straight with the bangs like Nicki Minaj. It fell perfectly and firmly along the arch in her back. I was even more impressed by the color of her eyes. They were olive green and slightly slanted as if she had some Asian in her. Her skin complexion was the color of toffee and appeared to be as soft as silk. The gold and platinum Versace dress she wore hugged tightly around her body, exposing the small waist and fat, wide ass. Not to mention her questionable double-D breasts. Besides the body and beauty, my eyes were fixed on the platinum diamond ring that lit up on her right ring finger.

Even if baby girl was married, I was willing to fuck up a happy home and family to get up in some of that pussy!

Quickly snapping out of the trance, I took the opportunity to get better acquainted.

"It will be a pleasure and honor to have you join me. It ain't every day that a man gets approached by a woman with such defined beauty," I admitted truthfully. My compliment had her blushing and flashing that pearly white smile of hers. That's when I placed her hand into mine and formally introduced myself.

"You can call me Boss. And what might your name be?"

"My name is Sophia, but my friends all call me Su-Su. Thank you for allowing me the opportunity to accompany you at the table. You're such a gentleman and a handsome one at that," she flirted before removing a large wad of big faces from her Gucci bag and cashing them in.

Only a true boss could hold up a table in Atlantic City for five minutes without being interrupted. Once the game continued, I began placing larger bets than I usually would. I was so busy trying to impress Sophia, win money, and earn a shot of pussy, that I lost focus. After hitting just a few numbers, I eventually crapped out, and went on a losing streak. Before I knew it, Sophia had stopped betting on my roll. Shortly after that, I lost all my winnings, including what I came downstairs with.

Having been sidelined from the game, I felt like a true sucker. From the looks Sophia was giving me, she must have been thinking the same thing. When she picked up a handful of her chips and offered them to me, it became apparent that she didn't think I was a sucker; baby girl thought that the casino had cracked my pockets. Her assumption was certainly premature. Two things had to follow: first, I politely rejected her offer and secondly, I had to show her that a true boss was *never* down and out and was winning even when he appeared to be losing.

I could have easily gone back upstairs to my room to retrieve the remaining stacks I had locked away. But I wasn't willing to risk leaving baby girl alone for some lame to come stepping on my toes, or for her to leave before we had a chance to get better acquainted. That's when the idea hit me that was sure to get me back in the crap game and up my chances of getting between Sophia's legs. Quickly removing my cell phone from my pocket I contacted my host.

One thing I learned over the years about casinos was that their employees had ways of functioning similar to your everyday hustler. They never turned down an opportunity to make some extra money. Minutes after contacting my host, I spotted him and two security guards walking toward me. One of them carried a metal silver briefcase handcuffed to his wrist. The gamblers at the table seemed to lose interest in the dice game and were focused on what was going on with me and my affairs.

"Boss, it's good to see you. How are you, buddy?" my host, Jerry Meyers, asked.

I cut straight through the small talk. "I'm straight. But I'll be much better the sooner I get back in the game and win my money back."

"Of course, buddy. I'm sorry for the delay, but I had to personally remove and count the thirty grand by hand before securing it and bringing it down to you. I assure you that it's all present and accounted for. If you wish, you may count it for yourself."

"That won't be necessary. It's thirty thousand, not thirty million. If a motherfucka needs to steal that little bit of money, he needs it more than me. That's shopping money!" I talked it how I lived it. From out the corner of my eye, I noticed that Sophia was watching my every move. When our eyes met, she flashed me yet another smile along with an approving head nod.

After cashing in for the second time that night, I decided to take it slow and gamble and bet at my usual pace. The results went in my favor. I ended up winning my money back plus a few thousand. From the looks of the chips Sophia had stacked up, it appeared that she had damn near tripled hers. As she walked over to the cash-out line, I followed close behind.

"Damn, Mrs. Sophia!" I spoke loud enough to get her attention, sarcastically adding emphasis on the "Mrs." to see how she would respond. "That's how the night's going to end? No good-byes or invites to a drink, dinner, or nothing, huh?"

"I'm sorry, Boss. I didn't mean to be rude, but I'm so tired. I at least owe you a thank-you for helping me win some money, but as far as dinner or a drink goes, I don't think my man would approve of me going out to eat or drink in the company of another man, especially one as powerful and handsome as yourself. Too many possibilities."

The way she put it didn't exactly deny my advances, nor approve of them. I believed she was testing me to see what I would say and do next. So I just waited.

"Think about it, Boss. If you were locked up, facing a lengthy prison sentence, how would you feel if your fiancée was out in the world mingling with another man?"

"Honestly speaking, I would be happy for you that a nigga was taking you out and treating you good. Especially if I was facing a lot of time. It takes a miserable motherfucka to try to keep his woman in the house writing letters, waiting on phone calls, and having no life because he doesn't have one. That's plain selfish." I kept it real. Seeing that my words were touching base with her, I continued speaking. "I tell you what. Won't you come up to my room? There we can smoke, drink, and talk about life. I won't bite you or expect you to do anything but keep me company and give me a chance to get to know you better. Is that too much to ask for?"

"Boy, you trying to get me in trouble. But since you're willing to share your weed, alcohol, and time to hear my problems, I'm going to accept your invitation. But before we go, I must forewarn you that I can talk for a long time. Especially when I'm grooving. Remember, you asked for this," she remarked before flashing a devious smile and leading the way toward the elevator.

Back inside my suite, we puffed on some exotic and popped a bottle of Dom Pérignon. The intoxicants seemed to loosen baby girl up. She began telling me her entire life story. I learned that her mother was of Middle Eastern descent and her father was Ethiopian. At two years old, she was adopted by an American family just outside of Philly. Four years ago they were killed in an automobile accident while on their way to attend her graduation ceremony. She admitted that she partially blamed herself for their deaths and was still grieving their loss.

Shortly after losing her parents, she moved to the city and began clubbing every weekend. That's where she said she met her fiancé, Victor. He was a Spanish cat from Camden and was currently locked up in the feds for trying to smuggle drugs back from out of town. He was supposedly facing thirty years. The level of comfort she achieved in my presence made her feel safe revealing that she had over $200,000 of her man's money stashed in the condo where they lived. She further explained that she was afraid living there because she believed it was only a matter of time before the police or someone else came looking for it.

Immediately, my conniving, scheming thoughts kicked in. I was strongly considering following her home and robbing her for every dollar she had. Especially if she wasn't trying to give me no pussy. But on second thought, I couldn't do that to baby girl. She was already down on her luck, not to mention the fact that I was feeling her.

But on some real shit, I wasn't trying to hear sob stories all night long. I would rather get up in those guts and hear her screaming and moaning all night.

In an attempt to get closer to my objective, I began slowly rubbing on her leg. But before I got too close to the inside of her thighs, she pushed my hands away. When I tried to kiss her on the neck, she turned her head away. That's when she stood up and explained why she was denying all of my advances.

"Hold up a minute, Boss. As I told you several times, tonight, you are a fine brother and all, but I never have and never will give my body up to a man I barely know. I'm a woman who requires commitment, provision, and stability," she addressed before walking over and standing directly in front of me. "Respect is everything. I listened to everything you said earlier about men in jail holding women back from living their lives. I agree. But I also knew what I was getting into when I started dealing with Victor. So, am I going to just call it quits and leave him for dead? No. But am I going to live my life and do me? Damn right!

"I would love to get to know you better, be friends, and see where things go from there. Women have needs and wants, just as much as men do. But there is a time, place, and process that must be considered before that happens. And if that does happen, I assure you that what I have to offer, you'll be beyond thankful that you waited. As the saying goes, good things come to those who wait."

Two things I never turn down is fast money or a fast challenge. That was exactly how I interpreted Sophia's little speech. The manner in which she presented and expressed herself showed that she had class and respect for herself as well as for her body. Honestly speaking, the fact that she didn't just walk out on her man because of the situation he was in or the time he was facing confirmed that she was a certified ride or die bitch. The average chick out here would have left that nigga in a heartbeat to spend a day in my life and a night in my bed. What I saw in Sophia was something real and special. Definitely something I wanted to keep around and get to know on another level.

Chapter 8

The long night that Sophia and I spent together was one of the best nights of my life, even though nothing sexual transpired between us. The conversation and company was compelling and satisfying in itself. Before it was all said and done and bond, an agreement and arrangement had been established between us. I opened my home to her with no strings attached. She agreed under the terms that she have her own bedroom and we remain on plutonic grounds of building a friendship. Whatever she was talking was all fine and dandy, but I knew deep down inside that once she seen how I operated, produced, and provided, her heart would choose me and demand her body to surrender to any and all of my needs, wants, and desires.

The following morning, there I was following Sophia down the Atlantic City expressway. She drove a money green Escalade. The big boy version. Yet she handled it as if it was a midsized car. We arrived at her Cherry Hill condominium in about twenty minutes.

It took us nearly two hours to pack up her shoes, clothes, and some other personal items she refused to leave behind. Her things took up every seat and compartment in her car as well as mine. But in the end, baby girl was coming back to Philly to live her life inside of mine and, hopefully, turn my house into a home in the process.

During the short ride back to Philly, my thoughts were on money and improving my living conditions. I couldn't change any fuck ups from the past, but I could damn sure step it up a notch so that my present and future consisted of success and 100 percent effort in everything I did. What I learned in the last day or so was that sometimes it took something serious or someone special to bring out the best in you. I must admit, Sophia inspired me to turn shit up on the streets to another level.

The neighborhood in which I lived was indeed "the hood"; however, it wasn't as dirty and grimy as some of the other communities around the city. In some places around Philly you couldn't even walk through the streets without ducking bullets and seeing niggas getting their brains blown out. Not to mention the open drug sales, prostitution, violent crimes commencing from broad daylight until the wee hours of the morning. Don't get it twisted, it went down where I lived, but not to the extent as it did in other places.

When we arrived on my block, I was relieved to see a few of the neighborhood kids playing football in front of the building across the street. I was prepared to offer them a deal they couldn't refuse: a hundred dollars apiece for them to carry all of Sophia's belongings into the house. Lifting and removing all of her things from out the condo had my back severely aching. When I got out of the car and waved them over with a few big-face hundred dollar bills, they raced over to see what had to be done to earn it.

As Sophia instructed the kids on how to carry her bags, I went up to unlock the front door and deactivate the alarm system. When I walked inside, I noticed a white envelope lying on the floor. I instantly became suspicious. For one, no mail ever came to my house; it always went straight to the Post Office box. Secondly, it had no postage or writing on it. Somebody had obviously walked up to my front door and slipped it through the mail slot. After picking it up, I carefully inspected it and discovered that there was a letter inside.

Before I got a chance to remove the letter, Sophia and the young bucks were coming through the door. Quickly tucking the letter away in my back pocket, I led the way to the master bedroom. It took about fifteen minutes for them to bring everything inside and upstairs. I paid them and they all ran out of the house hollering out something about new Jordans and Foot Locker. It felt good to know I had made their day.

Once we were alone, I gave Sophia a tour of the house. My crib wasn't balling out of control, but for a twenty-five-year-old street nigga, I was doing all right for myself. Better than most, yet striving to be the best I could be. My shit was indeed laid out.

The living room and dining room sat on top of onyx floors with an exotic Persian rug draped out in the center. A stretched black leather couch with a loveseat and marble table completed the living room with a homey comfort. Flat-screen TVs and monitors hung from the ceiling on a perfect angle so that one could comfortably view them from just about anywhere downstairs. I even had the fifty-gallon fish tank built into the wall with two baby sharks swimming around inside.

Besides the four-man Jacuzzi inside my bedroom, the rest of the crib was average. To say that I was up and coming would be an understatement. I was up and going! Sophia didn't seem to be all that impressed, but she damn sure didn't appear to be disappointed either. After the tour, I left her in the bedroom to tend to her unpacking.

Before I read the letter, I rewound the security surveillance in hopes of discovering who delivered it. The footage showed nothing but a masked man with a hoodie on dropping the mail through the slot before quickly leaving. Now why in the fuck would someone go through all these precautions just to drop some mail off? Somewhere in the back of my mind, something wasn't sitting right with this whole situation.

Upon reading the letter, I learned that it wasn't a letter at all. Someone had sent me a blackmail note. Many thoughts and people ran through my mind. With each second that passed, a rage of sheer violence was building up inside. The only thing that would relax my nerves was the shedding of blood and the death of my enemies. But since I was dealing with a faceless coward, everyone was suspect.

Reading the ransom note once more, I hoped to be able to read between the lines and figure out whose MO fit the contents of it.

It read:

The streets are watching your every move, little nigga! I must admit, that was some good driving the other day. I'm surprised you slipped away scot-free. Well, almost scot-free. Had you been on point, you would have peeped us following you and your goons around the hood all morning. Yeah, we seen the amateur work y'all put in, and we wasn't impressed in the least.

You ducked a lot of drama that morning. Had me and my people got our hands on you, shit would have been real ugly for you. And if the feds would have got their hands on you, they would have tried to give you a hundred years.

So, this is how it's going down. We figure had we hit you like we expected to, we would have easily got a few hundred thousand and a couple of birds. But now we're willing to quietly settle this for 150 stacks and four of those things. Or, we could just call the hotline, give up your name, and collect the reward money. That's right! You going to either pay us to shut the fuck up or them folks are going to pay us to talk. Your choice! You have forty-eight

hours to call this number or else we going to place a
call of our own. 215-555-0771.

   P.S. Don't keep us waiting!
   Remember we know where you lay, who you
fuck, and what you drive. You know nothing!

I could not believe the audacity of these niggas. What kind of shiesty shit were these clowns trying to pull off? I'd have rather they stuck to their original plan and try to succeed with robbery. But extortion and blackmail? They must ain't know who they were up against. These clowns talking about they been following me and watching my every move? Yeah, right! If they was watching my every move as they claimed to be, they must have been doing it from a satellite in space because there was no way I would allow a nigga to ever get the drop on me by following me. I watched the rearview mirror more than I did the road ahead of me.

After analyzing the situation, I strongly believed that the nigga who wrote and dropped the letter off was a crash dummy operating under someone else. The first person who came to mind was Shake. Reason being, he was the only person I told about the situation, and schemes like this was right down his alley. After the way he talked to me and treated me the other day, I wasn't putting shit past him.

Although I suspected that this extortion attempt was Shake's work, I wasn't exactly 100 percent certain. Something about that sneaky bitch, Felicia, just wasn't sitting right with me. The other day at breakfast, I believed that I may have exposed my hand by reacting as defensive as I did to her comment. The look she gave me afterward indicated that she suspected that I was involved. She definitely couldn't be ruled out as a suspect.

If anybody ever took anything from me, it was a bullet. That's the code I lived by and was willing to kill and die to maintain.

A true boss should always have two types of niggas on deck: a cold-blooded killer, and a strong man. My nigga, Gunner, was all of the above. He specialized in murder and shaking niggas down and was overly excited by those sorts of activities. With him, my life, health, status, and paper came before his own. To keep me ahead in life, and in the game, he was quick to take a nigga under, out, and over. This was definitely the kind of nigga to get kicked out of the zoo for scaring the animals! The nigga loved his work and was probably standing by his phone right now, praying that I called him with some business for him to go and handle.

If that was the case, then today was the day his prayers were going to be answered. Using a newly purchased prepaid cell phone, I gave Gunner a call. When he picked up, I spoke short and brief.

"Big fellow. You know who this is. I need to get up with you ASAP. Meet me over at the joint in ten minutes."

"Say no more, my nigga. I'm on my way," he replied. The tone of his voice was dangerous in itself. It was cold enough to breathe on a drop of water and turn it into an ice cube.

Chapter 9

The place I referred to as "the joint" was Big Sal's car wash on Fortieth Street. As I turned into the entrance, everything appeared to be running normal like any other car wash in the ghetto. That's exactly what Big Sal wanted any imposters and outsiders to think. Meanwhile, inside, all sorts of illegal transactions were being conducted. Criminals and drug dealers trusted to do their business here because Big Sal guaranteed that no one would be robbed, killed, or set up in any form or fashion while on his premises.

To ensure that his operations ran smoothly, there was a state-of-the-art system installed inside that could detect any and all irregular frequencies associated with wires or other listening devices. On top of that, he kept a dozen or so of his men on guard, covering the entire perimeter with heavy artillery in hand. If any of Big Sal's rules were violated or one was found to be in possession of a listening device, they wouldn't make it out to the other side. The fee for the service was one hundred dollars a minute, which also included the actual washing of your car.

As I pulled into the line, I was first acknowledged and cleared by the outside workers before being granted access inside. When I pulled inside, I saw Gunner getting patted down before they allowed him to get into my car. This was another practiced precaution that was respected and understood by all who used Big Sal's car wash to conduct business. Better safe than sorry, especially when discussing something as serious as murder.

After Gunner took a seat in the passenger side, he extended his hand and gave me a tight-gripped, manly shake. This big, black, Freeway-the-rapper-looking nigga was the closest thing I had to a friend. Our relationship and arrangements were mainly business, but the bond we established over fifteen years ago made us brothers by heart.

Me and Gunner went way back to our early days of adolescence.

Having come from a broken home with negligent drug-addicted parents, Gunner used to travel from his South Philly neighborhood down to my hood in hopes of catching a sweet vic to rob, just so he could get a meal for the night. If he couldn't find a young hustler to beat up and take their money, he would run up on someone's mother, push her to the ground, and snatch her pocketbook before he went home with an empty stomach. Most of the youngsters in my hood were scared to death of him.

Besides the stories I had heard about him, I didn't know him, never met him, nor did we ever cross paths. In the event that we ever did, I had a .25 Beretta with a nine-shot clip waiting on him to come try his luck with me. I didn't have to wait too long before we finally caught up with each other.

One afternoon, Shake had me watching his car while he went inside the pizza parlor to use the pay phone. Shortly after he went inside, Gunner came running out of nowhere with a brick in his hand, smashing it through Shake's car window. Immediately afterward, he snatched up the leather jacket that was hanging over the passenger seat, then took off running. With no hesitation, I pulled out my gun and ran after him.

I eventually caught up with him a few blocks away in an alley. As fast as he ran, I damn near lost him. Had

I not made a calculated guess that he had ran through the alley, he would've been long gone. Sweating, tired, and out of breath, I slowly walked up on him while aiming my gun in the direction of his face. I noticed a big sandwich bag filled with what I assumed to be coke hanging out of his front pocket. I also witnessed him pull out a large wad of bills from the inside pocket of the leather jacket. Either he didn't notice me walking up on him pointing a gun in his face, or he didn't care. Unfazed by me or the deadly weapon, I personally thought he just didn't give a fuck and had a death wish.

Moving straight past the talking and theatrics, I bust off two shots a few inches over the top of his head to see if that would get his full attention. It was enough to break him out of his trance, but still I couldn't detect a trace of fear or worry. I honestly thought that I was going to catch my first body right then and there. If the gun or warning shots weren't enough reason, then there simply wasn't any reasoning. I had to kill this nigga for violating my father's property.

I was prepared to do so, but scared to do it. Not that I feared the physical or spiritual consequences, but the mental and emotional aspects sort of spooked me out. With the gun shaking in my hand, I slowly began to apply pressure on the trigger. Suddenly, out of nowhere, this crackhead motherfucka named Jack emerged from a nearby abandoned car, interrupting the work that I was on the verge of putting in.

"Amin, is that you? What the fuck is going on back here?" he asked while wiping cold out of his eyes with his fingers. It became apparent that the shots had disrupted his sleep and probably blew his high as well.

"I'll tell you what's going on. This thieving-ass nigga broke into Shake's car and stole money, a leather jacket, and drugs. And if he doesn't give it back, I'm going to

leave his ass stinking back here." I gave one final fair warning, while extending my shoulder and repositioning the gun with a shooter's posture.

Upon the mention of drugs and money, Jack's eyes got as big as golf balls. Once he scanned Gunner and saw the possessions for himself, he volunteered to retrieve the goods for me.

"You don't need a gun for this young punk. When people hear gunshots, they call the police. I keep me a silent killer just for situations like this. Watch and learn, li'l nigga," he boasted before removing a switchblade and lunging toward Gunner full speed.

With one swift flick of the wrist, Jack slicked Gunner across the face and threw him to the ground. Afterward, he snatched the drugs and money and began kicking Gunner in the face and stomach. During the beating, Gunner made no attempt to defend himself nor did he utter a word seeking relief or mercy. He lay there and took it as if he was exempt from emotions, pain, or suffering. Until this very day, I'd never seen anything like it.

After Jack concluded the ass whipping that Gunner was sure to remember for the rest of his life, he walked over to me and handed me Shake's belongings. When I reached out to accept them, I got an unexpected surprise instead. In one quick motion, Jack smacked the gun out of my hand and began swinging his knife at my chest and neck. Had I not backed up, ducked up and down, and weaved, the nigga would have taken my head off.

Eventually, he backed me into a corner, leaving me with nowhere to run and no room to move. That's when his true colors came out.

"This ain't personal, young buck, but I got to cut you and kill you," he declared with a smile that showed his rotten yellow teeth. "This here is enough crack and money to keep me and one of my fine ladies high for a good long time. I might just drop by on your mother. I'm sure she can use the comfort after learning that her baby boy got his throat sliced from ear to ear. Now take it like a man."

At that point, all I could do was close my eyes and prepare to die. I just hoped that it would be fast. That's when I heard two gunshots followed by a loud thump. When I opened my eyes, Gunner was standing over Jack, kicking him in the face as he pleaded for his life.

"Please, young buck, don't do this to me. It's the drugs, man. They got me all fucked up. I never meant to hurt you. Just let me go get help—"

His pleas fell on deaf ears. Gunner stood over him, pointed the gun in his face, and emptied the clip into his head. Even as Jack lay bloodied and dead on the ground, Gunner still delivered a hard kick to his face before snatching the drugs and money from out of his dead hand.

Focusing his attention on me, he stared me up and down for a few odd seconds before throwing the sandwich bag filled with drugs in my direction. Once it was in my hands he stated the terms attached to it.

"This money and this pistol should compensate me for my trouble of saving your life and catching this body. Fair exchange ain't robbery, right?" he stated with a smile while wiping the blood off of his face.

"You right. But we need to get up out of this alley before the police come," I replied before tucking the drugs into my pocket.

"Cool! You go your way and I'll go mine. But if for some reason you feel the need to get up with me, just come down South Philly to Twenty-first and Segal Street. I ain't hard to find."

Shortly after that day, Gunner not only became my personal hit man, but also a very close friend whom I trusted with my life.

As I explained the dilemma to Gunner, he gave me his undivided attention and listened closely without interruption until it was his turn to speak. When that time came, he spoke his mind straight to the point without any sugarcoating or holding back.

"Damn, Boss. On some real shit, it ain't enough Tylenol in the world for these type of headaches. Me, personally? I say, fuck all the detective work. That shit for the police. I say we off whoever you suspect had something to do with it and let God sort them out. Real quick and easy, you dig?"

"I feel you, big fellow, but that will still leave the niggas who wrote the note breathing and able to do me the same type of damage or worse. So, I think we need to catch up with them first. I'm sure you can find a way to get the truth of the whos, whats and whys out of them," I knowingly insinuated.

"Say no more, my nigga. Go ahead and give them what they asked for. I'll take it from there. Just call me before you make the drop."

Chapter 10

Meanwhile, back over at the Boss's house, Sophia was already taking advantage of the luxuries of her new home. As she sat in the captain's chair inside the hot, relaxing Jacuzzi, the jet streams seemed to work magic as they shot up and down her back, providing a massage that temporarily relieved the tension and stress she had been under the last few months. She still found it hard to believe that she'd agreed to such an odd arrangement with a complete stranger in one night. But the way Boss laid his game down, he was hard to be denied. Besides game, she could deny neither his looks nor swagger, which were on a thousand plus!

What was most important and beneficial about this new arrangement of hers was the fact that Boss was a hustler making fast money. That alone made him a perfect replacement for Victor. In fact, it was Victor himself who had been trying to convince her for months to go out and find a baller who could provide her wants and needs with ease. He only asked one thing in return. She promised him she would fulfill his request but deep down inside she didn't know if it was something she could do. Only time could tell. But for now she had to do *her*.

"'My life . . . my life . . . my life,'" she quoted the chorus of Mary J. Blige's hit single. With all of the drama she'd been through and still had to overcome, the song reflected how she truly felt inside. With tears in her eyes she clearly realized that love was a motherfucka and life was a bitch.

"Well, Boss may not be Tony Montana with the mansion and the tiger, but he got the money, a nice house, and some sharks. I guess that's a start," Sophia thought out loud before allowing her hands to fall under the water and begin to caress the insides of her thighs.

Upon my arrival back home, the sounds of passionate moans and the Jacuzzi's motor awaited me as soon as I stepped foot in the door. Surprise, arousal, and curiosity overcame me all at once. I knew the sounds came from Sophia, but I needed to find out what was making her bring that freak side out. God forgive me for my perverted nature, but this was a must-see!

Quickly picking up the remote control for the security monitors, I cut the power on and immediately viewed the screen that fed live footage from the hidden camera in my bedroom. What I saw was better than any porno I ever watched in my life and she was on the solo!

With both of her legs spread over the rim of the Jacuzzi, she worked her middle with her right hand while the other lifted her breast up to her mouth so that she could suck and lick her nipple. The expression on her face was the sexiest thing I'd ever seen. The swelling in my pants was rock hard, begging to be relieved. I had no choice but to whip it out and masturbate right then and there as Sophia worked it out on the screen. It didn't take long for her to reach a climax, and the second I saw and heard the indicators I released one of my own.

"Damn, bitch! Yeah, take that dick!" I heard myself saying as I exploded all over the place. Although something like this was a first for me, I must admit I found it to be enjoyable *and* satisfying. On top of that, it made we want to fuck Sophia even more. Baby girl was a stone-cold freak. I had to have her. In situations like this, I always got what I wanted!

Later that night, me and Sophia had a few drinks, smoked a dutch of kush, and then ate some Chinese food. Afterward, we watched *American Gangster* on the big flat screen inside the living room. Sophia seemed to be fascinated by the movie, but to me, it was just another story about an old timer who had it before he ratted. Besides, I was really living through half of the shit they claimed to have done. My life was a movie in itself.

That night me and Sophia fell asleep on the couch. When I awoke in the middle of the night, I discovered that she was cuddled up in my arms, with her face pressed up against my chest. My right arm was around her waist, just below the arch of her back. The exotic smell of cucumbers and melons that lingered on her body left me to wonder if that "thing" tasted the way it smelled. The temperature seemed to have gone from sixty to one hundred in a matter of a few seconds. But the temperature wasn't the only thing on the rise.

Sophia must have felt my hardness pressed up against her because she woke up out of her sleep in a confused state. I lay there pretending to be asleep, just to see her reaction. I even snored lightly for added effect.

At first, she turned her body around as if she was trying to distance herself from the one-eyed monster's radius. At least, that's what I thought she was doing. But when I felt her hand reach down and measure my length from top to bottom with her fingers, I realized she was sizing me up. If I was hearing correctly, I thought I heard her say, "Ummm, umm, umm," before giggling and leaning her ass back up against it. This time, she positioned herself so that my hardness pressed straight through those black tight spandex pants she wore, and sat right on top of her vagina.

It took all the resistance inside me not to flip her ass over and fuck her until she was motionless. But there was a time and place for everything, and my day and time was sure to come, literally! Here it was she done made me come twice in one day and I ain't even touch the pussy yet. For that, she was going down in my books as the baddest bitch alive!

The following morning, I awoke to breakfast in bed. Even though I was still on the couch, it was the thought that mattered. It wasn't no ghetto-ass, hood rat breakfast either. Baby girl counted calories, protein intake, cholesterol, and all that other health shit. We ate cheese omelets, hash browns, fruits, and freshly squeezed grapefruit juice. It was different, but it was delicious and something I could definitely get used to.

Among the many other things about Sophia that I found special was how she woke up in the morning still as beautiful as she was when she went to sleep. Her natural beauty was so amazing. She could have jumped straight out of the bed, entered a beauty contest, and been crowned Miss America without even trying. Don't get it twisted, I'd had some of the baddest bitches from all sorts of ethnicities, and nationalities, but none of them could stand shoulder to shoulder with Sophia on her worst day.

Something about her presence gave me motivation and the belief that I could conquer anything I set my mind to. Baby girl was bringing out the best in me. My ambition was back; now it was time to remind the streets how and why I earned my position and the name to go along with it.

Chapter 11

That afternoon, Sophia went to the King of Prussia Mall to satisfy her "daily shopping craving" as she called it. Shortly after she left, I used a brand-new prepaid cell phone to call the number on the note. I was anxious to quickly get this shit over and done with so I could put it behind me and have those responsible put six feet underneath me. For these clowns to dare attempt to get in the way of my visions and set me back from chasing the American dream, I was about to send them a nightmare that didn't require them to be asleep. Yup, the end results would have them stretched out with their eyes closed, laid up in a box!

The nigga who answered the phone sounded so high and stupid, I doubted that he even remembered he was supposed to be expecting my call.

"Yo, who this?"

"Hold the fuck up!" Never mind the shock and disbelief, my *anger* started to get the best of me. "Y'all niggas putting notes in my mailbox and wasn't expecting me to call and straighten this out?" I barked into the phone receiver.

As I awaited a response, I heard some whispering in the background before someone else got on the line.

"Look, check this out here, nigga. Don't ever question our work. Who the fuck is you? Furthermore, the term is non-negotiable. Therefore, you have one hour to bring a bag with what we requested down to Fifteenth and York. In the middle of the block, there is an abandoned van.

Throw the bag inside and keep it moving," he instructed with authority. "Remember, your every move is being watched. So one wrong move, and it will be your last."

I could tell this clown done read one too many of El-Sadik Bank's books. It was unfortunate that niggas out here was inspired to make moves based on what people were writing, rapping, or filming. What they failed to realize was the fact that life was real and wasn't no coming back from death. Yet murder was the number one consequence for the actions that transpired on the regular in the hood.

I didn't appreciate the way the other nigga talked to me. That only added insult to injury. For that, I wanted to personally hear him plead for his life before he died, just to contradict the gangster he pretended to be.

When I contacted Gunner and gave him the scoop on what was about to go down, his reply was short and simple. "Say no more. I'm on top of it." Those words always provided me with security and assurance that the matter would be taken care of with promptness and priority.

After packing the money and work into a small book bag, I drove down North Philly to make the drop.

Once I arrived at the location, I approached with extreme caution. One hand on the steering wheel with the other tightly clinched around the Glock .40 sitting on my lap. The block was completely empty. Besides a few standing houses, the rest were either abandoned, boarded, or burned up. Junk cars and other garbage lined the streets and sidewalks. It was obvious why these niggas in North Philly was so scandalous and foul, they were bred and raised in filth.

Pulling alongside the van that the nigga described, I threw the ransom inside and kept it moving. Knowing that Gunner was somewhere in the cut watching everything unfold, I laughed at myself as I imagined the look on them niggas' faces before Gunner took their lives.

Chapter 12

From the second-floor window of Rudd's mother's house, he and Bey surveyed the block in close observation. Two fully loaded AR-15s were leaned up against the wall within arm's reach from where they sat. If Boss was to try anything stupid, the powerful assault rifles would see to it that he or his car didn't make it off the block. When they spotted his Porsche drive down the street, they were prepared to do any of three things: shoot it out, kill, or collect their ransom.

"That's what the fuck I'm talking about, nigga! I told you he was going to go for it. A threat of a federal beef will turn the hardest nigga softer than a cotton swab," Rudd boasted.

"That nigga went for the banana in the tailpipe!" Bey replied as the two shared a laugh and a high five.

For the next ten minutes the crime partners continued to watch the block from the window. They were looking for any signs that would indicate that a setup was in motion. They saw nothing that appeared to be out of the ordinary or otherwise suspicious.

"Grab one of those AR-15s and watch my back while I go get the bag. If you see something that don't look right, air it the fuck out," Rudd ordered. "I'm trying to hurry up and count this paper, and break it down before my mom's nosy ass gets home."

"Let's make it happen then, my nigga. I'm trying to hit South Street and pop a few tags, get a tat, and buy a piece of jewelry or two. We got to go out and stunt tonight," Bey declared before picking up the AR-15 and leading the way downstairs.

Just like the typical nigga, there he was spending money that wasn't even in his possession yet. On top of that, he talking about going out and splurging with the ransom money the same day he came up on it? How stupid, disrespectful and reckless could he be?

Immediately after receiving the call from Boss, Gunner was en route to North Philly. Murder was on the top of his agenda as he sped in and out of traffic through the inner-city streets. For the tasks that lay ahead of him, he brought along his three most lethal accessories of murder: Bloody Mary, Medusa, and his .500 Magnum, aka "the one hit acquitter." Bloody Mary and Medusa were his two treacherous female red nose pit bulls. They were highly trained killers with an attack so vicious they often would sever the limbs of their victims with their powerful, deadly jaws. And the .500 Magnum? It's one of the most powerful handguns known to man.

From a parking space on the corner of Fourteenth and York Street, Gunner sat slouched back in the driver's seat of his Yukon with a pair of binoculars. From there, he had a perfect view of the entire Fifteenth and York block. With his objective under close scope, he waited patiently for everything to unfold.

Once he observed Boss come through and make the drop, he knew that the moment of reckoning was approaching. A few minutes later, he spotted an unknown black male come out of one of the houses and retrieve the book bag while his accomplice stood at the door, holding by his side what appeared to be an assault rifle. The scene reminded him of a rat that unknowingly eats poison that satisfies his hunger for a moment, only to kill him in a little while later. If only they knew how short-lived their newly found riches would be, they would be trying to get closer to their Lord and seek His forgiveness for their sins while they still had a chance.

Not even thirty minutes later the two men emerged from the property with mighty fat pockets and extra swagger in their step. It appeared that they had nowhere near the entire ransom in their possession, just a small portion of it. That told Gunner two important things. For one, that the remainder of the drugs and money was still inside the house, and secondly, they were sure to return back for it shortly. Niggas ain't just leave that sort of money lying around for too long unattended, especially in North Philly.

After breaking down cash money as if they were Birdman himself, the two crime partners filled their pockets with over ten grand apiece before putting the rest up, and going on a quick splurging spree down on South Street. They purchased everything from the latest cargo pants, True Religion jeans, Polo shirts, Jordan shoes, et cetera. But, that was only the beginning. To further celebrate their biggest heist ever, they both went ahead and got tattoos that read GET RICH, THE FAST WAY! with a tattooed icon of the Looney Tunes Yosemite Sam underneath it holding two guns and a bandana covering his face. Their splurging spree wasn't complete until they went and paid Joe's Jewelers a visit. There they purchased iced-out TechnoMarine watches for a few thousand apiece.

In their minds, they were back. Therefore it was only right that they went out and stunted. The way they saw it, they had to show off their money in order to stay respected and relevant in their professions. In the hood, if you claim to be a crook and wasn't out every night buying out the bar, making it rain, or stunting in general, then people automatically assumed that you didn't have it to do so. In that instance you would be considered just another "broke, in-the-way-ass nigga."

"Don't go in here and be in this motherfuckin' bathroom all night like bitches do. Wash your ass, get dressed, and get out!" Rudd complained before they walked inside his mother's house.

"Stop bitching, nigga! I'm an ugly nigga, so it takes me a little longer to get myself together. Everybody ain't as pretty as you," Bey replied, as he set his bags down and went to switch on the living room light.

Before he could fully extend his arm to the wall, he noticed two pair of glowing eyes staring from the darkness. At first he thought they belonged to cats but on second thought, he didn't recall any cats ever being in the house or his mother mentioning anything about getting no cats. Slightly confused, he quickly flicked the switch on so he could get a better look.

At that moment, all hell broke loose!

"Get 'em girls!" Gunner commanded from the dark shadows of the hallway. Having removed the light bulbs from the fixtures, the darkness put the men at a great disadvantage, because the dogs could see just as well in the dark as they could in the light, while they couldn't see hardly anything.

Upon their master's command, Medusa and Bloody Mary attacked the would-be extortionists with astonishing speed and accuracy. Their method of attack was always straight for their enemies' necks, knocking the men down to the ground before tearing away their flesh with their sharp, deadly teeth. Had they been commanded to actually kill, they would have locked their powerfully strong jaws around their victims' throats and crushed them until they suffocated. But for the time being, Gunner wanted these guys alive.

While they were on the ground fighting to breathe and stay alive, Gunner frisked them down for weapons. One of them was armed with a holstered .357 Magnum. It was quickly removed and placed on his own hip. Surely it would be among his personal arsenal collection before the end of the night.

With the assistance of his dogs, Gunner was able to drag the men into the basement. The entire time, they screamed, hollered, and cried like bitches. Blood flowed profusely from the large puncture wounds and other injuries on their necks. But that wasn't even the half of it. Rudd's mother was already down in the basement, tied up with her eyes and mouth duct taped. She had been waiting all night for them to come and join the party.

Over the next five minutes, the pit bulls continued to carry out their fierce attacks on the two men. As they mangled, twisted, and mauled away at fingers, hands, arms, and ankles, Gunner watched on with admiration, excitement, and pride. It was as if he were a proud father watching his children walking down a graduation aisle with honor.

With only the clap of his hands, the dogs immediately abandoned their attacks and stood by their master's side with humbleness.

The after effects of the attack left the two men badly wounded and in excruciating pain. They lay there on the ground twitching and lightly moaning. They made sounds that resembled that of a woman who had just been raped.

For their exhilarating performance Medusa and Bloody Mary were rewarded with their favorite doggie treat and their master's affection.

"That's my girls! Yes, y'all are! I love my babies. Good job, girls!" He spoke in his best baby voice, while rubbing down the canines' bellies. In a split second he shifted his attention from the dogs to the former extortionists.

"So which one of you niggas going to be the first to talk?" he asked before taking the Magnum off of his hip. "Who sent y'all?" he yelled.

"Who the fuck is you? And what the fuck is you talking about?" Rudd asked with fear and confusion. He was in so much pain that it was a struggle for him to even speak.

"Oh, yeah? I guess y'all never heard of Boss then . . . huh? I guess the money and drugs I found in the book bag inside the bedroom ain't the same ones he dropped earlier either, right? You want to insult my motherfuckin' intelligence?" he shouted before lifting his pistol to Rudd's mother's head and pulling the trigger.

The shot that rang out resembled the sound of thunder clapping. Her head exploded open, leaving behind what looked like a busted-open watermelon.

"No! Mom . . . No!" Rudd cried out loud. "That's my mom, motherfucka! What the fuck did you do? Why the . . . You're a fuckin' dead man!"

"Hold up, homie." Bey spoke up for the first time since they had entered the house. "Ain't no sense in lying, we did it! But ain't nobody send us to do shit. We ain't no crash dummies. We put in our own work! Now you done already killed my man's mom and let your dogs go crazy on us. We willing to just charge it all to the game and let bygones be bygones. You go your way, we go ours," he suggested.

"Shut the fuck up, Bey! You stupid-ass nigga, can't you see that this nigga's gonna kill us regardless?" Rudd spoke reality to his partner before going haywire on Gunner. "Fuck you! Bitch-ass, coldhearted, coward-ass nigga! We ain't telling you shit. It's going to the grave with us. Kill us, nigga, 'cause I'ma be waiting for you in hell!"

At that point, Gunner had heard enough to determine that Shake was most likely not involved with these two characters. They were too unorganized and reckless. Boss must have been slipping big time to allow these savages to get close enough to him to pull off what they did. Had Shake been involved, they wouldn't have been able to spend a dime of the money until he got his cut off the top.

On the other hand, Felicia could not be exonerated, nor associated with the plot. It was Boss's call as to what was to happen next.

After contacting him and voicing his views and opinions concerning the matter, he was given his final orders. As requested, Gunner kept the call connected and on speaker phone, allowing Boss to hear the pit bulls as they went in for the kill. Both men were choked to death in a matter of seconds.

After the kill, the animals returned to their master's side to receive a treat. The faint smell of death was present on their breaths and the color of it was painted over their teeth and mouths. Together, they left the house as quickly and quietly as when they came in, leaving behind a scene so gruesome that it would put Charles Manson to shame.

Chapter 13

As the great hip hop legend Tupac Shakur once said and was later quoted, "Revenge is like the sweetest joy, next to getting pussy!" He never lied. Having heard these faggots breathe their last breath out of the same mouth they once talked that fly extortion shit with gave me great satisfaction. I don't knock a nigga's hustle, but when it's me who's being hustled, niggas are going to have a problem!

I agreed with some of the things Gunner said. I still had strong doubts that these niggas acted alone. I refused to believe that some local stick-up boys had enough sense or courage to get the drop on me without getting help from someone close to me. That meant from here on out everybody was under close scope, and getting treated with the same respect that I showed my enemies. I would never again put myself in a position where I could become vulnerable to another nigga's plot. From now on, my phone wasn't even getting answered unless it was strictly about money. No more social or recreational conversations, or visits.

I knew it was only a matter of time before somebody discovered those niggas' bodies. They were probably already decomposing and stinking up the whole neighborhood. I couldn't wait to stake out at their funerals. I figured if someone had enough courage to put batteries in their back and send them up against me, then they were likely to attend their funerals. Just so they could personally witness the aftermath of my anger.

Chapter 14

With everything that I had already been through this past week, I felt that it was necessary that I not only change the manner in which I conducted myself on the street, but the sceneries and vehicles needed to be switched up as well. With that at the top of my agenda, I headed to the suburbs to pay my man Alan, over at the Luxury Autos, a visit. He was the owner of one of the most prestigious dealerships in the area, and him and I had developed a respectable business arrangement over the past year or so.

For $15,000 every three months, I had access to every car on his lot. From the Bentleys, BMWs, Benzes, Porches, Rolls-Royces, et cetera . . . Whenever I got tired of the car that I was driving, all I had to do was take it back to the lot and trade it in for something else. With connections like these, who needed friends? Certainly not me!

The first car that caught my eye when I pulled onto the lot was the money green BMW 760i. If I ever felt like a car was personally designed for me, it would without a doubt have been this particular car. Picturing myself rolling in the spacious luxury machine was all it took. I was sold! This was definitely the car I was going to drive off the lot with.

Not once did I take the time to consider what type of message I would be sending to the streets when I drove through the hood in a big toy such as this. Truth be told, I loved to shit on every hater who possessed envy and jealousy in their hearts for me. I loved reminding them that I was doing better than them and that they could never do what I did. It was fascinating how their faces would break up when I came through in these toys and would always jump out with all this fly shit on. If looks could kill, I would have been dead a long time ago.

Niggas was going to hate regardless of what I did, so why not! With that said, I pulled that pretty motherfucka off the lot without a worry in the world. I know I was supposed to be trying to break bad habits, but it wasn't going to happen overnight.

Since I was right around the corner from my favorite jewelry store, Starlite Jewelers, I decided to stop and see if they had a nice new piece that I could purchase for a special friend. Having previously done business with the Colombian owners on multiple occasions, I was considered a regular customer and treated with the utmost priority the moment I stepped through the door. Just as real recognize real, so did money recognize money!

When I explained to the jewelers that I was interested in buying a gift for a female friend, they automatically assumed that I was looking for an engagement ring and pulled out a display of diamond rings. Although they were some mighty fine and elegant pieces, I had to let them know that marriage was not on my agenda; I just wanted something that would put a smile on a woman's face. That's when they produced a case of diamond bracelets. The stones inside were of all different shapes, sizes, and colors. I purchased the most expensive one. It had an assortment of multi-colored diamonds, including pink, and was as thick as a handcuff. It may have set me back twenty stacks, but it was sure to put me a few steps ahead with Sophia.

Upon my arrival back home, I was surprised to walk into the house and see that Sophia had turned my living room into her personal exercise gym. Ace Hood's club-banger "Hustle Hard" blasted through the stereo as my baby girl put her thing down with some intense aerobics. She had her hair in a long ponytail, and wore a bodysuit that was tight enough to cut off her circulation. The way she stretched, bent, and worked her body showed that she had flexibility and super endurance. I couldn't wait to find out.

As I stood there watching her, she seemed to step the intensity of the workout up a notch or two. I believed she saw me standing in the doorway, but was trying to pretend as if she didn't. It was as if she went from aerobics to exotic dancing in a single workout. I thought, *fuck all this foreplay, I want to fuck!*

When the song was over, I walked up behind her and put my hands around her waist. "Slow down, baby, before you hurt something. You up in here all hot and sweaty. Here, let me give you something to help cool you off." I had to smooth talk her before removing the bracelet from my pocket and placing it on her wrist.

She responded by jumping up and down and screaming at the top of her lungs.

Now that's what I call a chain reaction!

"Oh my God! Boss, this is the most beautiful piece of jewelry I've ever seen. It must've cost thousands and thousands of dollars," she estimated in a state of disbelief. "You went out and bought this for me? This is the sweetest thing anyone has ever done for me!"

That's when she gave me that look that I knew all too well, the one look where females would bite down on their lip trying to suppress their desires. As she struggled to fight her urges, I ripped her bodysuit open and made them irresistible. With her breasts exposed, I pushed them together and sucked on both nipples at the same time. Almost immediately, I felt her nipples swell up in my mouth. At that point, satisfying her desires became my number one priority.

That was when she pushed me against the wall and dropped to her knees. As she unbuttoned my pants, she licked her tongue across her lips with a profound hunger. Once she freed Willie, she scanned it from top to bottom as if it was the first time she had ever seen one. From there, she proceeded to lick the sides of it teasingly while staring deeply into my eyes. The warmth of her soft, wet tongue and heavy breathing sent chills down my spine.

Having had enough of the foreplay and the teasing, I grabbed the back of her ponytail with one hand, while the other guided my penis into her mouth. Surprisingly, she took the entire length to the bottom of her throat, held it in, then came up for air before going back under, repeating it over and over again. Each time she went down, she came back up faster. In no time, she had found her rhythm.

There was no way I could last under these circumstances. First my knees got weak; then my legs began to wobble. If I didn't hurry up and find a distraction to take my mind and eyes off of what she was doing (plus the way she was doing it) I was going to bust all inside of her mouth. I thought that staring at the ceiling would give me the strength to hold back, but I was wrong.

I tried to give her the courtesy of pulling out with the intentions of busting over her fully exposed titties, but she wasn't having it. She locked her lips tightly around me, hugged her arms around my lower back, and continued to deliver the best head I had ever had. From the way she moaned and the reaction of her body, I was able to determine two things: first, that she was so turned on by giving head that she'd also had an orgasm in the process, and secondly, that she was definitely a pro!

Even after benefiting from the amazing performance Sophia had delivered, I was still up and ready to go. But with me, taste came before touch, and my mouth was literally watering for it. Gently laying her down onto the Persian rug, I began ripping off the remainder of her body suit. My tongue had no patience in situations like this.

As she lay there completely nude, I took a brief second to admire the beauty of her face, body, and figure, before I went face first in between her thighs. There I encountered her fully shaved, glossy, peach-colored vagina. When I pushed her legs slightly back, the lips on it popped out in my face. With the tip of my tongue, I pressed it against the wet slit of her vagina, and stuck it inside as far as it could go. Slow and gently.

It was a bit salty at first because of the sweat from her workout, but once her natural juices began flowing, it got as sweet as honey. Turning my tongue sideways and up and down, I explored all the dimensions of her insides. From her reaction I knew that I was pleasing her in ways she hadn't been pleased in for a while. She moaned songs of pure ecstasy and pleasure while trying to escape me using her back and elbows. To prevent the escape, I locked my arms around her waist and directed all my tongue's attention to her clit.

Starting off with slow circles, I soon progressed to faster ones. Before I knew it, she was shaking and shivering as if she were suffering from hypothermia. With both of her hands behind my head, she scratched it, massaged it, and damn near pushed it up inside of her. Suddenly, the muscles in her pussy started to constrict and pulsate on and around my tongue. The orgasm she released soon afterward covered my mouth, lips, and beard with her feminine juices. Not one drop of it went to waste, as I slurped up as much as I could, before giving her a taste of herself with a juicy kiss to her mouth.

As I prepared to put the finishing touch on her, I first pushed her legs back as far as they could go, so far that her ankles were touching her ears. Entering her very gently, I encountered extraordinary wetness and tightness on impact. I felt her insides stretching to take on my full length and width. But after a few strokes, the fit was made. From there I was given more liberty to go faster, deeper, and harder.

To my surprise, she kept up with me, threw it back, and stayed wet the entire time. With a pussy as good as hers, there was no pulling out. Therefore, I extended as deep as I could into the back of her womb and came as hard and long as I ever had in my life. She came before, during, and afterward. Full of exhaustion, we collapsed right there on the living room floor and rested in each other's arms.

If that was how baby girl responded to gifts, I couldn't wait to see what she was going to do the next time I bought her something exclusive.

Chapter 15

As I had promised, later that night I took Sophia out to a local bar out by West Philly called Top Shelves. This place was a cross breed between a sports bar and a night club. Major niggas from all over the city of Philadelphia showed up to this place on a regular basis to flaunt their wealth by "poppin'" bottles, buying out the bar, and occasionally making it rain money. Besides the ballers, the "sack chasers" and "gold diggers" were always in the building, scheming on niggas while alluring them with their fat asses, tight clothes, and long weaves.

When Sophia saw that I switched it up from the Porsche to the big-boy BMW, she told me that I had a great taste for luxury. Once she witnessed the comfort and performance of the European-crafted machinery, she was set on purchasing one herself. If she acted right, I might just make that her next gift. But first she had to at least be on "wifey" status.

Dressed in the latest designer apparel, Sophia and I walked through the front door of Top Shelves hand in hand. She wore a tight-fitting red Juicy Couture sweat suit with a pair of four-inch high-heeled red bottoms. The way she was killing it in the sweat suit, it was only right that I became an accessory and murdered it in the black-on-red Prada suit with the matching footwear and sunglasses.

Besides the exclusive wardrobes, our jewelry had motherfuckas tucking theirs in. Not one cloud existed in either of our stones. They were as clean as HDTV. Fuck blinging, our shit was blamming! Especially Sophia's wrist. Her brand-new bracelet sparkled rainbow reflections over the walls and in the faces of the envious ones who stared with sheer hatred.

As we walked back toward the VIP section, we must have passed a dozen or so women who had shared my bed with me at one time point or another. There was "big butt Khalilah," "wet pussy Dana," "dick swallowing Angel," and "all night Ericka." Nicknaming all of my bitches based on their best sexual characteristics was the only way I could remember their actual names. They all were content with our arrangement and never stepped out of line. But tonight they gave me that surprised look, and stared Sophia down from head to toe as we passed by them.

There probably wasn't a bitch in the building who didn't wish that they were in her shoes, walking hand in hand with the one and only true Boss. The way she strutted across the floor with her head held high displayed such confidence and even a touch of arrogance. She knew with certainty that not one bitch in there could hold up with her on her worst day! She played her position as a boss bitch, and acknowledged that she was with a boss nigga.

As always, my guest and I were quickly seated at a table in the VIP section with chilled bottles of champagne awaiting our arrival. The bar buyout was five grand, which I paid with ease. Everybody got tipsy whenever Boss came out. I wouldn't have it any other way.

As I was sitting there sipping on a glass of Dom P, and enjoying the music, I watched all the hating-ass niggas giving me the ice grill, yet sipping on champagne, beer, and liquor that I bought for them. I just sat back and laughed at them. These grimy-ass niggas out there couldn't stand to see another nigga winning and celebrating their successes, especially if it "outshined" them!

Even in the company of all these haters, I still managed to have a good time, thanks to Sophia who was by my side the whole night. If she hadn't been with me I would have been gone.

Suddenly, out of nowhere, this bitch Felicia pops up and gets straight to screaming all in Sophia's face. This bitch was obviously drunk. As she talked she spit all over the place.

"Do you even know this nasty-ass bitch, Boss?" Sophia asked while standing up to defend herself. "You better get this ho, before I—"

"Have a seat, baby. Let me handle this," I replied before picking up a bottle and standing up. I shook the bottle up several times before spraying her down like a stray dog. Champagne shot in her face and in her weave on contact.

"Bitch! What the fuck is wrong with you, bringing your ghetto ass over here violating my space? Get your dirty ass the fuck out of here," I shouted as I continued to splash champagne in her face.

As the champagne began to fizzle down the bottle, it was as if the entire room, including Felicia, froze. After this bitch caused a scene, everybody in the bar was now looking at me like I had done something wrong. When in all actuality she was the one who had started the fiasco. I heard a few people in the crowd talking shit like, "That's fucked up!" and "Why is he doing that to that poor girl?" But, for all I cared they could get some too! To make matters worse, Sophia was now looking at me with disgust, as if to say, "Damn! These are the types of bitches you out here fucking?"

Before I even had the chance to explain myself, here came this lame-ass nigga running over to play super save a ho! After asking Felicia if she was okay, he pushed her aside and directed his full attention toward me.

"Spray me with some champagne you bitch-ass nigga," he challenged before reaching toward his waist.

Big mistake! At that point the "shoot first, ask questions later" policy was in full effect. I had no more champagne in the bottle so instead I decided to pull out the Glock .40 off my hip and squeezed off a few shots in his chest. Those who knew who I was took flight first, long before it was even a possibility for the confrontation to escalate to violent shooting. Those who ain't know any better had to learn the hard way.

As the frightened partygoers ran and dove for cover, we quickly got up and blended in with the large crowd. Once we made it outside, the police and ambulance sirens could be heard approaching from a distance.

Before we got into the car Sophia made the oddest request. "Give me the gun, Boss," she urged without further explanation. Seeing that I was reluctant to pass over my pistol to her, she went on to explain, "If the police were to pull us over there is no need in being in possession of a possible murder weapon. Now give me the gun!"

She was right. If the police had no gun, they had no case. Quickly placing the gun in her hand, she wiped it down thoroughly before throwing it into a storm drain nearby. Meanwhile, I slid over to the passenger's seat and set it back as far as it would go. This way it would appear that she was alone.

As we began to distance ourselves from the bar and the bloody scene I had left behind, we drove in complete silence. My thoughts took me back to the very moment I saw that clown approaching me. He looked like the type of nigga who was trying to make a name for himself by stepping to a nigga with status and respect. That's how most of the niggas out here got down. Always looking to gain rank and position on another nigga's account, instead of putting in the work to get it themselves. He would have made it out better if he had just asked me for a job.

There was no telling if I had left bodies behind. Somebody could have given my name to the police. I was indeed disappointed with the way I handled the situation. That was extremely reckless of me. Especially with all of my drama I'd been through this whole week.

It goes to show how dangerous pride can be. It was the leading cause of niggas getting killed, and one-way tickets to the penitentiary. After the night's events, I could've easily fallen victim to any of the statistics. I don't know what I was thinking to even take my baby girl to a local establishment like Top Shelves. Incidents like this were always prone to happen at these types of places. I felt it was only right that I gave her an apology to end the silence.

"Sophia, baby, I'm sorry for the way I reacted back there. I could have probably taken care of that situation a lot better than the way I did." I took responsibility for my actions. "You have my word that I will never again put you in any kind of danger unless it is unavoidable; in that case I will always protect you."

"Boss, listen to me very carefully!" She spoke with stern sincerity. "I know you're out here doing your thing and that's the sort of shit that comes with the territory. But you have to be careful of the type of people you allow in your circle. Your associations with others, especially females, should never be subject to those sorts of situations. Let's keep it real: if you go to jail behind your actions from tonight, you're going to be mad as shit that you're in there because of an incident that involved a dirty-ass hood rat. I'm a loyal woman and I really like you but don't leave me out here by myself. Tighten your game up, babe!"

"Damn that's some real shit, Sophia. I ain't surprised though. I knew you was a real bitch the second I laid eyes on you. Everything you do and say testifies to it. I fucks with you heavy and before it's all said and done, I'm gonna make you love me, baby!"

That night marked the first time that we actually slept in bed together. And for the second time, we made slow, passionate love until we were both overcome with sleep.

First thing the following morning, I was awoken by the loud banging coming from my front door. My first thought was that it was "the boys" coming to lock a nigga up in relation to last night's shooting. On second thought, had it been police, there probably would not have been any knocking at all. They would have kicked the door in and sent the task force and SWAT team in to get me.

Quickly stepping out of bed, I retrieved a robe and headed downstairs. Upon checking the security monitors, I seen that it was Shake standing at my front porch. I was curious to learn what led to this unexpected visit, especially after all the shit he talked about the last time we saw each other. He didn't want me around him or his crew anymore, yet, this nigga was there standing at my front door?

The second I opened my door and invited him inside, he started fussing and complaining about last night's shooting.

"Amin, what the fuck's gotten into you? Have you lost your fucking mind?" He snapped on me.

I could tell by the look in his eyes that he was extremely upset. But fuck it! So what? My problems were my problems. They didn't have shit to do with him. But, here he stood in my house ranting on and on about something that he had no concern with. Hadn't he turned his back on me? So what did he care?

"I've got people calling me all over town telling me how you done shot three niggas up over some bitch. What if one of those niggas died? Do you think it's going to be hard for them to find a witness among a club full of people? A nigga's gonna snitch you out, Amin!" He began to shout.

Here we go again! Another person blowing up the scene in my house talking some rat shit. This was the main reason why I snapped on Felicia the other day. I didn't give a fuck who he was, nobody was going to disrespect me in my house.

"First of all, Shake, if we're going to continue this conversation, then you're going to have to keep your voice down. It's too early in the morning for all of that hollering, plus I have company upstairs." I put him in check.

The look he gave me was one that a father may give his rebellious son after standing up to him for the first time.

"Now I don't know where you got your information from, but whoever it was need not worry about me. As you suggested about the snitching shit, it will probably be one of those people who's calling your phone and giving you these bogus reports. They the ones you need to be worrying about, not me."

Before I could continue standing my ground, Sophia walked halfway down the steps to see what was going on.

"Boss, is there a problem down here? All the screaming and hollering done woke me out my sleep with a migraine headache," she complained, as she stood there dressed in nothing but a red silk Victoria's Secret nightgown. The robe hugged and exposed her voluptuous figure and large breasts. With her hair hanging over her shoulders, she was one hell of a sight to see.

"Sorry about that, baby. We will keep it down, beautiful. Go 'head and lie back down. I'll be up there in a minute," I assured her.

"Thanks, baby. Can you hurry up please? Because it gets cold lying in that big ol' bed by myself," she insinuated with a smile before going back upstairs.

As she walked up the steps, her wide heart-shaped ass swayed from side to side, bouncing and jiggling every step along the way. Two things were sure to wander and wonder whenever she was in one's presence: that was a person's eyes and mind. That was exactly how Shake responded to her profound beauty. He stood there mesmerized with his mouth and eyes wide open in a state of disbelief. He probably was trying to figure out how I pulled a bitch better looking than any he ever had.

"Anyway!" I chimed in, interrupting his reckless eye-balling and fantasizing of my lady. "As I was saying, I ain't provoke that situation at all. You know how these clowns out here like to jump in nigga's business. He happen to jump in mines and had to suffer the consequences. You dig?" I spoke with arrogance, refusing to admit that I was wrong, or consider what he was saying.

Instead of responding to my comment, Shake just stood there and stared into my eyes. It was as if he were trying to read my thoughts and beyond. Then suddenly he smiled, as if he had it all figured out.

"I see what's going on, Boss man. You feel as though you're big enough to spread your wings and go fly away on your own, and as you please right?" He spoke with disappointment. "I mean you got the money, power, and a gorgeous woman to go along with it. You don't need me anymore. Shit, you don't even want to hear what I got to say. You're moving around on these streets as if you're invincible, and exempt from death and the pen.

"I still love you as a son, but since you think you have life all figured out, I'm going to get out your way and allow you to travel in your own lane, at your own speed. Some things in life can't be explained or understood until you personally experience them on your own. But when you get in a jam because of your actions, don't come running to me. Stand on your own two, and be the man you claim to be.

"With that said, I ain't got nothing else to say. Go ahead back to bed. I wouldn't keep that pretty young thing upstairs waiting too long if I were you. Just watch yourself," he warned with a smile before leaving.

In a sense I was happy he put it like that, because on some real shit, he'd been giving me bad vibes ever since he walked through the door. The way he kept talking about jail and snitches made me wonder what his real agenda was behind showing up at my house at eight in the morning talking about a shooting. Was he wired?

If it was ever discovered that Shake intended to harm me in any way, I wouldn't hesitate one second to kill him. It seemed like the more he exposed himself, the more I began to see his true colors. I had a strong feeling he was up to something, I just couldn't put a finger on it. But when I did, that same finger would be around a trigger, squeezing it over, and over, and over again. All in his face!

Chapter 16

DEA Agent David Sheen was one of the most highly respected federal agents in the field. When it came to conducting sting operations and intense investigations, he was the number one man for the job. He had a reputation of breaking some of the hardest suspects down and getting confessions and cooperation out of them. As a DEA agent, he loved his job, and was dedicated and committed to fight the war on drugs with every resource available.

Inside the federal building on Sixth and Arch Street, Agent Sheen stood patiently outside of his supervisor's office. He was waiting for his boss to finish a meeting with another agent so he could speak with him face to face. While waiting, he opened up the brown folder he held in his hand, and scanned the investigative report once more. The subject was an alleged kingpin by the name of Amin Hussan, aka Boss.

Thanks to a confidential informant close to the subject, the feds were able to obtain sufficient information that immediately grasped their attention and interest. So much so, they had personally requested that Agent Sheen lead the investigation. Having spoke with the CI (confidential informant) himself, he felt the information was reliable, valuable, and worthy of taking a closer look. But before doing so he had to first brief his boss and get approval. That was the proper procedure whenever conducting intense investigations that required wiretaps, surveillance, or any other forms of government funding.

After a short wait, the fellow agent came out of the office and informed Sheen that the boss was waiting for him. When he went inside the boss was seated behind his desk, shuffling through a stack of papers. It appeared that he was overwhelmed with work.

"Good morning, sir. I just need a few minutes of your time if possible," he requested respectfully.

"Sure, Dave. I'm sorry to have kept you waiting, but as you can see I have a lot on my plate," he explained while motioning his hand over the papers and files that lay spread across his desk. "In fact, I have a meeting over at the United States attorney's office in fifteen minutes, so we need to make this fast."

"Thank you, sir. I'll be as brief as possible," he replied before opening the folder and passing it to his boss.

"On the mug shot picture before you is an individual by the name of Amin Hussan, aka Boss. Based on information provided by our informant we have reason to believe that Mr. Hussan is involved in narcotic trafficking and distribution. He may have also committed and participated in several acts of violence. Those crimes are currently being investigated by the locals and ATF.

"With the influence and alleged connections Mr. Hussan is reported to have, I need to get a closer look into his affairs. I'm requesting that you assign me another agent, and possibly pull a few strings to keep our informant happy. I'll take it from there."

"Sounds like you may be on to something. How long do you suppose it will take you to build a strong case, if I back you on this one?"

"Give me a month, boss, and I assure you the best results possible. I might even get this guy to talk," he spoke with assurance.

"You have exactly one month, starting right now. Stay safe, and be sure to keep me posted," he advised him before concluding the meeting.

Chapter 17

After coming off a week of sidetracks, losses, and disappointments, I woke up Monday morning to a new day, but the same shit. Straight to the kitchen with the Pyrex pot, dope, and a triple beam scale. I was anxious to put the work together for distribution before putting it on the streets. I didn't realize until this morning that in the last few days, I done ran through close to $100,000. That wasn't really shit, but with no money coming in, that was moving backward.

As I was packaging the work up in Saran Wrap, Sophia walked in on me in the process.

"Boy, what you in here cook . . ." She stopped in mid-sentence after glancing at the drugs spread out across the counter. "Oops! I'm sorry, baby, I thought you was in here cooking breakfast. If you go out with all that stuff on you, please be careful. Remember your promise," she reminded me before kissing me on the lips then leaving me to finish up my business.

I respected the fact that she knew her place and position, and didn't try to interfere nor question the way I earned my living. For her to support me even while I was doing wrong further revealed that she had wifey characteristics, and was a true "ride or die bitch" all the way around the board. Her presence in my life only pushed me to do better.

Within an hour after leaving the house I managed to move five kilos like it wasn't nothing. Nigga would've thought I had that coke on a diet the way I got rid of that weight. Although I should've made at least $120,000, I wound up with only forty-five of it up front. Mainly because this generation of hustlers was a bunch of lazy, cheap niggas who thought they had all of the sense in the world.

Most of them were expecting handouts. Although they would have the money to buy a brick or two, they would rather get work fronted to them on consignment, or only pay half of it up front. That way they had grounds to complain that the coke didn't come back right, hoping that would lower the price they originally owed. If it wasn't that, then it was the story of how somebody got locked up, and they took a major loss and needed a few weeks to get the money together. Meanwhile, they were flipping that off your dope over and over again.

The drug game was really a headache, which was why I would never solely depend on it to get me on top. Too many crabs in the bottom of the barrel. They would pull a nigga back down the second you even looked like you was ready to take off.

Unsatisfied with my financial earnings of the day hustle, I decided to make up the difference by resorting to what I did best. Take money!

That led me to revisit the home of a prominent hustler by the name of Mummar. Although the lame had a profound ability to move work and get money, he was nonviolent by all means. The nigga wouldn't bust a grape in a fruit fight. Where I'm from, we refer to those individuals as sweet vicks. In fact, the few keys that I moved this morning had previously belonged to him.

About a month ago, me, Buddah, and Ryddah ran in his crib and found twelve bricks and about $90,000. To be sure that nothing of value was left behind, I did a double check of the entire house. While doing so, I stumbled upon a hidden compartment located in the back of his bedroom closet. Inside, there was about two more bricks and a couple thousand dollars. I didn't touch none of it. Instead, I closed it back up as it was, and kept the discovery to myself.

Reason being, I knew that once Mummar returned home and discovered that particular stash spot had kept all of the valuables secured, he would continue to use it under the belief that it wouldn't be found in the event that another burglary or robbery occurred. It was basically the same strategy practiced by farmers all over the world. Fatten the turkey up all year long and keep it nice and healthy, and when it's Thanksgiving, bust it over side the head and have yourself a feast!

That was my exact intention when I placed the crowbar between the locks on Mummar's back door and gained immediate entrance. I already knew he wasn't home because before I came there, I rode by his girlfriend's house and seen his car parked out front. Still I proceeded with caution. Personally, I wouldn't give a fuck if he was home or not. I specialized in home invasions just as well as I did burglaries.

Two minutes after forcing entry into Mummar's home, I walked out with a Nordstrom bag filled with drugs and money; from the look of it, I estimated it to be about 250 stacks and seven or eight bricks. When I imagined the look on Mummar's face when he came home and discovered that he'd been completely cleaned out, I pictured him crying and literally kicking himself in the ass for not investing in a better stash spot.

I think that even the most successful individuals in the world will have to agree that it takes a true boss to take a few days off from hustling, only to return and make over a quarter million dollars on the first day back. And it didn't even take but a few hours. It really came easy, but just imagine what I could do if I put my all into it.

When I arrived back home, I encountered Sophia sitting in the living room in complete darkness. The blinds were still closed and the entire house seemed to be deprived of light and sound. Once my eyes adjusted to the dark, I noticed that she was holding her cell phone and appeared to have been crying. My first thought was that she had talked to her boyfriend, Victor, and became emotional during or after the call. My jealous nature was instantly exposed.

"What's wrong with you? Your man Victor got you up in here crying?"

"Don't be foolish, Boss. Victor's in jail. What on earth can a man do or say to me in jail that would make me cry?" she responded harshly. "It's not Victor that made me upset, it was you. Do you realize how worried I was up in here, knowing that you're out there on those streets driving around with all those drugs? And you wasn't even considerate enough to call me and let me know that you're all right? That's the same shit he used to do! I knew that you two were just alike. All y'all niggas is!"

"Now hold the fuck up, Sophia! Don't you ever compare me to another nigga." I put her in check before cutting on the living room light. "You're right, I should've called, but I didn't. That's only because I was too busy making all this money so we can be straight," I boasted before turning the bag upside down and letting the money and the bricks hit the floor. That got her full attention.

"Oh my God! Boss, that looks like much more than what you left here with. How did you do that?"

"I think it's best if you not know everything that I'm involved with. The less you know the better." I quickly separated my business from our relationship. "But here is something you do need to know. Your skin looks like it can use some sun. And I know the perfect place we can go get you some. Now take this money and go get us some luggage and a few fly outfits to wear on a cruise."

After peeling off at least $10,000 for her to go to the mall, she slightly delayed the shopping spree to take a few minutes to thank me with her mouth. She did it so good, I dropped five more stacks for her to treat herself to something nice, besides what I was already paying for. It ain't tricking if you got it. And I had it!

Chapter 18

The very next day we boarded the Carnival Cruise ship in Miami, Florida. Among the many accommodations and luxuries that the ship offered its guests, it included spacious cabins, over ten swimming pools, a spa, gym, casino, five-star restaurant, and dozens of scheduled concerts and entertainment events.

That afternoon Sophia and I took advantage of the beautiful weather while tanning in the sun, sipping on ice-cold piña coladas. I kept it casual in a pair of all-white Louis Vuitton shorts, the matching boat shoes, and a V-neck. But of course, Sophia looked extravagantly beautiful. She wore a gold and white Chanel thong bikini set, with the sandals and glasses to match. Her hair was styled in two long French braids, giving her that Pocahontas look.

After soaking up enough sun to turn our skin complexion a shade darker, we decided to cool off in one of the pools. I was like a big kid in the water. I kept going underneath, playfully biting and kissing on Sophia's ass. She eventually caught my head between her thighs and held it underneath. She only let me up for air after I stuck my finger inside her pussy. All in fun, we were just enjoying our vacation and having a good time together.

Later that night Sophia dragged me out to the deck of the ship to attend a live reggae concert. The band was actually good. The way they were putting their thing down with the music had those in attendance mimicking the best Jamaican dances they knew. Sophia happened to know all of the freaky ones! With her ass pressed up against my crotch, she slowly wound her hips before touching her hands on the ground and doing the X-rated version of the butterfly. I may not know how to dance, but I sure did know how to fuck. So while she was putting her moves down on me, I responded with a few of my best bedroom moves, in the form of a dance.

While Sophia and I was deeply caught up in our dirty dancing, a white couple came out of nowhere and tried their hardest to copy our moves step for step. It was the funniest shit I ever seen in my life. They were stiff as an ironing board, and had no rhythm whatsoever. It took all composure for me not to be rude and laugh in their face. Instead I gave them the thumbs-up and cheered them on. From there it got even funnier.

Being away from the hood, and all the shiesty, no-good niggas who dwelled there, gave me a sense of stability, but most importantly, peace of mind. Having left all of my worries back home, I was able to lower my guard and really enjoy myself. Here wasn't nobody going to shoot me for stepping on their shoe, or try to rob me for my money, or any of the other foolishness that occurred day in and day out back in the hood. That's what getting money was supposed to be about. Having means to survive, shelter, nice things, and being able to enjoy life.

If a nigga couldn't do that, then what was he hustling for? This vacation helped me realize a lot of things that were essential for me reaching my goals. I just had to get back home and apply them to my everyday hustle. But for now, I was going to continue enjoying my vacation.

Chapter 19

DEA Agent Murphy Malloy was assigned to assist Agent Sheen in the ongoing investigation of Amin Hassan, aka Boss. Ever since they began conducting around-the-clock surveillance on the subject, they'd witnessed him make several suspected drug transactions, and even pull off a brazen broad daylight burglary. For now, their job was to document his crimes, associates, frequently visited places, habits, and anything else they considered essential to their investigation. Not to arrest him, nor blow their cover.

Thanks to the constantly provided information from their CI, they were able to stay a few steps ahead of his every move. The informant had already agreed to plant a listening device on Hassan's property, person, or car the next time the opportunity presented itself. With that in place the agents were confident that Boss would be in their custody long before their thirty-day deadline was up. He already committed enough crimes to take him off the streets for thirty years. But at the rate he was going, they figured he'd be at life before it was all said and done unless . . . ?

Chapter 20

As it turned out, the white couple with the funny dance moves turned out to be the coolest white people in the world. We ended up inviting them out for dinner and drinks, and in exchange they shared some of their personal stash of weed and ecstasy with us. Now I never took an X pill, but since I was on vacation, I figured it couldn't do me much harm. Sophia felt the same way, so we popped them together at the same time.

The effects really didn't kick in until we smoked a few jays behind the deck in an isolated area. That's when things started to get weird. We were both singing, dancing, laughing, and feeling like we were the only two people in the world. The view of the ocean, moon, and the sky suddenly went from amazing to breathtaking. Everything was magnified.

Feeling like an invincible daredevil, Sophia sat backward over the railing, miraculously yet dangerously defying gravity. Had she not thrown her arms around my neck, she could've easily fallen into the dark depths of the ocean. She seemed to find her flirt with death amusing and was turned on by it. After climbing down from the railing, she began to lift up her dress. "You saved me, baby. If you wasn't as strong as you are we probably both would've fallen into the ocean. I'm a very bad girl, Boss. Teach me a lesson!" she requested slow and seductively.

Thanks to the short sundress she wore, I was able to put my hand underneath it and find her wetness with ease.

With my most gentle touch, I glided my finger back and forth over her slit. She began to moan lightly as she put her head back and stared into the moonlit sky. Along with the warmth and wetness that covered my fingers came the fragrance of coconut and raspberry. My mouth began to water as I wondered if it tasted the way it smelled.

Following the scent like a hound dog in search of an escaped slave, I buried my face into her, and ate it like a savage. For the first time ever, she took it without running. This time she fucked my face until she came over and over again. Somehow, we ended up in the sixty-nine position. From there it was on.

Although Sophia gave me head a few times in the past, tonight she gave me brain. I felt her mouth go all the way down on me until her top lip was touching my nuts. There was no gag reflex, choking, or throwing up, which usually resulted whenever a bitch attempted to deep throat me. While she was busy using her mouth as a weapon to drive me crazy, I was licking her from the top of her pussy down to the crack of her ass. The more I licked the faster she sucked.

We must've stayed in the sixty-nine position for close to twenty minutes straight. I had lost count of how many times Sophia came while I ate her pussy. But for some reason, I couldn't cum. I mean, I wanted to, and I should have, but it just didn't happen. It must have been the X. Regardless of what it was, I was determined to get my shit off. It was time to switch positions.

By the time I got Sophia back on her feet, she could hardly stand. Her body was still shaking from the massive orgasms she experienced. Leaning her over the railing for support, I prepared to drive it inside her from the back. That's when I noticed a shadow standing there behind us. I shouldn't have been surprised to see that it was the white couple watching us once again. These motherfuckas was some perverts! My delay of entry had Sophia wondering what happened.

"Baby, why you ain't put it in? I want you inside me right now!"

"Hold on, baby. I'm about to smack one of these white motherfuckas upside they head. I ain't into all of that peek freak shit!" I voiced while pointing in their direction. Before I could do or say anything else, Sophia reached back and guided me inside of her.

"Let's give them something to watch. You still owe me a spanking, and I want it now!"

Since she put it like that, I had no choice but to give her exactly what she asked for. I fucked her with hard, power-ful, deep strokes that damn near sent her overboard for the second time in one night. To keep her from falling over, I locked my hands around her small waist and continued to unleash a mean beating on that pussy. Each time I drove it inside of her, that wide, fat ass of hers would form a wave that clashed against my abdomen. Making that booty clap.

The orgasm that was approaching felt as if it formed in the bottom of my spine. Sophia was also on the verge of busting again. She was moaning loud and throwing it forward. The pleasure and satisfaction that followed may have lasted only a few seconds, but those few seconds felt like forever.

For the remainder of the trip we shopped, gambled, partied, and made love as if we invented it and had it patented. When the ship stopped in the Bahamas for a day we went out to eat, did some more shopping, and explored the many tourist attractions the island had to offer. The quality time we spent together bought us closer than what we were prior to the trip. The degree of love, appreciation, and respect I developed for her had the potential to grow into something deeper.

Having accomplished and received everything out of the trip that I intended to, I slept the last day of it away, with Sophia lying asleep in my arms. It was some of the best sleep I had in a long time. Peaceful, comfortable, and relaxing.

They say you have to go away to make a comeback. I was now a believer. I was reenergized, focused, and ready to go ten times harder than I ever went. Actions exceed beyond words. Therefore, I was going to show them better than I could tell them.

Chapter 21

The first thing I did once I got back to the city was switch cars up once again. Since it was still summertime, I upgraded to the SL Mercedes-Benz convertible. It was gold with the tan top and peanut butter leather seats. This pretty motherfucka had a 402 horsepower bi-turbo V8 engine, which meant it went from zero to sixty in about seven seconds flat.

When I rolled up on some of the niggas who owed me money, they reacted with excessive dick eating, turning from hustlers to groupies right before my eyes. Most of them had never driven a Benz, or could afford one, yet they asked questions like, "How much will one of these cost me?" I was thinking, *nigga, please! Most of y'all fleas couldn't even purchase a brick without getting it on consignment, yet you want to converse Benz prices?*

Because I had to deal with these niggas for the time being, I kept things on a respectable business level at all times. I wasn't trying to make friends or enemies. I just was trying to make some money. Therefore, I collected money, dropped work off, and kept it moving. Nothing less, nothing more.

Part of the proceeds that I accumulated that day went to Sophia so she could put a down payment on a new house for us. She'd already found a nice three-bedroom townhouse out in the suburbs, so now it was only a matter of handling the paperwork and clearing the checks. No problem! I wasn't feeling the fact that a bunch of snakes knew where I rested my head at. On top of that I had to worry about Sophia's safety. These niggas out here would snatch her up in a heartbeat, and put a six-digit price tag out for her safe return. Situations like that I'd rather prevent before they happen.

In fact, I wasn't too far from leaving the streets alone and venturing into a variety of legitimate investments. Being a hustler my entire life allowed me to develop the skill that it took to market, communicate, produce, and sell. Those elements combined were ingredients to success in any business.

Hoping to reach my goals a little faster, I decided to drop the price on the remaining dope I had left. Being that the drugs were stolen, it was impossible for me to lose either way. If I was to only make a dollar off it, it was still a come up. It took me nothing but a crowbar and two minutes to acquire. Once the streets caught wind of the drastic decrease on the prices, them hungry niggas would be coming out the woodwork to cop as if it was Black Friday!

When it came to getting the word on the streets, Shake was always well informed. Nothing seemed to get past his knowledge. Just today, he'd already received a dozen or so phone calls from his associates all around the city. All of them had similar reports. Boss this, Boss that. Boss! Boss! Boss!

The name in itself was starting to leave a foul taste in his mouth. His patience had grown thin with the young man he once loved and cared for as if he were his own child. It was his belief that Boss had gotten way beyond himself. The power and position he had was inherited through him. The lessons and understanding of life were obtained through him. Without him there would be no Boss.

Where was the homage and respect at? Who was Boss to lower the prices on kilos without his approval? Was it an open challenge to take over the city? That's exactly how it appeared to be, and Shake wasn't going for it. It was time to bring Boss down to size and throw a major loophole in his plans. It was the same situation when one had a dog that no longer listened nor could be reckoned with, it had to be put down for good.

"I bet it's that bitch who turned him against me. From the moment I saw that whore I knew she was going to be trouble," he voiced out loud before placing one of many calls that was sure to put a monkey wrench into Boss's plans.

Chapter 22

Meanwhile, over at the Federal Building, Agents Sheen and Malloy had just wrapped up an informative call with their confidential informant. The information they received from this particular call was enough from them to brief their supervisor and hopefully get a warrant to indict. And that was just the tip of the iceberg. They also had pictures of the subject in the act of committing crimes from robbery to numerous drug transactions. If that wasn't overwhelming enough, they had actual wiretaps from incriminating conversations that took place inside the subject's car.

Their CI had somehow managed to place the bug in the subject's convertible without his knowledge. How and when the CI was given that sort of access was beyond their comprehension. Same with the information that the CI provided. It was if the CI was watching the subject's every move just as much as they were. Strange, but very substantial.

As expected the supervisor was well pleased with the conducting of the investigation. A sting operation was immediately set up that was designed to catch the subject red-handed. At the time, they would come from every angle and bring him down as quiet and humiliating as possible. Their CI would be the key factor in the success of the operation. If things went smooth for them, they'd go smooth for the CI and likewise.

Chapter 23

If my priorities wasn't in order, then I wasn't in order. With the line of work I was in, that could be detrimental to my health, wealth, and freedom. Therefore, I dedicated my entire day to moving and making sure the new house was comfortable, secure, and decked out from the ceiling to the floor, and everywhere else in between. To ensure that my requirements were handled correctly, I had a group of professionals on hand consisting of a security specialist, an interior decorator, and a certified locksmith.

My instructions and suggestions were adhered to and executed without delay, resulting in the house being correctly transformed into a home. Along with the added appliances, luxurious furniture, and stylish designs, the place was well suited for a true boss such as myself, and a fly queen as my lady friend.

This was my first taste of the American Dream, and I was loving every bit of it. I soon discovered that when you lived among legitimate, middle-class citizens there was a comfort level that eliminated the fears and worries that developed from living in the ghetto. There was no more locking doors, circling the block, looking out the window at every car that passed by or any of the other survival tactics that one was forced to adapt to. Sadly, but fortunately if you were an unknown black face in this neck of the woods, the police would be over you like flies on shit. That's why I was making it my business to get acquainted with my neighbors.

Chapter 24

Now that my living situation was in order, I was able to hit the streets and finish up where I left off at. On my way down to the city, I received a text message from Gunner. It was a simple question mark, and nothing more. Whenever he didn't hear from me for a few days, he would send this exact same message. I replied to his text that I'd get with him later on tonight and that everything was cool. I knew down inside that in this particular instance his true intention of sending the message was because his trigger finger was itching and he was looking for a way to get a good scratch.

That reminded me that he still had the money and dope from the random drop. Even after giving him his fee for service, there would still be a large lump sum for me to put up in the safe. Now that's what I called a win-win situation!

Since I was in West Philly, I decided to drive to Big Sal's car wash to get the convertible detailed. It was a beautiful sunny day outside so I wanted them to put that Turtle Wax shine on the whip. It wasn't fair to the Benz that my neck and wrist was gleaming so hard it made the gold paint on the car look dull. I figured a nice shine on it would give it an equal comparison with my jewelry.

When I pulled up into the entrance, I was greeted by a few of Sal's workers. Although they were used to me pulling up in all sorts of luxury vehicles, it must have been their first time seeing the new SL convertible. They did and said everything but worship the motherfucka! I understood clearly. I mean it wasn't every day that typical car wash employees got the opportunity to get so close to a mighty fine German-crafted vehicle such as the Mercedes-Benz.

Compliments were usually good, but when done excessively it could be rather embarrassing. But that was the sort of attention that exotic cars attracted. I was used to it.

It was nearly ten minutes later before my car finally made it to the drive-thru. While coasting through the machine, everything suddenly came to an abrupt stop. The next thing I knew, the driver-side door flew open and I was forcefully snatched out and dragged off like an animal.

I ended up inside a room covered in plastic. Inside there I was stripped completely naked while several men held me at gunpoint. It became apparent to me that I was about to be killed. But for what?

As I was lying on the floor asshole naked waiting for the gunshot to end this humiliation, Big Sal finally came storming into the room.

"Youngster, why in God's name would you bring that hot-ass car into my place of business? You working for the feds, ain't you, motherfucka?"

I was confused. What was this nigga trying to say? What, that because I drove fancy cars on a regular basis I was working for the feds? Or was he indicating that my ride was stolen?

"Sal, what you trying to say? Working for the feds? Do you realize what you're saying, and who you're saying it to?" I questioned his offensive accusations.

"What am I supposed to think when you come into my place of business with a wire in your car? How I know you weren't sent to plant it in here?" he inquired suspiciously.

"Hold the fuck up, Sal. You found what in my car?" I responded in a state of disbelief. "If that shit was in my car, I swear on everything I love I had no knowledge of it. Either it was in the car when I got it, or somebody put it there. You've known me for years, Sal, and for you to assume that I'm a snitch is a very offensive label to tag me with. Don't you think that if I was working for the police, they would've raided this motherfucka by now? We need to fix this up before it goes too far," I warned him as I started to become inpatient.

"Even if what you say is true, I'm in a fucked-up position either way. Things done went too far, son, and if I was to give you a pass on this, I have to worry about you and your people bringing me a move in retaliation for this misunderstanding. I'm stuck between a rock and a hard spot," he insinuated.

"Now wait a minute, Sal! I know how things work here, and I respect the game. This was all a big misunderstanding. If anything, I should be thanking you. Knowing me, I would've eventually said some shit that might have got me the chair. You have my word that what happened here today will never leave this room."

Big Sal stared me directly in my eyes as I spoke, searching deeply for truth, lies, sincerity, and deception.

"Not once in my life have I ever gone against my usual protocol. Please don't make me regret it," he voiced before snapping his fingers. Immediately, his men helped me up to my feet and gave my clothes back.

"From here on out, you're never to show your face in my place of business ever! We understand each other?"

"Indeed. I respect you regardless, and this situation doesn't change that. I'm just thankful that we were able to resolve this without going to extremes."

Although I had just been violated in the worst way ever, I drove out of Big Sal's car wash grateful that I'd come out of the situation alive. Shit could've gotten ugly back there. But right now that was the least of my worries. Figuring out who was responsible for putting this wire in my car was more important.

I was suddenly overcome with a case of paranoia. Among suspicion and confusion, equaled a combination for disaster. I needed my medication like yesterday! I drove straight down Eighteenth and Master Street looking forward to copping some syrup and an ounce of haze to calm my nerves. To play it safe, I parked around the corner from the block and walked over on foot. I was strongly considering just leaving that hot-ass car right there in the middle of North Philly. I damn sure wasn't getting back in that motherfucka with no drugs on me.

Walking onto Eighteenth and Master Street was like entering the stock exchange building on Wall Street. Hustlers flooded the block from corner to corner, taking orders and serving customers out in the open as if it were legal. With the cop-and-roll policy in effect, incoming and outgoing traffic flowed like clockwork. I'd never done business with any of the workers, so I walked straight past them in search of the boss, a middle-aged hustler by the name of Squally.

I finally caught up with Squally in the middle of the block. Him and a few other hustlers were engaged in a game of craps. When he noticed me approaching, he picked up the dice and walked over to greet me accordingly.

"Boss! What's happening, my nigga? You ain't driving?" he inquired surprisingly before extending his hand to me.

"Yeah, I'm always driving. I just parked my car around the corner. One of those days, you know how the shit go. Plus I could use the fresh air. You dig me?"

"I hear that. What you want me to get for you, your regular?"

I nodded in agreement before pulling out a stack of money and passing it to him. As he walked across the street to fulfill my order, one of the hustlers at the dice game began to complain about Squally putting the game on hold.

"Hurry the fuck up, dog! Who the fuck is dude supposed to be that we got to stop what we doing so you can serve him?" he shouted.

Before I could reply to the slick remark, Squally put the nigga in his place before he allowed his mouth to get him put in a grave.

"Shut your bitch ass up before you get your little ass killed out here," he warned him. "You don't even know who you in the presence of, stupid! That's the problem with you young niggas. You best to be respectful whenever you see my man's right here. I ain't going to tell you again!" He checked him.

Fortunately Squally's words had talked sense into the young fellow. Certainly enough to humble him, and keep his mouth shut. It probably saved him an asshole full of problems.

"Don't mind these young niggas, Boss, they just stupid and reckless by nature. I apologize on behalf of him. In fact, the next time you come down, it's on me," he offered before passing me a brown sandwich bag that held an ounce of haze and eighth of yellow syrup.

"It ain't about nothing, homie. These pups out here don't know no better," I spoke loud enough for the young punk to hear me. "But I'ma get up with you later." We shook hands once more before departing.

As I walked away, I cracked the seal on the eighth, and start sipping right then and there. The promethazine was sweeter than honey, and numbed my tongue and throat as it went down. Its effects seemed to kick in immediately. Those familiar feelings of being superior, unstoppable, and untouchable came back ten times stronger than what they usually were. And just like that, my fears and worries were gone. My swagger was back like it never left.

Fuck that wire, the nigga who put it there, and the motherfuckas who listened in on it! That was my attitude as I pushed the keyless entry feature and approached the driver-side door of the convertible.

"Pussy! I know you ain't think I was going to let that shit ride did you?"

That's all I heard before a sharp pain shot through my shoulder. I turned around just in the nick of time to catch Felicia's hand before she could stab me with the razor again.

"What the fuck is wrong with you, bitch? You been following, me huh? What else you been doing?" I demanded to know while struggling to get the knife out of her hand. At the same time, my mind was piecing shit together with each second that passed.

"Ain't no talking, nigga. You wasn't trying to talk when you was shooting motherfuckas the other day. Was you? Now let me go!" she screamed as she put all her strength and energy into stabbing me again.

At that point, the signs became clear. This was no coincidence that she just happened to pop up out of the blue talking reckless about me shooting people. She was wired for sound. There wasn't a doubt in my mind that this bitch had been following me around all day. It was her who put that wire in my car. And once the feds discovered that their wire had been found and removed, they sent the next best thing. This bitch!

Now I really was trying to get the knife out of her hand. I had zero tolerance for snitches. My policy was catch a rat, kill a rat! And that's what I intended to do the second I got my hands on that knife.

As I was out here tussling with this bitch, I never noticed the black-on-black Cadillac pull up alongside of us until those flames of burning metal came flying out the passenger-side window. The first shot caught me in the upper back and spun me all the way around. Fortunately, I never let go of Felicia's shirt. If I had, I would've never been able to swing her in front of me and use her body as a human shield. The gunman wasn't impressed in the least. He didn't stop shooting until the sounds of sirens were approaching from every direction. Only then did he cease fire and pull off.

If only Felicia was bulletproof. I pondered as I lay on the ground, suffering from multiple shots to the upper body. I was in bad shape indeed, but not like Felicia was. She was stretched out on the side of me, with her head leaking like Ancha Momma! Her shit got pushed back.

Even in my current condition I wanted to see the proof with my own eyes. Mustering up all the strength I had inside, I managed to reach under Felicia's bloody shirt and feel for the wire. Just when I thought I felt it, I was suddenly overcome with severe dizziness. Followed by complete darkness.

Chapter 25

The casket was wooden oak, outlined with black and gold trimming. There lay the Boss in an all-white tuxedo, with hundreds of flowers and other ornaments spread out around the area where the casket sat. Thousands showed up to pay their final respects to the man whom they considered a legend of their generation. Many hearts suffered behind the loss. Their pain was evident through their loud weeping and raving during the service.

In the front row of the church, there sat Sophia, Shake, Gunner, and few other close associates. Among them, there were faces of happiness, sadness, resentment, and envy. This group of individuals was the first to approach the casket. Starting with Shake.

Leaning as close to the body as possible, he whispered, "My little nigga, Boss. Ummm umm. Here you was suppose to be a product of me. Now look at you. You're nothing but a failure and a disappointment," he voiced coldly before walking away.

Dressed in an all-black suit, gator shoes, and a pair of dark shades, Gunner approached and stood directly over the casket. He spoke as if he were conversing with someone among the living.

"I told you to watch these niggas. All these mother-fuckas is snakes! If God Almighty was to remove every last one of them from the face of the earth, there would be not one person left behind. You can't trust a motherfucka. That's one mistake I'll never make," he addressed before walking away.

When Sophia approached the casket, she did so with extreme caution. It was as if she was hiding from someone, and in fear that something was going to happen to her. Her hands shook frantically as she placed them on top of the body.

"I'm so sorry, baby. This wasn't supposed to happen to you. It's all my fault. I should have warned you. I wanted to, but I didn't know how," she claimed tearfully. "I should've never . . ." She stopped in mid-sentence and began to look around nervously. "I'm sorry, Boss. But I have to go."

Afterward, she turned around and walked away. At that moment the entire congregation began singing a song of forgiveness and mercy before closing the casket.

When I opened my eyes and viewed my surroundings, it was as if I'd escaped from one nightmare only to wake up to another. There was all sorts of tubes running down my throat, inside my body, and into machines. One of them monitored my vitals, one fed me, and the other helped me to breathe. Although I felt heavily medicated, I was still in excruciating pain. But unfortunately for my enemies, I was still alive.

As I lay there trying to count my blessings from the previous day, I easily lost count. I wasn't one to ever question God's plan, but I wondered why He kept sparing my life. With all the dirt and mischief I was responsible for, I should've been dead a long time ago. But I guess it's true when they say, "Only the good die young." In that aspect that would probably explain why my sneaky ass was still alive. Wasn't shit good about me!

As much as I tried not to think about the dream I just had, the flashbacks of me lying dead in a coffin were too realistic for me to ignore. I honestly believe that the dream was a message sent with meaning, warning, and purpose. I just had to interpret what it all meant.

The flushing of the bathroom toilet interrupted my thoughts, and informed me that I wasn't in the hospital room alone. After the sink water ran for a few seconds, the door opened and Sophia came walking out. Still feeling a little odd by the dream, I wasn't yet ready to confront her. Instead I closed my eyes to a slight peek and watched her every move.

When she walked over to the bed and stood over me, I noticed that her eyes were puffy and swollen from crying. Just the sight of me being in my current condition brought tears to her eyes. Rubbing her soft hands down the side of my face, she cleared her throat and in her softest voice began whispering in my ear.

"Amin. Baby, if you can hear me. I love you and I miss you. You have to keep fighting, baby. It's gonna take more than those five shots to kill my boo! Don't make it easy for them." She spoke words of encouragement before leaning over and kissing me on my forehead. "You promised me you'd never leave me. And true bosses never break their word. I need you now more than ever. Please, baby, don't die on me."

Every word she expressed was delivered with sincerity and devotion. I felt it deep down inside, and my heart never lied to me. The next time she leaned down to kiss me, I poked my lips out and beat her to the punch. My kiss landed right on her lips. She reacted by turning into a born-again Christian right there in the hospital room.

"Oh my God! Thank you, God! Dear Lord, who created the heavens and the earth, thank you so much! Thank you, Lord!" She praised loud enough to wake up the hospital and heavens above.

Several doctors ran in the room and immediately began checking the charts, monitors, and other equipment. Meanwhile, I was lying there as calm and cool as the other side of the pillow. Besides the pain I was in, I felt as if I could've hopped out the bed and walked away right then and there. While the doctors were running their tests on me, I kept a smile on my face the entire time. Now I could better relate to how the legendary Tupac felt when he said, "Five shots couldn't stop me, I took 'em and smiled!"

I later learned that a major part of my survival was thanks to Felicia. Had the bullet not been drastically slowed down after going through her body first, my injuries would've likely been fatal. The syrup I was drinking moments before the incident took place also played a significant role in me surviving the hit. It actually slowed my heart down enough to prevent me from going into shock and losing too much blood. And they say drugs kill? I beg to differ.

The average nigga who got hit like I got hit ain't live to talk about it. Yet, instead of me praising a higher power and giving thanks to Him, I credited myself for my fast thinking and quick reaction. Having been close enough to death to kiss it in the mouth twice in one day, and still breathing after the fact, gave me all rights to dumb myself, "the untouchable Boss!"

Although the police didn't like the fact that I threw Felicia's body in front of me in order to protect myself, I committed no crimes by doing so. While they called it an act of cowardice I considered it a cold-blooded survival tactic. As far as they knew we were both targets and victims of a drive-by shooting. Unfortunately for them their investigation received not the least of assistance by way of me. I refused to say one word to the cocksuckers!

Through their one-sided interrogation, I was able to find out a few useful things. Such as there was no arrest made, nor did they have any suspects in the shooting. That was a good thing. That meant that Felicia's accomplice who drove the black Cadillac was still out there somewhere.

Whoever he was, if he did his homework on me, he should be moving himself and everything dear to him far away from Philadelphia while he still had a chance. He'd already underestimated me once. But after seeing the great lengths that I went to in order to survive, he probably realized that he was fucking with a professional. He would soon see for himself. Again!

Against all odds I was discharged from the hospital after a short two-day stay. And that was mainly for observation purposes. All of the injuries I sustained were basically flesh wounds. There was no internal damage, missing limbs, or anything else associated with serious gunshot wounds. I was just as healthy leaving as I was coming in.

Although hospital policy required that all patients being discharged from the intensive care unit be wheeled out, my pride wouldn't allow me to do it. Instead I was on my feet limping away on my own two. Having chewed up two Percocet beforehand, the aches and pains were numb to a point they didn't exist. To be a true solider, the boss of all bosses, I had to represent it and demonstrate it at all times and to the fullest degree.

As Sophia and I walked side by side out of the hospital, I couldn't help but notice the way she kept her right hand inside her pocketbook, and proceeded along with extreme caution and alertness. If something or someone was to try to hurt me at that very moment, there was no doubt that baby girl would pull that thing out and lay something down to protect her man. In that instance, I honestly trusted my life in her hands.

Once we got inside her truck, she removed a small Glock 9 from her pocketbook and placed it on my lap.

"Carry this with you wherever you go. It may be small, but it will back a motherfucka down," she assured with the conviction of a certified arms dealer. "By the way, I had the Benz towed back home. You and I know that had it stayed down North Philly too long, them crackheads would've stripped it down to the frame."

Sophia never ceased to amaze me. She was constantly proving her worthiness. Always going the extra length to make sure things were in order, and I was straight. The term "ride or die bitch" was an understatement in reference to her actions, in how I viewed her.

On the ride back home, my thoughts went back to that terrifying dream I had after being shot. As the signs became more apparent, I interpreted them to be a warning that if I continued living as I did, then death will be my ultimate destination. That may have been enough to scare the average nigga straight, but after what I done survived, it was going to take a lot more than a dream to stop me from getting this money.

Chapter 26

On the cold streets of Philadelphia, niggas in the hood always kept count on the shootings and numbers of bodies that dropped. These statistics rendered what neighborhoods were most violent and unsafe. It was a big game that earned the thugs and the goons bragging rights to claim their hoods as the most dangerous. The winners usually ended up with a permitted stay in the box, while the losers were the ones laid in the street, leaking out their brains.

When word hit the streets that I got shot, the rumors began to circulate immediately. Niggas claimed I got killed by a bitch. They said Felicia got shot five times in the head. Another rumor said that some young buck from North Philly killed me after an argument at the dice game. Them haters was fast to count me out for dead. Word had it that a few nobodies from around the city was even taken credit for my murder. Biggie said it best when he said, "Niggas would rather see me die than see me fly!"

Fortunately for my enemies' sake that meeting with Gunner never took place the other night. If it had, Shake may have ended up on the "list." Now that I knew who the root of all my troubles was, and having already dealt with her, I needed to swallow my pride and go clear the air between me and Shake. Regardless of our disagreements, that was my father, and I was dead wrong for even entertaining the thought that he would ever do anything to harm me. For me to accuse him of being a snitch and wearing a wire on me only proves that I'm one paranoid motherfucka!

Being deep in those streets will do that to a person. However, being paranoid and following your instinct wasn't such a bad thing at all. It could actually be the difference between living and dying. I'd rather be safe than sorry on any day. Look at me. It took for me to get shot five times to catch a rat, kill a rat, and save me the time and energy of killing someone real close to me. That worked out good!

Along with a prescription for Percocet, the doctors also recommended that I remain on bed rest for at least a week. Sophia volunteered to play nurse and see to it that their orders were followed to the fullest. She even took it a step further, by feeding me my meals in bed and giving me a sponge bath two and three times a day. Wanting me to focus all my energy recovering she put all of my phones up so that there wouldn't be any distractions to slow down my progress.

Of course I thought she was being a little extreme and exaggerating my injuries, but since her intentions were pure and this was her way of showing her love and loyalty, I let her do her. But lying in the bed wasn't paying the bills. I still had moves to make and money to collect.

With the rumors and speculations that were surfacing, I just knew that niggas who owed me money was praying that they were true and I was really dead. That way they wouldn't have to pay their debts. Too bad their prayers were in vain, because I was coming for every dollar of mines, plus some! Sadly, these was the niggas I had to deal with, and put on to some money.

I gave Sophia's little program just two days before I decided that I had enough. When I broke the news to her that I was going out to take care of some business, I was surprised that there was no complaints or objections. Instead, she retrieved this heavy-ass Teflon bulletproof vest, and dropped it in the floor in front of me.

"I can't stop you from going out and doing your thing, but please wear this just to have some reassurance in an event that you get shot again. I'll feel much better about you going back out there so soon if you wore it." She voiced her concerns. "And please take my truck, baby; you don't need to be in that hot-ass Benz."

Just to make her happy I agreed to wear the bulletproof vest, and use her truck, but the vest was coming off as I drove down the block. Baby girl was such a G, she made sure the clip of the Glock was fully loaded and there was one in the head before I put it on my hip. Before leaving the house hugs and kisses were exchanged, but Sophia's last-minute request made me want to drop to my knees and marry the bitch right then and there.

"Baby, let me come with you," she asked with tears in her eyes. "That way I can have your back or take a case for you if need be. Just let me come, baby," she begged.

"Girl, you going to cum as soon as I get back home and let you count this money while I eat your pussy. I'm good out there on them streets, Sophia. These motherfuckas caught me slipping once, but never will lightning strike the same place twice. I do circles around them niggas out there day in and day out. You just have that thing ready when I get back."

When I walked out of the house I felt like my old self, but a new man. After tossing the duffle bag in the far back, I adjusted the driver-side seat and scanned through the iPod at the same time. Through the rearview mirror, I noticed her standing at the front door with one those "please don't leave" looks on her face. When she came out of the house and started walking toward the truck,

I blasted "99 Problems" by Jay-Z, and pulled off as if I didn't see her.

I felt bad about giving her the cold shoulder, but at that moment she came second to my money. As soon as I turned off the block I took off that big goofy-ass vest, and threw it on the floor in the back. The Glock 9 on my lap was all the protection I needed. I wasn't on the highway but for a minute before I heard howling sirens coming over the music. When I looked in the rearview, a redneck state trooper was directly behind me with the lights flashing. Being as though I hadn't broken any traffic laws, I put my right turn signal on and eased over to another lane, hoping that he was just trying to pass. Why did the cocksucker switch lanes right along with me? Pulling up inches away from the back bumper, he repeatedly honked the horn, which sounded off concurrently with the sirens.

Having just listened to Jay-Z's "99 Problems," I figured I was armed with enough legal knowledge and tactics to pull over and handle the traffic stop accordingly. But not before dropping the gun on the floor and kicking it under the seat with the heel of my shoe.

As the trooper approached the truck, he kept his right hand over the holster of his service pistol. I cracked the window three inches as the law required, and held my ground. "What seems to be the problem, Officer?"

"I need to see a license, registration, and proof of insurance, and a separate photo ID, sir," he requested without acknowledging my question. Everything from his demeanor, speech, and posture confirmed that he'd spent majority of his life in the military.

This redneck was asking for a whole lot, but it wasn't nothing I couldn't produce. After passing the requested information to him, he walked back to his patrol car and began to process it. I guess when a nigga was driving a vehicle that cost more than ten grand, it was out of the ordinary, and more than enough reason for suspicions to arise. Although his profiling of me in particular may have been accurate, how many hardworking, honest-living black people was he harassing every day because they appeared to be successful? America was still giving the KKK badges, bullets, and courtrooms.

My political thoughts were interrupted when suddenly another state trooper approached my car from the front, boxing me in between both patrol cars. I couldn't recall ever seeing this routine being used during a traffic stop, but I guessed it was some sort of new safety precaution they had in effect. So I hoped.

After a long half-hour wait, the trooper who initially pulled me over exited his patrol car. In his hand he carried what appeared to be a few traffic tickets. Relief set in almost instantly. I promised myself that once I got out of this, I was turning my black ass around and going straight home. A women's intuition should never be ignored, especially when they react unusual to your departure. Sophia felt something inside that she wanted to come tell me, but instead of me being patient and hearing what she had to say, I pulled off on her.

When the trooper walked up to the truck and passed me the tickets, I thought that would conclude the traffic stop. I was wrong. He made a request that I refused to comply with when he asked, "Sir, I'm going to need you to step out of the vehicle and follow me back to my cruiser. This will just take a moment."

"Step out the vehicle?" I responded in disbelief before reading over the traffic ticket. "Man, this ticket for a broken tail light, so why does that require me to step out of the vehicle?"

"Boy, I'm going to ask you one more time! Step out of the vehicle. Now! And right now!" he demanded before snapping the button on his holster open.

All type of shit was running through my mind as I tried to decide what to do next. Here these crackers had me boxed in on the middle of the highway while I'm riding dirty as a dump truck. The would've, should've, could'ves were too late to reason with. My options were limited, and all had the same results.

Shoot it out? I'm dead! They search the car? It's over! What was a nigga to do? Hoping to buy some time until I decided which way to approach this situation, I got on my NAACP, and began protesting, and making any racial accusation I could think of.

"I ain't stepping out of shit! You racist, motherfucka! What's the charge? Being black in America? Or is it the fact that you're mad because you can't afford this Cadillac Escalade, and a young nigga such as myself own one? Get the fuck away from my car! We'll see what my attorney, Denis Conan, has to say about this illegal traffic stop." I checked him harshly before rolling the window back up.

He may not have called me a black nigger to my face, but the look he gave me displayed just as much hatred as the word itself. He flashed a wicked smile before snatching the radio from his waist and yelling a bunch of police codes. Afterward, he drew his service pistol and pressed it against the window, aiming it directly at my head. Within seconds I was surrounded by dozens of state troopers. They responded to the scene as if it were a hostage situation.

Once they pulled the bullhorn out and warned me to surrender or else, I realized that these racist rednecks were itching for an opportunity to personally see to it that there was one less nigga on this earth. The wise words of Shake suddenly came to mind, when he said, "A true solider always picks his battles and decides when and where to fight them."

Here I was outnumbered, outgunned, and out-colored. I ain't never picture it all ending like this. And I wasn't about to let it happen. I'd rather be judged by twelve than carried by six any day. With that said, I looked forward to having my day in court.

Complying to their demands, I stepped out the truck with my hands up, kneeled down on my knees. The cocksuckers still Rodney Kinged my black ass for general purpose. Once they had me cuffed and placed in the back of a patrol car, all the troopers except for the first two left the scene. To my surprise, my car was never searched, nor did the troopers attempt to interrogate me. Something wasn't right.

Shortly afterward, two tinted-up Dodge Chargers pulled up behind the patrol car. Four white men emerged wearing those familiar blue jackets bearing yellow logos that read DEA and FBI. Three of the agents approached the troopers, while the other got inside the Escalade and pulled off. When they walked past the patrol car, they looked inside and greeted me with a wave and a smile, as if we were old friends. After a brief discussion with the troopers, they took me out of the patrol car and placed me in the back seat of the Charger.

I couldn't believe this shit! As long as I'd been ducking the alphabet boys, they done caught me with enough dirt to seal my fate forever.

They had to be watching my every move. Damn! Here I was trying to get it all, and done fucked around and lost it all in the process. That bitch Felicia done spoke from the grave.

My thoughts were interrupted when one of the agents addressed me. These cocksuckas had the nerve to refer to me by my street name.

"How you doing there, Boss? I see you don't waste no time. You were just shot five times last week, but yet you're back on the streets ready to hustle like there's no tomorrow," he said. "Now that's what I call a man who's about his business. Anyway, you just sit tight and relax. We're going to go downtown to Sixth and Arch Street to have a little meeting. By the way, my name is Agent Murphy, and this here is Agent Sheen."

"The introductions ain't necessary. I don't know y'all, don't want to know y'all, and I damn sure don't know who Boss is," I replied firmly. "The only thing I want to know is when am I going to be able to contact my attorney?"

"Calm down, Mr. Hussan." Agent Sheen spoke for the first time. "It's not as serious as it looks. At this point you're not charged with any crimes. We're not going to search your car, or any other of your personal property. However, if that remains the case all depends on you. You're in control of your own destiny. If our meeting goes okay, you'll be just fine. We'll take those handcuffs off of you in a minute here."

For some reason the agent's words seem to bring me a sense of relief. But I knew better than fall for the good cop, bad cop trick, or the courteous "help us help you" tactic he thought he could run on me. Regardless of what evidence they had, or claimed to have, I wasn't saying a word. I knew enough to know that if they had a strong case against me they would be arresting me, and not questioning me.

These *federales* must've thought they were fucking with an average nigga off the streets. They had a better chance of breaking the da Vinci code before they broke me!

Once we arrived at the Federal Building on Sixth and Arch Street, we pulled into the building and they removed the handcuffs as promised. Along the way, we walked past the Escalade. It was parked up, and didn't appear to be searched yet. Just the thought of the illegal contraband concealed inside there made me shiver as if a breeze from the Arctic had hit me in the face.

After a long elevator ride up to the seventeenth floor, they led me to a small office where I was offered a seat and a cold bottle of water. I took the seat, but refused the water. Water was for dry mouths. Dry mouths came from too much talking. I was ten steps ahead of these fuckers!

While Agent Sheen was attempting to make me as comfortable as possible, Murphy was busy going through folders and pulling out pictures, receipts, and a tape recorder. Placing the pictures in front of me one at a time, he stared into my eyes and studied my reaction very closely. The photographs displayed me making numerous transactions in various places around the city, while others showed me getting in and out of different luxury vehicles, carrying large duffle bags, and even pulling off the burglary on Mummar's house.

These *federales* had copies of receipts from jewelry stores, trips, house, cars, et cetera. How did I let these motherfuckas get close to me without me knowing? Probably the same way that sneaky-ass bitch Felicia was following me around, putting bugs in my car. Too fucking comfortable, always underestimating people. The anger and disappointment in my shortcomings sent me over the edge.

"So what the fuck is y'all saying? This don't prove shit but that y'all should've been paparazzi instead of *federales*," I remarked sarcastically. "Either charge me, or let me go. But I ain't saying shit. I want my lawyer now!"

"I don't think you understand what's going on here, Boss, but before you say another word I suggest you shut the fuck up and listen for a change," Murphy snapped. "Personally, I don't give a shit about you. If it was my call, I'd go down to the garage and search your truck. As a matter of fact that's what I am going to do. Fuck this shit!" he threatened before jumping out the seat, walking to the door.

"Hey! That's enough!" Agent Sheen intervened. "Come on, guys, let's not jump the gun before we have the opportunity to at least have this meeting. Mr Hassan, Agent Murphy, let us please put our disagreements to the side and be gentlemen. If we're not able to come to an understanding then, afterward, Agent Murphy, you do what you need to do, and, Mr. Hassan, I'll personally allow you to use my phone to contact your attorney. That sounds fair, right?"

I said nothing. But I did find the classical good cop, bad cop act funny. I was laughing my ass off on the inside, but on the outside I held my poker face firm and sharp. Agent Murphy seemed a little reluctant at first, but eventually sat back down at the table. What a theatrical performance. They deserved applause.

Shortly after restoring the peace, Agent Sheen started the meeting. "I'm going to be straight up with you, Boss; we work completely different than the state or any other law enforcement agencies you previously dealt with. Unlike those other agencies and courts, we don't care about how much money you have, or what high-powered lawyers come running to your rescue. Our agencies and courts will not be influenced nor corrupted.

"What matters in our eyes is what kind of information you can bring forward. Your willingness to be our eyes and ears on the street. And most importantly, if your assistance personally makes an impact on the war on drugs, and putting away violent offenders." He revealed the process of initiating a rat.

"Think about it, Boss. You'll be a hundred times more powerful than what you are now. We become your connection. That means you'll have an unlimited supply. Droughts? Don't exist. Competition? Just give us the word and we'll get them out of the way for a few years.

"Every bust you set up, you'll get forty percent of whatever we find and whatever assets we seize and liquidate. Let me make it clear for you, Boss. We don't give a fuck what you do or how you do it; as long as it brings results we're looking for we are happy. You keep us happy, we keep you rich, free, and virtually untouchable," Murphy added.

I couldn't believe what these *federales* were sitting here offering me.

They made the shit sound as if it were morally correct. This was a major insult to everything I stood for. Besides that, I was already untouchable, and I didn't have to be no rotten piece of shit to get that status. I guessed Murphy thought that his little speech could somehow break the ice that was represented by my demeanor and strength. I wasn't the least impressed. I let it be known by lifting my hand and looking at my watch.

"You want to be a fucking wise guy, huh? Well here are your options, Boss: either you serve us on the streets, or we'll see to it that you serve a life sentence in the state penitentiary! You're not as slick as you think you are. Do you think we don't know about the shooting at the bar? Or that you were the mastermind behind the kidnapping of White Mike? You do realize that two federal agents were injured in the commencing of the crime right? That means, conspiracy, attempted murder on federal agents, robbery, interference with a federal investigation. Should I go on? Or do you get the point?" Murphy held back no punches.

The bomb that he just dropped on me had stolen my breath away, and had me sweating like I was sitting in the sauna. For that moment I reflected on all the dirt I did in the duration of my lifetime. All the money, power, respect that I acquired couldn't even get me out of this jam. On some real shit, I wish that I never had it, or that I could somehow give back. All of the killings, shootings, robberies, drug deals, et cetera, had finally caught up with me. Karma had sent the FBI to do her dirty work.

These *federales* were up in my head, and they knew it. At that point they refused to let up.

"Come on, Boss, I know you don't want it to end like this. You have a beautiful woman back home, a lovely house, money, cars, jewelry, and status, which you hustled so hard to maintain. Don't make us take it away from you," Sheen reasoned. "We know you're not a rat and we'll never look at you as one. We respect you as the boss you are. If you were anything lesser we wouldn't have wasted our time.

"You're a man of strong influence, leadership, and determination. With us behind you and you behind us we can take each other straight to the top. Look at Sammy da Bull, Alpo, TI, Frank Lucas, Nicky Barnes. These guys helped the feds and they're still respected. Frank Lucas is being acknowledged as an American gangster, for crying out loud! TI still goes platinum and has fans out of the ass.

"Before we leave you to decide your fate, consider this. If you don't cooperate, we're going to take your house, your money, your lady, and anything else that holds value for you. We'll charge you with a hundred-count indictment, and push for a speedy trial. We'll make sure that you have a jury of middle-class white citizens who have only seen blacks on television. We'll present pictures, a few witnesses, wire taps, and a couple of us good federal agents who will paint a picture better than Picasso.

"More than likely you'll be convicted and sent to a federal penitentiary. In there, you're not going to be looked at like a hero because you didn't cooperate. What do you think, you're going to get a fucking reward and celebration because you didn't snitch? You'll be treated no different from the rest of those assholes in there. A strong-minded young man such as yourself will remain hopeful for a few years, praying that you find a loophole in your case, so that the court of appeals will over turn your sentence, or grant you a new trial. You'll be one of those guys working out to stay fit, reading, writing to keep your mind occupied, and telling your stories of how you had this and had that over and over again until the crowd of listeners can tell them back to you word for word. One day you'll realize that no relief is coming, and the very things that kept you strong will begin to slowly break you down. Suddenly the homosexuals will appear attractive to you. Gambling and drinking will be your temporary escape from reality. Meanwhile your mind is deteriorating piece by piece," Murphy concluded with his finishing touch.

"We're going to give you a few minutes to think this through. For your sake we hope you make the right decision," Sheen advised, before they stepped out of the room.

As soon as they left the room, I stumbled over to the garbage can and threw up everything in my stomach. I was experiencing a severe case of bubble guts like never before. Who the fuck did these *federales* think they was? They were basically playing God. Giving me an option of life or death! Heaven or hell!

As I stood there trying to gather my composure, their voices and offers echoed repeatedly inside my head. Becoming more tempting with each second that passed. I stuck my index fingers in my ears hoping to block them out. Consequently, they got even louder.

To my surprise, I began to consider their offer. I thought about my freedom, my wealth, my status, Sophia, and everything I had going on with my life. There was no way I was going to choose death over life. Who would? At that moment everything I preached, practiced, and honored was contradicted. Since I couldn't beat the feds, fuck it, I decided to join them.

If I was going to play their game, I was playing it to my advantage. My rules, my way, or no way. If all that powerful untouchable shit they said was true, then I was about to take over the entire city. Sure, I'd agree to work for them, but in reality they would be working for me. This would be better than having police on the payroll. I could see it now. Just like that, my visions and schemes began to unfold right before my eyes.

About ten minutes later the door swung open, and the agents stepped inside. Sheen held a pen, and what appeared to be some sort of contract, while Murphy played with a pair of handcuffs.

"So what's it gonna be, Boss man?" asked Murphy with a conspicuous smile on his face. It was as if he already knew what the answer was. "Are you going to be serving us, or will you rather serve life?"

Refusing to allow them the satisfaction of seeing the shameful look of defeat in my eyes, I kept my head down low as I spoke. "This is how it's going down. I'm not testifying at no trials, nor will I outright set anybody up. I'll deliver the niggas to y'all my way and my way only. Under no circumstances will I allow my reputation to be tarnished because of this arrangement of ours. That goes for y'all as well. I don't care what y'all have to do to keep this shit top secret, but it needs to be done or else we have no deal." I stated my nonnegotiable terms.

"We wouldn't have it no other way, Boss. As far as we're concerned you're the same person you were before all this took place. We expect you to put that same hustle and energy you put into the streets into this. No one besides us in this room will ever know about this meeting, or what we agreed to. The only difference between how you conducted business then and now is that we're your employers. We want reports, names, addresses, telephone numbers, et cetera. All you have to do is lure them in with the bait, and when they bite we'll hook them and pull 'em up. Understood?" Sheen inquired. One would've thought he was talking about fishing, if they didn't know any better.

"Yeah. Whatever you say," I answered nonchalantly. I still couldn't believe that I had agreed to be a rat. This was unreal. I strongly questioned, was this shit always in me, and just waiting for the opportunity to present itself, or had their mind games bought it out me?

Over the next three hours, I was taught the deceptive tricks and techniques of a low-down dirty rat bastard! Some of the things they revealed was unbelievable. It made me wonder where and how they even came up with this shit. When they said that I'd be a hundred times more powerful and virtually untouchable that was an understatement. They should've added extremely dangerous to the equation.

If I played my part right, I could make this shit do what it do! Behind the scenes I could still get a nigga killed, robbed, and extorted. While on the other hand, I'd use the *federales* to get rid of the competition, my enemies, or anybody else who stood in the way of my progress. With that kind of power intact, that made me a quadruple threat.

Before my induction as a federal confidential informant became official, I first had to sign my soul away. The terms stated that I would be given a five-figure yearly salary, not including the percentages and incentives from the confiscated money and other assets; the last line informed me that if I was to ever renege on my end immunity would be reversed and used against me as an admission of guilt.

After the signing process was completed, they pulled yet another trick out of their hats. This one was by far the best of them all. After stepping out of the office for a minute or so, Murphy returned with the duffle bag that was in the back of the Escalade. Setting it down on the table in front of me, he went on to explain to me what was now inside of the bag.

"Whatever you had in here earlier is no longer here. It has been replaced with a synthetic form of cocaine. It can be snorted, injected, and can even be cooked up to a crack-like substance. It may not be actual narcotic, but it's just as good, potent, and extremely effective," he revealed.

"By law, we can't legally distribute or manufacture an illegal substance. Therefore, we've created our own version of it," Sheen further explained. "Fortunately for us, federal laws allow us to still charge suspects in possession of the synthetic cocaine, because of their intent in having it in their possession. Meaning that when they buy it, possess it, and sell it they're doing so under the pretense that it's actually cocaine.

"This stuff is similar to the spice incense that people all over the world are smoking in place of marijuana. It has the same effects, reactions, and smell, but it doesn't show up as marijuana in the bloodstream or the urine. The weed came first, cocaine came second, and our chemists are working on heroin as we speak. It just goes to prove that every negative can be made into a positive."

Before I was set free, they gave me a cell phone that had a device installed that when activated would allow them to listen in on a conversation, plus be able to pinpoint my exact location. Its purpose was to entrap criminals, and also be my blanket of security in the event something went wrong and they needed to get to me fast.

While we were on the elevator going back down to the garage, Murphy advised me that I was on the clock the moment I drove out of there, and they were expecting immediate results. He called it the first of many tests.

Sheen's last minute advice was more comforting. "Boss, if for some reason you're ever pulled over by the police, alert us immediately so that we can straighten it out."

Surprisingly, when I got back in the truck, the gun was still under the seat as I left it, and so was the bulletproof vest. I knew for certain that they searched the car and came upon the items, but since they didn't mention nothing about them, or confiscate them, I guessed that meant they didn't care that I had them.

With gun on my lap I drove out of the garage feeling like a born-again Boss. I don't think there was a nigga in the city who done ducked as many indictments and bullets in their lifetime as I did in the past week alone. I had a reason to be here on the streets. Therefore I would remain on them by all means necessary.

Chapter 27

On my way over to West Philly, I decided to check in with Sophia. I knew she was probably going crazy over the fact that I hadn't called nor answered my phone in the past three to four hours. But if only she knew the sacrifices and compromising I just went through all in the name of love, life, position, and freedom, she'd understand why, and should be appreciative.

When I called her she picked up, but didn't say anything before disconnecting the call. When I called back the second time, she forwarded me to voicemail. My third and final attempt, she decided to answer like she had some muthafucking sense.

"Yesssssss! What do you want?"

"What do I want? Girl, what the fuck is wrong with you?"

"Don't fucking cuss at me, Amin," she shot coldly. "Where are you at and where have you been?"

"I got caught up in something. I'm all right though. I'll be back home in a little bit. All right?" When she didn't answer, I sensed that there was still a problem. "What's wrong, Sophia? You ignoring me now?"

"You want to know what's wrong with me? When the person I love gets shot five times and returns to the streets not even a week later, and I don't hear from him all day, and can't reach him, my mind starts to think the worst-case scenario. So wherever you was at, and whatever or whoever you was doing, go back and finish up!" she asserted before hanging up in my ear.

I understood where she was coming from, but she was dead wrong for hanging up in my ear. She ain't know any better. I'd deal with her later, but for now I had to fulfill other obligations.

Chapter 28

Parked on the corner of Arlington Street, I watched for nearly twenty minutes straight as Tamir served crackheads nonstop. The block was jumping like a pair of Jordans. The little slick nigga must have had a new connect, because I hadn't seen or heard from him since the last time I hit him off. Just like these typical niggas out here. When they money fucked up, and they trying to get put on, they seemed to forget how they got there.

I really wanted to smack him upside his head with the burner and run in his pockets, which was my usual routine for keeping these niggas in check. But out of the thousand ways to kill a coward, in this instance, it would be established by throwing him to the feds.

Before making my presence felt, I activated the phone that the feds had given me. When I stepped out the truck, Tamir's face looked like he just seen a ghost. Forcing one of those fake smiles of his, he motioned for me to come across the street with a wave of the hand. *What? This nigga done bumped his head!* Clearly he'd forgotten who was the Boss and who was the worker. I saw I had to remind him.

"Nigga, who the fuck you think you is, waving me over to you? I'm the Boss, nigga. You think that I will be caught dead standing at the spot where you serve crack and stash packs at? You better walk your bitch ass over here, before I smack your fuckin' teeth out your mouth!"

His pride was so damaged all he could do was laugh it off and pretend he thought that I was only joking. But I never played those types of games with any of these niggas, nor was there a smile on my face. He knew deep down inside I was a serious as a heart attack. That's why he walked his ass across that street and extended his hand with humility.

I ignored the gestures and left his hand hanging in the air.

"Nigga, don't come over here smiling and fronting like we friends and this shit a game," I barked harshly. "I see now that you got your weight up and done lost my number, huh?"

"Naw, Boss, it ain't even like that. I heard that you just got shot, and plus the last time we done business, you carried me like I was a sucka or something. You must've thought that I was talking out the ass, but as you can see, I'm doing me out here," he boasted proudly.

"Doing you, huh? Okay, I tell you what, since you got the balls to stand up for yourself, I'm going to forgive you for the disrespectful treatment you've been showing me. And I'm sure that since you been 'doing you' you got a few dollars to cop these things at twenty a pop. Right?" I reeled him in with a slight bit of intimidation.

"Twenty a pop?" His eyes lit up with surprise. "Man, if you got them in for that cheap, can I get three for fifty and owe you a dime? You know I'm good for it, Boss."

And that fast, he was back on my dick, swinging on it like Tarzan. Not only that, the setup was in full motion.

"For you? No problem. Go ahead and get the money together. I'll be sitting in my car waiting for you," I replied with the same smile he'd given me earlier, but the difference between his and mine was his was out of fear, and mines was based on cruel intent.

Chapter 29

From there it was only a matter of time before he was taken out of the game. At that time, his position would be replaced by another one of my expendable soldiers. Like Denzel Washington said in *Training Day*, "This shit is chess not checkers!" I already had a few young niggas in mind who would turn this gold mine to a diamond in the rough.

Before I could take a seat inside the Escalade, I was sidetracked by the sight of pure beauty. Mommy had the sexiest hips, legs, ass, and the walk to go along with it. As she got closer, I was surprised to see that it was scheming-ass Corrinne. She was one beautiful bitch! At five feet two inches, 130, she looked like a younger version of Pam Grier.

With each step she took, her long black hair bounced concurrently with her perfectly shaped ass and titties. Although I had never actually hit it, she did give me head one night after I drove her home from the bar. Had it not been for her period being on, I would've taken her somewhere and fucked her brains out. I still tried to hit it, but she wasn't that "type of woman," so she claimed.

The last thing I heard she was locked up for credit card fraud and identity theft. That explained the extra thickness that was complementing her body. Milk may have done a body good, but jail did one better! Damn!

As soon as she spotted me, she recognized who I was and ran up to me with open arms. While embraced in a hug, she took it upon herself to place a kiss on the side of my mouth.

"Hey, Boss! Long time no see. With your sexy self," she complimented appropriately. "Since I've been home I done heard a lot of shit about you. People are saying you was dead and everything. That's why I don't believe nothing that I don't see for myself. And I still don't believe half that shit," she joked before cracking up laughing.

"You know how it is, when a nigga out here winning, misery has the tendency to make shit appear worse than what it really is. I'm not only living, but I'm alive and doing better than the best of them." I discredited the haters' account, before boasting my status with honor and pride. "You just came back home, huh? Yeah, I can tell. But anyway, what you about to get into?"

"You're funny. But yeah, I just came home the other day," she confirmed. "I just came up here to visit my grandmother. I live in Southwest now, and I'm about to catch the bus back home. Do you have a number I can reach you at? We do have some unfinished business to attend to," she insinuated seductively before licking her lips.

"Oh you remember, huh? I tell you what, if you sit tight for a minute or two. I'll take you home and put some money in your pocket so you can go buy yourself a little car or something. A bitch as bad as you should never be on the bus." I spoke the truth.

"All my life I've been getting money and taking care of myself. I've never depended on a nigga for his money. But since it's you, I might take you up on that offer, but only if you allow me to pay you back when I get on my feet."

I respected the fact that she wouldn't allow her independence to be compromised to a degree that it couldn't be returned to her. Although I agreed to the terms she presented, I would never accept a dollar back.

As we were sitting in the Escalade catching up on old times, Tamir finally came out of his house and walked over holding a large brown paper bag. I'd honestly forgotten that I was in the process of setting this nigga up. Quickly excusing myself, I hopped out and went to the trunk to make the transaction. It took but ten seconds to make the exchange that was sure to get Tamir a ten-year sentence or better. To me, it was all business, never personal.

Before I could pull all the way off the block the "fed phone" began ringing. At first I was a little hesitant about answering because I had company, but on second thought, I decided that it may not be a good idea to put "my employers" off on the first day of work.

"Yeah, what's up?" I answered nonchalantly.

"That was a hell of a job back there, Boss man. It's like you're a natural the way you handled your first assignment. We'll meet up later to collect the money. At that time we'll have an eighteen thousand dollar check for you. We'll be in touch."

That must have been the easiest money I ever earned in my life. What was most surprising of all was the fact that I didn't even feel bad afterward. Not a bit of sympathy, shame, or guilt existed throughout my mind, body, and soul. In my perspective, this was chess using real people. And as a true chess player should know, to be a winner one must make the right moves for the best position, and be willing to sacrifice without hesitation to keep himself (the king), secured and in the game.

Before parting ways with Corrinne I gave her five grand, my number, and a kiss with the promise of linking up with her in the very near future. Women were so used to niggas taking advantage of them while they were at their lowest that she seem surprised when I didn't make any advances to get her in the bed. Of course I could've easily walked her inside and had my way with her, but I let her know I had a woman back home I needed to attend to, and I would catch up with her some other time. As expected, she respected the fact that I kept it all the way one hundred, and that I wasn't pressed to hit it. It actually made her want me even more.

"You something else, Boss. Most niggas out here will rather lie and play games just to get some pussy, but I see that you're much different from the rest of these clowns. I respect that. And soon as you're ready, hit me up and let me show you better than I can tell you," she implied before getting out of the truck.

As she walked toward the entrance of her apartment building, that ass was like an audience after a good performance. It clapped with every step she took. I was tempted to get out and walk her upstairs to her apartment. But that's what she wanted me to do. When the time was right, I was going to fulfill her every fantasy and desire she ever mustered the thought of. But on my time.

After the crazy day I been through I couldn't wait to get back to the crib and relax with my feet up. At least that was the plan. But the second I walked through the door Sophia's constant ranting and nagging prevented that from happening.

Where was I? What was I doing? How? Where, and why? I'd never seen her upset. But fuck all that. I ain't appreciate being interrogated in the comforts of my own home. Especially after all the interrogations I'd been through. It was time for me to lay down law before she started thinking that it was permissible to inquire too deep into my business. Bad enough she knew too much as it was.

"Check this out, Sophia. When I'm out there on them streets I'm taking care of business. Nothing more, nothing less. I have enough headaches dealing with those motherfuckas out there. I don't need to come home and have you contributing to the shit. It's not enough Tylenol to go around," I spoke in my most serious voice.

"What I'm doing out here pays the bills and keeps you laced up in that top-of-the-line name-brand shit that you love to flaunt in," I reminded her. "If you can't accept what I do then leave the bank books and credit cards and take everything you came with."

My comment left her frozen with the surprise, and seemed to instantly restore the belief and support she usually had in me. As she started to apologize, I placed my index finger over her lips, indicating silence. There would be no further argument, conversation, or clarification on any of the issues I addressed. They weren't up for discussion.

Since I wasn't a physically abusive nigga, I removed her clothes right then and there and disciplined her with a hard dick and a mean fucking. During the process, I had her screaming at the top of her lungs how she would never question nor second-guess me again. The way I put it down on her, I strongly doubted that we would ever have to revisit that subject again.

Chapter 30

During the course of the next few weeks, shit was coming together as beautiful as they ever been. I'd already thrown the feds enough suckas for them to stay off my ass for the time being. In between time, I was making more moves than U-Haul trucks. I was eating good, shitting even better, and sitting on dirty money like Ben Franklin's grave. The haters could say what they wanted to say, but yet couldn't none of them tell me nothing. Come to find out the feds took Tamir down a week or so after I lined him up. Not only did they catch him with four keys of coke, but he also led them to his supplier. They ended up arresting him as well. They didn't discuss the specifics of all that they confiscated from the supplier; however, they did mention that the bust was a major success, and that the little double-dealing nigga Tamir was out there cutting side deals like he was Gee Money in *New Jack City*. As good as I was treating him with the cheap prices, he still showed no loyalty or respect for the game. His actions only further justified the decision I made to work for the feds. There wasn't no loyalty out here on these streets. It was every man for himself. Therefore, why wouldn't I be armed with the most powerful dangerous weapons a nigga could have? Some have AK-47s, others had AR-15s, I had the guns and the FBI! Who or what could fuck with that?

Now that Tamir was out of the way, his block was currently under reconstruction. The young hustlers whom

I put out there hugged it from sundown to sunup. They easily doubled the numbers Tamir did, and was looking to triple them before the month was out.

While I had some spare time on my hands, I decided to put my pride to the side and go holla at Shake. The visit was way overdue. We needed to iron out our differences before somebody's feelings really got hurt and one of us acted out on them. That could be dangerous for either one of us, especially Shake.

Besides all that, if anybody had the word on the streets it was Shake. I might have fucked around and walked up on something or someone I could line up if I could get close to him for a few hours. Shake was like the bridge that all hustlers and gangsters used to network through. He was a coach, the connect, and the advocate of the game.

When I pulled up to the shop, I caught up with Shake just as he was getting into his Lexus LS 450. I beeped the horn twice before pulling up on him and rolling down the window. I seen niggas kill they brothers, girlfriends, and homies for pulling up on him and rolling down the window without identifying themselves first. Niggas had no choice but to assume it was an enemy coming to kill them. Unfortunately, all gangsters here lived by the "squeeze first, ask questions last" policy, and that's why mistaken identity cases were on a constant rise.

When Shake saw that it was me, he reached down at his waist as if he was ready to draw his pistol on me. I reacted by quickly retrieving the Glock 9 from off my lap. Luckily Shake came to his senses a split second before he was ready to get fired on.

"Boss? Is that you, son?" he inquired as if he was unable to recognize me.

"Damn, OG, it's been that long you done forgot what I look like?"

"As much as you switch those damn cars up, how could I keep up? You know better than to be creeping up on me."

He shot me a smile that made my skin crawl.

"But anyhow, what brings you down this end of the city? You decide to get back on the team, or do you still think that you could carry this city on your back without your father's guidance?"

"I'm just trying to holla at you, pops. We may not always agree with each other, but I'm going to love you forever regardless," I declared sincerely. "Now the question is, do you have some time for your boy, or are we going to continue carrying on as if we're strangers?"

My request seemed to put him deep in thought for a brief moment before he responded. "Go ahead and park your car, then come back and take this ride with me."

It wasn't exactly what I was planning, but it was sure to keep me close to him for an hour or so at the least. After parking the convertible up, I put the Glock on my hip before getting out and joining him.

As soon as I sat in the passenger seat, I spoke what was on my mind and in my heart. "First and foremost, I want to apologize for my behavior and disrespectful ways. You're the closet thing I had to a father while growing up. You taught me how to be a man and a provider. For that alone, you have my love and loyalty for life," I promised him. "Sometimes a nigga get too far caught up in these streets, and that shit starts to take a toll on how one thinks, and acts. I assure that I'm focused and back like I never left. Those five shots to the chest was warning for me to get my shit together. All of my affairs are in order with the exception of this minor little bullshit we going through. The sooner we get past this, the sooner we can get back to normal. The way it should always be, and the way it needs to stay."

"I couldn't agree more. You put that so perfect I can't even add nothing to that. That's the Boss I raised talking now. I don't know who that other nigga was. But as long as he stay away, I forgive you and welcome you back to the table with open arms. I love you, son," he expressed with tears in his eyes, before opening his arms and embracing me with a tight bear hug.

Just like that, the father and son duo was back in motion. With his connections my reach was expanded by at least a football field or longer. It wasn't shit I couldn't talk my way into or out of!

Chapter 31

Meanwhile back over at the house, Sophia had just returned from CVS. She was in a rush to make it to the toilet. As she ran up the steps, she ripped open the box of the pregnancy test. Once she finally made it to the commode, she put the test screen underneath her, and emptied her bladder. After cleaning herself up, she set the test down on the sink and waited for the results.

When her period came late for the second month straight, she began to suspect that something was wrong. The thought of being pregnant had her nervous and more sacred then she'd ever been in her life.

"Baby, whatever you do keep that special place for me in your heart, and don't let no nigga put no baby up in you." Victor's words echoed through her mind, reminding her of the two major requests she promised to uphold no matter what.

It wasn't long before guilt kicked in and had her crying her eyes out. Disappointments and failure were starting to become a habitual occurrence in her life. She picked up the test stick and read the results. The test confirmed her worst fears. She was pregnant! The news only added to the stress that she was already dealing with. There was no way she was going to have this baby. Before she even left the bathroom, she called the clinic and scheduled an emergency appointment for an abortion.

Being in love with two men at the same time wasn't easy. Even though Victor was in jail, it was still very difficult to balance the two relationships. Both of them had special needs that required a lot of her time, patience, and attention.

On one hand, she had to sneak behind Boss's back and take Victor's phone calls, write and receive his letters, plus send him money. Luckily, there was a post office around the corner from the house where she was able to set up a private Post Office box address, or Victor would have talked her into giving up the house address. She stayed hopeful that he'd get relief from the courts and be on his way home soon, but from the looks of things it didn't look like that was going to happen at all. It appeared as if the courts and the system were selling him dreams, and had the both of them believing a bunch of bullshit. That's exactly why, with each day that passed, she was losing faith in Victor and the system, and falling deeper in love with Boss in the process.

On the other hand, Boss had her on a constant emotional rollercoaster. At times she hated him, but her love for him exceeded the hate. What she couldn't stand the most about him was that he was the first man she loved before she had him figured out. Besides that, she hated the fact that he allowed his arrogance to dictate his thinking and how he conducted himself on the streets. She was surprised that he'd survived this long without being killed or put underneath a jail. But after getting by this long, she assumed that he was truly the Boss of all bosses, as he claimed. Either that or he had a rabbit's foot up his ass.

Fearful of getting caught up in the middle of a deadly love triangle, and tired of living a lie, she promised herself that if things continued as they were, then she would simply get rid of the excess baggage.

Chapter 32

I ended up riding around with Shake throughout most of the afternoon. In that frame of time he must've made a dozen stops, held over a hundred conversations, and given me a thousand different speeches on life. If I had a dollar for every time I done heard the shit, I would have been a millionaire. The sad thing was, I used to believe in all that bullshit. But altering experience, all the honor and loyalty that was instilled in me my entire life went straight out the window in the matter of a few hours.

Hoping to avoid hearing anymore of the bullshit he was preaching, I closed my eyes and pretended that I fell asleep on him. Still I was on constant alert of my surroundings. Just when I thought the day was a waste, Shake received a telephone call that changed it all around. I listened in closely to every word he said.

"Hearing from you is like music to my ears . . . Really? Now that's what I'm talking about . . . Okay, I'll see you at the shop at seven o'clock on the dot . . . Be cool."

The phone call seemed to have changed Shake's entire mood. He was so excited he couldn't even sit still. He went from tapping on the dashboard to checking his watch every few seconds. I had a feeling something big was about to go down. But I couldn't put a finger on it. These were signs that were far too familiar. Whenever Shake carried on like this, he had something major in the making.

His boastful arrogant ways wouldn't allow him to keep the news a secret. It wasn't but a few minutes after the initial telephone call before he was hitting on my leg, trying to wake me up.

I opened my eyes with a start and annoyance as if I was really sleeping.

"Wake up, son. You know true hustlers don't sleep; we rest one eye's up!" he reminded me.

But if only he knew.

"It's a good thing you choose today to come fuck with you daddy, li'l nigga. It might turn out to be the best decision you ever made in your young-ass life! Tell me something. What do you know about that H?"

"What? You talking about heroin?" I played stupid.

"That's exactly what I'm talking about," he confirmed proudly.

"Not that much. But from what I heard it's rumored to get a nigga rich in six months or less, and dopefiends can't live without it. Why you ask?" I fished around.

"You know me, I'm always looking to venture into other investments. From what I know about that H, if you got that number ten dope, your money will come ten times faster than it ever came! Look around, everybody and they mother getting high off that shit!" His voice grew loud with excitement.

"The only reason I kept the team away from it for so long is because of the time they given out behind it. But if we play it smart and get a quick six-month run, we can do some beautiful numbers and step away unnoticed." He spoke the OG rule. "In the next few days I might be able to get us a nice line that could get us that number ten dope unlimited. Keep your eyes and ears open, and see if you can find a place to move it. If it come through as I expect it to, you going be the first motherfucka I hit off. You already know!"

The entire time Shake was revealing his get-rich-quick scheme, I was piecing together the connection between the phone call and the sudden mention of heroin. Once I thought I had it all figured out, I began constructing a plot of my own.

As soon as Shake dropped me back off to my car, I called Corrinne up to see if she was available to do me a quick favor. When I reached her and explained the dilemma I needed her assistance with she stopped everything she was doing without hesitation. I wasn't surprised that she agreed so easily. I was a boss, and I've always had that type of effect over woman. What wouldn't a bitch do to get next to a nigga like me?

Since I was already in Southwest Philly, it only took me about ten minutes to get over to her spot. Shortly after I pulled up out front, this bitch came walking out wearing a pair of Daisy Duke cut-offs that were so short and tight, they left very little for the mind to wonder. To top it off she wore a tight wife beater and a pair of red bottoms. If she ain't look like a black Wonder Woman, my name wasn't Boss. I was loving the fact how she kept it classy yet hood at the same time.

Before she could make it over to the car, I jumped in the passenger seat, and gave her an open invitation to push a spaceship without having to go through NASA.

"Go ahead and drive, ma. I'm going fuck around and crash trying to keep my eyes on you and the road at the same time." I kept it one hundred.

"Look who's talking? Nigga, you know you be having my juices flowing all crazy. Even though you be holding back with that dick!" She flirted while staring directly at the erection that'd been in the making ever since she walked outside of her apartment. "This is the biggest convertible I ever been in. But don't worry, I'm a rider. The bigger the better for me," she insinuated. Clearly she was talking about my Johnson, and fronting like she was referring to the car.

Two hours later, I was following Corrinne back over to her apartment in a triple black Dodge Charger with the V6 Hemi engine. She'd put the car in her name on the strength of who I was and nothing more. But because she did the favor for me without delay or questioning, I figured the least I could do was go upstairs to her apartment and catch up with our unfinished business. I did have two hours to kill. And what better way to kill time?

Fortunately, I had bought an ounce of exotic weed upstairs with me, because Corrinne was trying to kill my lungs with some of that backyard boggie. Once again, I had to invite her into the life of a true boss. In this instance, that meant smoking how bosses smoke. Only the best!

There was no cutting up or rolling cigars up when I smoked. All I did was pour the tobacco out and replace it with high-grade marijuana. I barely even broke the buds up. I just stuffed them into the cigar.

After Corrinne threw on a Prince CD, we relaxed and treated our lungs to one of the finest exotic plants marijuana had to offer. While Prince was singing about how much he adored his special lady, Corrinne's hand went fishing down my pants. She eventually freed Willie.

As if it were on fire and burning up, she extinguished it inside of her mouth; suffocating it with her wet, warm saliva, and soft tongue. Next, she wrapped her arms around my legs and proceeded to give me head that was so good it should've been against the law. Mommy used no hands whatsoever, strictly neck, lips, tongue, and throat. She was the first woman I ever seen show strong gag reflex discipline as she did. I was so far down her throat the head of my dick was touching her esophagus. Yet she handled it like a pro.

Before I allowed her to get the best of me, I had to put the dutch in the ashtray and defend myself. Quickly sliding my fingers through the small opening in her shorts, I followed the warm moisture until I came upon her honeycomb hideout. Slowly I circled my finger over the silky, soft lips of her wet vagina. My very touch seemed to hypnotize her most intimate body parts, subjecting her hips and thighs to rotate in the same motion and direction as my finger.

Once the teasing became unbearable, she worked the muscles in her vagina to suck my fingers up like a vacuum cleaner. Almost instantly her pussy began popping and overflowing with juices. Her hole was so tight, I could literally feel the rhythm of her pulse as it raced along with her heartbeat. The way she was winding and grinding that thing on my finger made me wonder if she'd still be able to handle it in that manner once I put this dick up in her. With that thought I dropped my pants and prepared to find out.

Bending mommy straight over the sofa, I pulled her shorts and panties down to her ankles. When I entered her, the tight confinements of her vagina seem to constrict around me with a grip so strong, I feared that it might cut off my circulation. Hoping to get some leverage with my stroke, I gripped the sides of her ass cheeks. It was so soft that the tips of my fingers sunk into her skin. Unable to balance the pain and pleasure, she gave up and buried her face into the pillow and bit down on it.

As I was long stroking her from the back, I put the twist in my hips and touched every wall inside of her. While one of her hands caressed my nuts, the other went to work on her clit. It wasn't long after that before she caught her second wind; with a sudden burst of strength and energy, she began bucking backward so hard that I lost my balance and fell on my ass. Through it all our bodies remained connected intimately.

No sooner did we land on the floor than she was already riding me with the position, motion, and speed of a jockey turning the final lap at the Kentucky Derby. Only I was the horse, and the finish line was the rewarding orgasm that we achieved together.

"Damn, Corrinne! Your pussy on a thousand," I complimented her as I struggled to catch my breath. "If I would have known that thing was that good, you probably would have been my bitch a long time ago."

Usually when I came out of some pussy, I would either roll over and go to sleep, or hit the streets. Yet here I was kissing and massaging all over Corrinne's back on some romantic shit. I stayed cuddled up with this bitch for damn near forty-five minutes. The time was six-thirty, and although I didn't want to leave, I had to go right now!

"Go ahead and get your freaky ass up, ma. I got to get ready to bounce and go take care of this business," I advised with a smack on the ass.

"Damn, boy! You should've waited until later to put your thing down on me like that. My poor little coochie all swollen and throbbing," she revealed without shame. When she went to stand up, a small waterfall came gushing out of her pussy onto my lap.

"Goddamn! All that? What was you trying to do, get me pregnant with triplets?" She stared at the puddles with disbelief. "Let me clean you up before I send you home to your woman."

Just when I thought she was going to retrieve a washrag as a normal woman would've done, this bitch drops to the floor, licking and slurping every drop of it up off of me. That put the icing on the cake and officially made her my number two bitch. To make her feel of importance, I left her with the keys to the Benz, a few stacks, and told her to go do her. To my surprise, she dropped to her knees again and tried to unbutton my pants. I had to literally push her down and run up out of that motherfucka! This bitch was a real live nympho! But I wasn't mad at her.

Ten minutes before seven I was parked up a block away from the shop conducting surveillance like I was the *federales* fo'real fo'real! In a sense I guess I was. So far, Shake's Lexus was the only car parked outside the shop. It wasn't until a little after seven that a money green Benz wagon pulled up behind the Lexus and parked.

The man who emerged appeared to be either light skinned or of Spanish descent. He walked with phenomenal swagger, and dressed like a corporate dope boy. His jewelry was kept to a minimum. A basic yet rather expensive Audemars Piguet watch complemented his wrist. He carried a small package tucked underneath his arm. The secure manner in which he held it indicated one of two things: that it was either something illegal, or very valuable. Possibly both? Heroin was the first thing that came to mind.

About twenty minutes later, the nigga came back out accompanied by Shake. There was no sign of the package that he originally went inside with. At that point I was almost 100 percent positive that he was either the connect or was sent by him to deliver it. That meant that he would eventually lead me to the dope!

With a smile, a handshake, and farewell greeting, Shake saw the man off to his car. As soon as he pulled off, he rushed back into the shop in an obvious hurry.

From the direction in which the Benz traveled, I knew a quick shortcut that would allow me to catch up with him a few blocks away. My estimates put me exactly two cars behind him. That was when I noticed he had New Jersey plates. It also explained why he was driving toward the Ben Franklin Bridge.

As I followed him into New Jersey, I maintained a respectful distance of at least two to three cars behind him.

He got off at the Cherry Hill exit and turned down Maple Tree Street. About two miles down the road, he turned onto White Hill Avenue. I noticed that there was a No Exit sign posted right next to the one that read 24-HOUR TOWN WATCH. I continued up the road, knowing that since he turned down a block with a No Exit sign, it was obvious that he lived somewhere on that street. After driving another mile or so I came upon a Texaco gas station. I filled up the tank before traveling back in the direction in which I came. When I reached White Hill Avenue, I cautiously turned onto the block. With the exception of the little bit of lighting coming from the large single homes, the neighborhood was rather dark. The structure of the homes and driveways were almost identical to the ones in my community. It showed that the nigga had taste.

Each house I passed I closely surveyed the premises, looking for that money green Benz wagon as if it had owed me something. There was no sign of it. Maybe the nigga had parked it in one of these garages? Just when I started to think that my efforts were in vain, I spotted the Benz parked behind a BMW X5 in the driveway of the last house on the block. Jackpot! I could almost smell the come up.

Before exiting the block, I made a mental note of the property and its surroundings. From there it was only a matter of time before I ran up in that bitch and tossed it up from the floor to the ceiling, and everywhere in between. But first I had to get a few motherfuckas out of my way! *That should be a piece of cake.*

When I got back over to Philly I stopped over Corrinne's crib briefly to trade cars back. As I tried to leave, she blocked the door and begged me to put her to bed before I left. How could I deny her? Not only did I put her to sleep, but I gave her something to dream about before, during, and afterward.

Chapter 33

First thing the following morning I got an unexpected call from Shake. He told me to get out of the bed and come straight down to the shop, claiming something urgent came up. The way he put it didn't sound as if he was requesting it. It kind of made me wonder what angle he was on. I had to remind myself what type of nigga I was dealing with.

I wouldn't be surprised if Shake had staged the phone call and the drop that was made just as a test to see what I would do. If I would cross him and go after his connect. What if he wanted me to hear that telephone call?

The more I thought about it, the more I realized that if Shake didn't trust me that much, he would have just got me out the way. It was him who once told me, "If one's loyalty is in question, then he's unworthy of the living." Therefore, I didn't think he would go through all the theatrics just to test me. I figured that these sudden worries was just my conscience eating away at me. With everything to gain and nothing to lose I shook off my worries and fears and headed over to the shop. All of my life I'd been dancing with the devil, ducking police, and popping my collar. It was too late in the game for that scary shit. I realized one thing about this street life: every situation had the potential to either better your life or take it away. With the advantages I had, I could risk the chance.

When I entered the shop I had my poker face, and the Glock 9 on my hip locked and loaded. One of the barbers informed me that Shake was in the back office. Two quick taps on the door got me immediate entry. When Shake opened the door, he had that devious smirk on his face.

Nodding toward the desk, I looked over to see several sandwich bags containing a golden brown powder substance. I knew exactly what it was, yet, I stood there staring at it with amazement as if I didn't. Just as expected Shake did the honors of introducing me to the product before me.

"This here, son, is what I've been telling you about. Us old-timers call it smack, and you young niggas call it dope or diesel," he schooled me. "The difference between this right here, and that bullshit call that they serving on the corners all over the city, is this is pure, and could take more hits than Muhammad Ali in his prime. I only copped a few ounces for now, but if it do the numbers I project it to do, then we can start buying keys. Go ahead and take a few bags and see if you can make it do what it do."

"Damn, pops! You wasn't bullshitting was you?" I replied while picking up three bags. "I got a few peoples waiting on my phone call right now about getting they hands on some of this shit right here." Sadly, I was actually referring to the feds. Shake ain't have a worry in the world, but I definitely couldn't say the same for his connect.

After giving me one of his thirty-minute speeches on the ethics of hustling, he finally allowed me to part with the dope. Having made it out of there still breathing with my plots undetected reassured me that I was in complete control.

With a dutch of cush and an ounce of syrup as my advocators, I was able to easily brainstorm the finishing touches necessary to perfect my plan. Bobby Fisher and

Einstein together couldn't have come up with a better strategy. Quickly removing the "fed phone" from the middle console, I connected to the agents.

"Well! Well! Well! If it ain't ol' Boss man," Murphy answered sarcastically. "We were starting to think that you don't love us no more. You give us a few fish out of the sea and think that's enough? Please! Those guys were all corner boys. We want someone just as major as you are. As the saying goes, fair exchange ain't no robbery. Do you understand what I'm saying?"

"If you shut the fuck up for just one second, you would've heard what you wanted to hear when you answered the phone!" I shot back what he ditched out. "Now listen! Within the next twenty-four hours or so, I should have some solid information about a big-time heroin supplier out of New Jersey. If my sources are correct it's going to be a big shipment coming in some time tomorrow. I just need y'all to be on point and prepared for it to go down. I'll be in touch."

After giving instructions I hung up right in the cracker's ear. I had to make it clear to him who was running the show. Who the fuck did he think he was talking to? It was obvious that he had me confused with one of their other CIs, who allowed them to put their hand up his ass and control him like a puppet. I was the muthafuckin' puppet master! I was a boss coming into the game and played it only to win and secure my status. To be a great thinker, one must be able to think through the beginning, the middle, and the ending of every situation he involves himself with. Then he has to be prepared for what comes afterward.

Having set high expectations in this particular heist giving me the financial stability to live well beyond comfortable possibly forever, it was time for me to step back and play Phil Jackson. And what would Phil Jackson be without great players like Michael Jordan, Shaquille O'Neal , or Kobe Bryant? The same as I would be without my nigga Gunner.

With that under consideration, I was prepared to offer Gunner position as my underboss. His loyalty toward me has been 100 percent since he came into the picture. I done lost count of how many niggas he done aired out and murdered on my orders. If there was anyone I could depend on to come through during crunch time it was him.

It may be difficult task transforming a stone-cold killer into a prominent hustler, but for a nigga who done turned whores to housewives and ounces to bricks, difficult takes a day and the impossible less than a week. When I called Gunner and told him that I was coming to pick him up, he seemed confused. But when I told him to dress casual, he acted like I was speaking a foreign language.

"Where we going? You know I don't do the club scenery," he reminded me. "You talking about dress casual? For me that's a pair of Timberlands and some army fatigues."

"Nigga, wear whatever you want. We just going to have a few drinks, and talk some business over. When you're with me, you're going to be good regardless."

After picking Gunner up we drove to the Clock Bar just off Germantown and Erie Avenue. During the ride over he asked me a hundred questions about the shooting that left me with five bullet holes in my chest. He didn't appreciate the fact that I hadn't called him not once since the shooting incident took place.

"Some shit I had to handle on my own, big fellow," I explained. "When it comes to putting that work in, I'm just as dangerous as you are," I reminded him.

Once we made it inside the Clock Bar, Gunner suggested that we sit at a table that gave us a clear view of everybody coming in and leaving. There was only one table in the place that offered that particular arrangement; however, it was being occupied by a group of females.

With my swagger on a thousand, I approached the ladies and offered them a deal they couldn't refuse. "Excuse me, ladies, I don't mean to interrupt y'all night, but this here table is me and my man's favorite place to sit. If you ladies would allow us to sit here, I'll make it worth your troubles," I assured them while pulling out a stack of hundred dollar bills and throwing it in front of them. They were sold faster than a dildo on a faggot street.

After throwing back a few shots of Patrón, Gunner appeared to be a little more relaxed. Only then did I reveal my reasons for bringing him out tonight. "My nigga, you know we go back a long time. We've been doing this since we was little kids. Look at us now. We done came up nice huh?" I looked him straight in his eyes as I spoke.

"Hell yeah! But it ain't come easy. A lot of blood, sweat, and tears," he replied.

"You ain't never lie, my nigga. But check this out: I'm thinking about getting married real soon. I'm even considering having some kids and doing the family thing. That means I need to start stepping away from the game. You dig me?"

He replied with a nod.

"I know you done made some nice money over the years, but not as much as I have. As my brother and my nigga, I want to see you on my level or better before I walk away completely. It ain't no catch, homie; all you have to do is pick up where I left off.

"It's the perfect time, G. I just got a connect on some good dope and all we need is a six-month run. On some real shit if we went and took over one of those Poppie's blocks down North Philly we could do it do it in three. But it's your call, my nigga. What you think?"

"Damn, homie. It touch my heart that you're concerned enough about my future to make sure I'm well off before you move on with your life. That's some real shit, homie, and I thank you for that," he expressed his appreciation. "Of course I'm down, but I don't know if I have the patience to deal with a bunch of niggas. I ain't going for no sob stories and the bullshit. I been done killed a nigga quick! But anyway, what exactly would I have to do?"

"It's easy. All you have to do is pick money up, and drop work off. Every now and then you may have to put a nigga in line, but for the most part you'll be fucking with all official niggas." I stretched the truth a little bit. "I tell you what, keep the coke and money you owe me from the clowns you dealt with down on Fifteenth and York, and go ahead down North Philly and get us a dope block. You do that, we split all proceeds fifty-fifty."

"Nigga, we on!" He accepted the offer. "Give me a day or two and I'll have us a block. Or else my name ain't Gunner."

To celebrate our new partnership we popped a few bottles and toasted to the good life. It was amazing how my mouthpiece put thoughts in niggas' heads that allowed them to envision the success that they would die to live.

Before dropping Gunner off, I gave him the three ounces of dope Shake had given me earlier and promised that there will be much more where that came from. We agreed to link up again in the next day or two.

When I arrived home later that night, I found Sophia in bed with a box of tissues, and eyes full of tears. It broke my heart to see her in that condition, so I climbed in the bed and tried to comfort her. When I went to put my arm around her, she pulled away from me.

"Damn! I can't touch you?" I shouted with frustration.

After a few odd seconds she raised her arm in the air and showed me the blue hospital band on her wrist. That's when she broke down crying and started punching all over me.

"You stress me out, Amin . . . I've been worrying about you so much since you got shot . . . I . . . I . . . I was bleeding earlier, and I wanted to call you. I needed you, but I ain't want to call you and get cussed out, so I drove myself to the hospital," she revealed through tears.

With her hand rubbing across her stomach I already knew what she was going to say before she even said it.

"I was six weeks pregnant, and I had a miscarriage. Why? Why God take my baby away from me?"

Her words were like a sharp dagger stabbing me deep in the heart. Unfortunately, I couldn't explain why, nor answer her questions. What it all came down to was the fact that my lifestyle and selfishness had caused her to lose my unborn child. The hurt and sorrow bought me to tears as I sought comfort in Sophia's arms.

That night I made a few promises to myself and Sophia. For one, I was going to start spending more time with her, and showing her love and affection she deserved. I explained to her that I'd already handed down my status to a close associate, and that my role in the streets would be at a minimum. Furthermore, I assured her that after I officially wrapped up all my business affairs we were moving far away from Philly. Afterward, we could give the pregnancy thing another chance. Those sincere words of assurance put a smile on her face and seemed to make her feel much better.

Realizing that a good night's sleep was essential to my well-being physically, and mentally prepared for the challenging day I had ahead of me, I went into the bathroom to retrieve my reserve eight-ounce bottle of syrup that I kept in the medicine cabinet. While there I noticed two prescription bottles bearing Sophia's name. What caught my attention was the name of the doctor who prescribed them.

Sam Shults? The name was definitely familiar to me, but I couldn't remember for the life of me why. Fuck it! I wasn't going to dwell too hard on it. Knowing me, I done probably seen his name on one of the thousands of bottles of syrup I done drank throughout the course of my life. After throwing back an ounce or two of syrup, I returned to the bed, wrapped Sophia's leg around me and fell straight asleep.

Chapter 34

The following morning, I woke up to one of man's most favorite treats. Sophia's head was deep underneath the covers slobbering me down like there was no tomorrow. It wasn't one of those fast, sloppy blow jobs; baby girl took her time and allowed her lips and tongue and jaws to become one with the dick. The sensation and pleasure had my body in full submission. When I started to cum in her mouth, she sucked it faster and jerked me off at the same time. The experience left my toes curled up and had me calling out her name with satisfaction.

Now that's how a boss is supposed to start his morning off! To top it off, she hooked up a mean breakfast. Not only did she serve it to me in bed, but she fed me strawberries and cherries from her very hand. The feeling I had when I walked out the house made me a firm believer that some good head and a hot breakfast was an essential part of having a wonderful day.

On my way down to the city I contacted Shake, and briefly explained that I had some good news, and needed to speak with him face to face as soon as possible. He urged me to meet him over at the shop in fifteen minutes.

When I arrived, business was up and running as usual. Every barber's chair in the establishment was occupied and the waiting area was filled to capacity. The barbers who cut there were known to give some of the freshest, sharpest haircuts in the city. After shaking a few hands of those whom I knew, I headed to the back office where Shake was patiently waiting for me.

Upon being invited inside the office, Shake greeted me with the handshake that extended into a hug.

"What's the situation, son?" he inquired with great wonder. "I know if you're up at this time of the morning, it gots to be something of major importance."

"There you go. Always got your boy figured out," I admitted, only to stroke his ego. "Anyway, I got to give you your props on this one, pops. This has to be your most brilliant idea yet," I dragged him before dropping the news on him. His face was covered with curiosity and anticipation.

"That dope was fire, pops! The shit was all gone two hours after you gave it to me. Here's your money. Twenty-five thousand to be exact." I pulled the money from my front pockets and dropped it on the desk in front of him. "I just hope you got enough left to cover this hundred thousand dollars. I got a nigga trying spend that right now as we speak for some of this."

"Didn't I tell you, son? You going to learn to listen to your father, boy. I got some good news and some bad news. The bad news is everything is gone. Sold. Finished. But the good news is more is only a phone call away. I initially was gonna wait a few days, and have the dopefiends running around like chickens with their heads cut off, because they can't get their hands on that good shit. Let them get a li'l dope sick then pop back up and cure them. But since the streets responded the way they did, we might as well go ahead and flood them. Give me a second in private so I could make this phone call, would you?"

Five minutes after being excused he called me back inside. He then informed me that everything was in order, and we'd be back in position by the afternoon. That easy Shake had unknowingly thrown his connect under the bus, subjecting him to be robbed of his freedom, money, and dope, all at one time. That's what I called a lose-lose-lose situation for him, and a triple win for me.

Shortly after leaving the shop, I placed the call to the agents. Thankfully it was Sheen who answered this time, because I definitely wasn't for Murphy's bullshit.

"Hey, Boss, how's it going? Tell me something good. I have over twenty agents on standby as we speak. Please don't make me look bad."

"Come on, Sheen. You should know better than that. If I say there's cheese on the moon you better get yourself a spaceship and some crackers," I remarked defensively. "Now check it out. There's going to be a green Mercedes-Benz station wagon coming over the Ben Franklin Bridge from New Jersey between now and this afternoon. The license plate number is FXF 9680. I'm a 100 percent positive that dude will be transporting a large quantity of heroin, and possibly a few guns. I'm expecting a big payout from this one. Make sure you hit me up later and let me know how it went."

"If your information nets us a successful bust, you'll be the first person to know it. I'll call you personally," he suggested before hanging up.

Immediately afterward, I drove over to Corrinne's apartment to switch cars up once again. While stopped at the traffic light a few blocks away from her spot, I happened to glance in the rearview mirror. The sight of my own reflection caused me to slightly jump back and reach for my Glock. It was as if I was staring into the eyes of the devil himself. For that split second I hardly recognized my own self.

What was I becoming? Or better yet, what had I become? Who was I kidding? I was who I was before I got here. I just hoped that Shake didn't see the person I saw when I looked into the mirror.

Thirty minutes later, I was turning the Charger down White Hill Avenue. As I drove to the house I noticed that neither the Benz nor the BMW X5 was parked in the driveway. With nothing to lose and everything to gain, I turned inside and drove up to the open garage. With crowbar in hand and Glock on my waist, I was prepared for either a burglary or a home invasion. But from the looks of it, the house appeared to be unoccupied.

Inside the garage there was a door that connected to the house. How convenient. That provided me the perfect cover, and easy access to gain entry without having to worry about no nosy neighbors watching. As a precaution, I covered my face with the bandana and wore a fitted hat cocked slightly over my eyes. Fifteen seconds later I was inside.

Chapter 35

Around the same time on the New Jersey side of the Ben Franklin Bridge, Spanish Eddie was stuck in the middle of a traffic jam in the E-ZPass lane at the toll booth. The overhead sign informed drivers that the E-ZPass booth was experiencing technical difficulties, and the E-ZPasses were being scanned manually while repairs were being made. He noticed that there were several workers on site working vigorously to correct the malfunctions.

"These fucking idiots pick the perfect time to do this bullshit," he mumbled under his breath, after glancing at his watch. At the rate the traffic was flowing in the E-ZPass lane, he was sure to be late making drops. The thought of his impeccable reputation being tarnished because of lateness seemed to worry him more than driving across state lines with fifteen keys of heroin, ten bricks of coke, and a fully loaded MAC-11.

After a twenty-minute delay, he finally made it up to the booth. When he rolled his window down and went to hand his E-ZPass to the worker who was scanning them, he got an unexpected surprise. The "workers" who were supposed to be repairing the malfunctions drew weapons and surrounded the car from every possible direction. Instead of his E-ZPass being taken and scanned, he got a Glock .45 placed against the side of his temple.

"DEA! FBI! Let me see your fucking hands! You try anything slick, I'll blow your fucking head off," the agent warned him before he was violently pulled out of his car and thrown to the ground. As he was being hog tied with plastic restraints, the agents were already tearing through his car.

In a state of disbelief, Spanish Eddie lay there face down on the highway trying to come to terms with the fact that he'd been set up. Here he'd been dealing drugs for over ten years straight without so much as one infraction with the police. But as soon as he started doing business with a nigga, he just so happened to land on the *federales'* radar and in their custody.

He would've never dealt with Shake had a respected associate of his not vouched and referred to him as a trustworthy, honorable businessman. Trusting another person's judgment and backing was about to cost him everything he worked hard to acquire, and some. Right then and there he vowed that he would see to it with every resource he had, and every favor owed to him, that Shake paid dearly for crossing him.

His thoughts of vengeance were interrupted by the agents celebrating their findings.

"Well! Well! Well! What do we have here? Who are you, the fucking resurrection of Tony Montana?" the agent asked while slamming kilo after kilo on top of the hood of the Benz.

Spanish Eddie ignored him.

"Oh let me guess, you don't speak no English? Well if I was you, I'd learn the language real fucking fast, because you're going to have to do a lot of talking to get out of this one."

Still, Spanish Eddie refused to acknowledge the agent or offer them any cooperation. At that point he was hauled off to the federal detention center in downtown Philadelphia.

Meanwhile, Agents Murphy and Sheen were headed over to the federal courthouse armed with a search warrant. On the title for the Mercedes-Benz there was a New Jersey address where they believed the suspect lived and stashed his drugs. They were sure to find out.

Chapter 36

After ten minutes of searching turned up empty-handed, I was on the verge of abandoning the mission and walking away. That was until I noticed that there were surveillance cameras in nearly every room of the house. That gave me a hell of an idea. But first I had to find where the feed was going.

Having recalled seeing a computer inside the master bedroom, I raced back upstairs to see if the feed was being captured there. Upon pushing enter on the computer's keypad, the screen displayed every room that had a surveillance camera in place. The system was almost identical to the one I had at my old house. Lucky for me, I knew how to work it.

After estimating the time span from when Shake made the call and placed the order, and how long it took him to get everything together and leave, I rewound the disk to ten o'clock in the a.m. Just like magic, there was the same light-skinned nigga from the other night standing inside the living room talking on his cell phone. After a five-minute conversation, he put the phone in his pocket and went through a door that led to the basement.

Following his movement to the other screen, I watched him closely as he pulled the chain on the light switch up and down three times. In turn, the drop ceiling opened up, revealing his secret stash spot. That was all I needed to see. Quickly ejecting the disk, I placed it in my back pocket before running back downstairs.

Once I was inside the basement, I activated the stash spot, just as I saw him do it. Just like clockwork, the ceiling slowly fell from the wall, granting me full access to the contents it held. Inside I discovered three large gym bags. I quickly removed them, closed the stash spot, and carried them out to my car.

Once I placed them in the trunk of the Charger, I couldn't resist the urge to take a peek inside one of them. I decided to unzip the biggest one. It was packed to capacity with rubber band–wrapped big faces. That was enough reason for me to get my ass in the car and distance myself as far away from there as possible.

Chapter 37

Once the search warrant was signed, a flock of agents assembled and headed over to the property to execute the order. Their preliminary search turned up absolutely nothing, but once they turned the specially trained German shepherds loose, they ran straight to the garage and began sniffing and scratching at the floor. Their reaction indicated that there was some form of illegal contraband hidden beneath it. After removing the floor panels, they discovered a sophisticated floor safe with a hydraulic lift reinforcement. With no knowledge, experience, or tools to get inside of it, they had no choice but to call in a specialist.

Shortly after the safe specialist arrived, the safe was compromised, revealing a small bunker below. Inside, they recovered millions of dollars in cash and hundreds of kilos of suspected heroin and cocaine.

Such a huge bust was destined for the history books. Not only that, but the agents took dozens of pictures while holding it, standing on top of it, and packing it up as evidence. These pictures and the story behind it were sure to make the front page in newspapers, and breaking headlines all over the country.

Chapter 38

As soon as I got back to Philly, I stopped over at Corrinne's apartment to switch cars back. I assured her that the Charger was now hers and she could do with it as she pleased. When I requested permission to keep a few things over at her spot for a few weeks, she removed a spare key off of her key ring and advised me that her home was mine, among many other things. Man, was this bitch fighting hard for that number one spot. Who wouldn't?

Feeling above the law, I push the Mercedes down the highway at top speeds. No regard for other travelers, police, nor the possessions in my trunk. With the feds in pocket those worries no longer existed.

I played by my own rules and made the shit up as I went along. Now I knew how Tony felt when he said the world was his, because not a nigga in his right mind could tell me that it wasn't mines.

I wasn't about ten minutes away when this cocksucking state trooper pulled behind me blasting his sirens and honking the horn like I done killed the president or something. This was the perfect time to test my juice card. I slowed down and pulled over to the side of the road, but didn't come complete stop until I had Sheen on the phone. When he answered I could hear the excitement in his voice, as well as laughter and yelling in the background.

"Boss, you're the fucking man, dude!" he yelled into phone. "Because of you, we took down a major kingpin and confiscated mountains of drugs and money. This is going to get you the biggest payday of your life."

"All that sound real good, but right now I got a real fucking problem," I announced with concern. "This fucking racist-ass state trooper is pulling me over on the same stretch of highway as the last time. He picked the wrong time, because I was just on my way to meet up with another big time kingpin to see if I could possibly reel him in, but if I'm late, it's out of the question. The guy's not going to want to meet up with me," I lied.

"What? Put that asshole on the phone and tell him he's interfering with a federal investigation."

When the trooper walked up to the driver-side window and saw that it was me, he snapped the button to his holster open, spit his tobacco on the side of the road, and prepared to talk some bullshit. I cut him off before he could say anything.

"Officer, you're interfering with a federal investigation. My supervisor wants to have a word with you right now," I declared before passing him the phone.

He didn't budge. In fact he seemed to be growing impatient. Until I put his ass on speaker phone.

"Sheen, it's the same muthafuckin' trooper from the traffic stop. He acting like he don't want to get the phone, so I got you on speaker."

"Officer Andrews. This is DEA Agent David Sheen. You are interfering with a federal matter. If I have to contact your supervisor Mr. Gilmore, he's not going to be very happy with this. Is that clear, sir?"

"Yes, sir, Agent Sheen. I had not the slightest clue that this young man was affiliated with the federal government. I'll see to it personally that he's never again inconvenienced on my highway." He kissed ass as if his career was on the line.

"Thank you, Officer," Sheen replied. "Boss, be sure to give me a call in an hour or so. My hands are full right now, but we'll go over the details of the bust later on."

"That's what's up. I'll holla at you then."

After disconnecting the call, I was wondering why the trooper was still standing at my window. As I began rolling up in his face and preparing to pull off, he motioned for me to stop. Reaching inside his shirt pocket, he produced a business card and passed it to me. On the card there was a name and a number.

"I think we might have gotten off on the wrong foot. The name is Officer Andrews but you can call me Bob," he suggested before extending his hand inside my window.

I left it there for a few odd seconds, before I decided that it couldn't do me any harm in having a state trooper in pocket. You never knew when he might come in handy. I accepted his hand and introduced myself. "Okay, Bob. The name is Boss. Nice meeting you, but I got to get going."

"I apologize for the inconvenience. If any state troopers ever give you a problem, please don't hesitate to call me, and I'll fix it immediately," he assured me. "If it's not too much to ask, if you hear about anything illegal coming down this highway, please give me call. Have a nice day."

If that was the case, I might as well have called him on my motherfucking self. As I pulled off, I burned a little rubber, honk the horn twice, and threw Bob the peace sign. The day's events, and all the moving around I was doing, gave me a severe case of the bubble guts. In an effort to hurry up home and get on the toilet, I pushed the Benz at speeds of a hundred miles per hour.

Upon pulling up in the driveway, I noticed that Sophia's Escalade wasn't present. Good! That meant I could take a peaceful shit, count up my proceeds, and not have to worry about her being all up in my business.

Carrying the bags into the bathroom along with me, I unzipped them and turned them upside down. The other two bags were filled with bricks. Fifteen keys of dope, and twenty bricks of coke to be exact. The money looked to be anywhere between two hundred, three hundred grand easily. The sight of the fortune lying there before me, made my guts bubble even more. Quickly dropping my pants and boxers in one motion, I sat down on the toilet and let it rip.

After ridding my system of the waste, I discovered that there was no toilet tissue whatsoever. I never been an environmentalist, so in my mind paper was paper. I heard rappers and dope boys talk about they had so much money they could wipe their ass with it, but I don't believe none of them actually did it. That s what made me different from the rest of these niggas. I backed up whatever I talked. Picking up a stack of money, I removed a few fifties and hundred dollar bills and wet them until they were soft enough to wipe my ass. It seem like I was living out a new fantasy every day. It just goes to show that half the shit these niggas was talking, I was really living.

The grand total of cash was $260,000. The money went into the safe, while the drugs were packed back up inside the gym bags and prepared to be taken over to Corrinne's spot. A true boss should never keep the drugs in the house where he rested his head at. Too many things were subject to go wrong.

By the time I finish counting and securing the money, it was about that time to give Sheen another call and see what the hell he was talking about. From what he was saying, it made it sound like the nigga was driving around with a thousand keys and $100 million. That was highly unlikely. So what the fuck was Sheen talking about? In search for answers, I speed dialed him on the fed line.

When he answered his phone he was still amped up. "Boss man! My main man! Did everything go right with that traffic stop?"

"Yeah, I'm straight. But the question is, what went down with the New Jersey cat?" I cut to the chase.

"What! You haven't heard?" he asked with surprise. "Every news station across the Delaware Valley is covering the story. Hell, a news reporter from CNN was here just a little while ago."

"Wait a minute, Sheen, I must be missing something here. What the fuck could he have possibly been driving around with to get this type of attention?" I asked with frustration.

"We did find a substantial amount of drugs and even a gun inside the car, but when we went over to the guy's house, that's where we found the mother lode. The guy had two sophisticated stash spots. There was one in the basement, which was empty. But the one we discovered underneath the floor had enough dope to get the whole state of New Jersey high! In addition to the drugs, we also recovered millions in cash," he bragged proudly.

"As soon as we get an accurate count of the money we confiscated, we'll get you a nice fat check. Definitely somewhere in the six-figure margin. Anything else you need? If not, I have to get back to work here."

"Naw, it's all good. I'm glad it worked out for y'all," I lied. "But I do need that check as soon as possible because my money is kind of funny."

My objective was to always keep the *federales* under the impression that working for them was my only source of steady income. That way they had no need to worry about me ever crossing them and running off. In their minds they fed me, protected me, and basically owned me. Similar to a dog. When the master gets comfortable with the animal, he eventually removes the leash and allows it to roam freely. That's exactly what I was doing.

As I sat back on the leather sofa puffing a dutch of cush, my thoughts went back to the conversation I just had with Agent Sheen. The fact that I'd left behind millions in cash, and enough work to reverse a drought, had my mind filled with the what-ifs, how-comes, should'ves, and could'ves. It was like having a winning multimillion dollar lottery ticket in my possession, losing it, and discovering that someone else had found it and cashed in on it. It was still a win-win situation for me either way. But just the thought that I was so close to it, and missed it by a few inches was something extremely difficult for me to accept. But fuck it! I was still winning even though it seemed like I was losing. At the end of the day I still looked to profit in multiple ways from the situation. In my books, that's all that really mattered.

By the time Sophia made it home later that night, I was starving, lonely, and horny. Here she came walking through the door, clenching several shopping bags bearing logos from Saks Fifth Avenue, Nordstrom, and Neiman Marcus. As always her hair was done, nails were pedicured, and she looked absolutely beautiful. However, I wasn't feeling the tight, short DKNY dress she wore. It exposed way too much titties, ass, and thighs for my liking. My jealousy got the best of me.

"Where the fuck was you at dressed like that? What, are you a stripper now?" I insinuated harshly while staring her up and down with the evil eye.

"Don't start your bullshit, Amin," she argued while returning the look. "I'm already having a fucked-up day. I got some bad news that my grandpa is real sick and he's in the hospital. I need a drink," she announced before walking over to the mini bar in the dining room and pouring herself a glass of vodka and cranberry juice.

"First my parents, then the baby, and now my grandpa's health is taking a turn for the worse. What, am I cursed? If I didn't have you, I don't know where I'd be."

Hearing the pain in her voice and seeing the tears in her eyes was more than enough reason for me to get up and comfort her in my arms. After learning of her latest misfortune, I felt bad about the way I talked to her. I was so touched by the last statement she made, that at that very moment, I dropped to my knee, prepared to take our relationship to the next level.

"Baby, I know that the timing may be off, and you're going through a lot right now, but I can't let another day go by without me expressing how much I truly love you." I spoke from the heart while staring into her eyes. "It's real, baby. I feel it inside. I want that feeling to last forever. The only way that will be possible is if you be my wife. So will you marry me?"

"Oh my God! That was so sweet, baby. I love you too, Amin, and I feel the same way." She smiled. "Of course I'll marry you."

To celebrate the plans of our future, and spending the rest of our lives together, we opened up a bottle of champagne and cheered glasses for our love, loyalty, and longevity. We set a wedding date for a few weeks away. Neither of us wanted a big wedding, so we agreed to have a small ceremony with just the two of us.

Before going into the bedroom to consummate our engagement, Sophia informed me of her plans to go visit her grandfather in the hospital in Los Angeles. She invited me to come along on the trip with her, but also gave me the option to stay behind. Only after reassuring me that she'd be okay traveling alone did I agree to the arrangement.

If it was necessary for me to go, I would've gone without question, but because I had a lot of important business to tend to, I decided to stay behind. Surprisingly, Sophia didn't argue nor protest. Her only request was that I take care of some of the wedding preparations while she was gone. No problem! I'd rather pick out tuxedos and dresses any day than sitting up in the hospital, smelling the foul stench of decaying bodies and sickness.

The following morning, after dropping Sophia off at the Philadelphia International Airport, I made one of two important phone calls. The first one was to Shake. I didn't want him to get suspicious and wonder why I suddenly stopped calling out of the blue after being so pressed and eager to get my hands on some more dope. Fortunately I got his voicemail.

"Shake, what's good, OG? I'm still waiting on your call. Is everything still a go? Hit me back and let me know what's up as soon as you get this message." I recorded with the same hunger and anticipation that I possessed when I stood before him the other day.

My next phone call was to Gunner. He informed me that he'd been expecting my call and suggested that I come pick him up so we could discuss the progress of the projects that we were in the process of putting together. I drove straight over to his house to see what he had in store. If I liked what I heard, I had three keys of dope in the trunk for him right now!

As soon as he got in the car, he wasted no time putting me up on game.

"The last time we met up I told you that I was going to have a dope block for us in a day or two, or else my name wasn't Gunner. Well, what's my name, nigga?" he boasted with arrogance. "Yeah, nigga! I went down Fifth and Luzerne and took one of those Poppies under for their block. Those niggas pumpkin pie. Check out how I ran down on them cowards."

"After watching three young hustlers move dope out there all day I was able to determine who was the strongest and weakest among them. Later that night I let the dogs go loose on two of them and left the weakest nigga alive. First I made the nigga help me put his dead homies in the trunk of one of their cars; then I gave him the option to either live and work for me or join his homeboys. Of course he chose wisely.

"He eventually told me the ins and outs of their whole operation. But that wasn't shit. You know I wasn't letting him in the circle that easy. In order for a nigga to get close to me he gots to put that work in first. Guess what I had this little nigga do?" he asked with that wicked smile of his.

"After learning that his boss came to pick up the blocks profit every day around midnight, I gave shorty a twenty-two long and instructed him to go outside and kill him. For insurance purposes, before he went outside to do the deed, I let him know that if he crossed me or failed to do the job correctly, I was going to pay his baby mother a visit, and it wouldn't be a pleasant one. The little nigga ain't never kill nothing a day in his life, but in the position I put him in, he went out there and gave his boss six to the head. We put his ass in the trunk with the rest of them before burning the car up. He been moving dope out there for me ever since. In fact, those three ounces is just about gone. I done played my part; now it's your turn to do yours."

"What? Nigga, you know better than anybody that anything I stamp you can take to the bank and cash in on it," I reminded him. "I'm still the same ol' Boss. But let me show you better than I can tell you."

Pulling the Benz over to the side of the road, I got out and removed the three bricks from the trunk. When I got back inside I tossed the work on his lap and watched as his face lit up like a Christmas tree. Still I had another surprise in store for the big fellow. It required us to take a ride over to Luxury Autos to holla at my man Alan.

Fortunately for us, Alan had just got his new inventory in, and was giving out super deals in hopes of getting rid of many cars as possible. That led him to make me an offer I couldn't refuse. When it was all said and done, I was able to trade in the Benz along with $30,000 cash and drive off the lot with a platinum-colored Maserati for myself, and silver big-boy F350 for my nigga Gunner. If I ain't know how to do nothing, I knew how to keep a nigga loyal, honest, and motivated!

Chapter 39

The second Shake learned of his supplier's arrest, he knew that it would be in his best interest to leave the city immediately. From the outside looking in, he realized how suspicious it looked that his connect just happened to get stopped and busted with a car full of drugs moments before they were scheduled to meet up. In the hood, being labeled a snitch or a suspected rat came along with grave penalties, especially when it caused a highly connected man like Spanish Eddie his freedom. That alone gave him every reason to believe that his life was in great danger.

Until he was able to clear his name, he disconnected all forms of communication and laid low over at his condo in Maryland. Not even his closest, most trusted associates knew anything about the place. All with the exception of one. This specific person was far beyond just an associate; he was more so Shake's extra set of eyes, ears, and brains behind the scene. It was because of this associate's sources, networking, and connections that he had prospered to the level of success and power he possessed.

One of the many advantages that came along with being connected to this specific associate of his was he always kept ten steps ahead of the individuals whom he conducted business with or around. From day one, this associate had promised him that his life, freedom, and status would never be in jeopardy, as long as Shake kept him informed on who was who, and what was what.

That's what made this entire situation with Spanish Ed-die so confusing. Usually before something that big was carried out involving a business associate of his, he would know at least a day or two in advance.

With his empire on the verge of collapsing, Shake needed to figure out what went wrong, and fast. Or else the damage to his name and reputation would soon be complete. In search of answers, he called his associate from a landline, hoping to somehow clear his name.

Chapter 40

Snuggled up comfortably in the first-class section of the plane, Sophia sat back, relieved that Boss decided not to come along. Fortunately, her lie was convincing enough to get away from him for a few days without him becoming suspicious.

Her real reason for traveling to Los Angeles was to visit Victor at the federal detention center in downtown L.A. where he was being held. For the past month he'd been begging her to come down, claiming that there was something important that he needed to talk to her about face to face. She was reluctant at first, until he started bringing up all of the things he did for her during the course of the relationship. He knew that it would make her feel bad, and the guilt would eat her up, and influence her to make the trip down.

Regardless of his reasons for wanting to see her, she had a few of her own motives for flying down. The most important one of all was that she wanted to see if the love she once had for him still existed, if it was strong, real, and worth the deceitful lies she was living. This trip would decide if she walked out on Victor and down the aisle with Boss, or continued to play both sides of the fence with the two of them. . . .

Chapter 41

Over the course of forty-eight hours, Gunner had the block doing mighty impressive numbers. Competition was blown away by the highly potent heroin, and the large quantity of dope stuffed inside the bags. They were coming from all over just to get a slice of the devil's pie. I was proud of my nigga for being able to make the transition from a cold-blooded killer to a certified dope boy.

In just two days he had already gone through half of the three kilos I had given him the other day. At the rate he was moving the work I'd be out by the end of the month. More than likely, I would have to eventually find Gunner a real dope connect in order for him to maintain the block. I'd cross that bridge when the time came, but for now I was kicking my feet up, as a true boss should.

As if things couldn't get no better, I was given a $200,000 check for the New Jersey bust, with the promise of another two once all assets belonging to the suspect were seized and liquidated. On top of that these cocksuckas gave me twenty more bricks of the synthetic coke, suggesting that I stay busy. What the fuck was I going to do with all this shit? I already had enough of my own! I was starting to feel like the more I did for the *federales* the higher their expectations got. I had to get away from all of this madness before karma found out my secrets and came for my ass.

Now that I had some extra time on my hands, I decided to catch up a few things that I been neglecting to do. First thing first, I had to go get all of the drugs out of my house. Along with that, some of the money had to go as well. My safe was already filled to capacity, and there was hundreds and thousands of dollars scattered all over the house.

Until I figured something else out, I would use Corrinne's apartment for the time being.

When I called to inform her that I was on my way down, the bitch start playing with her pussy and sucking on her finger all up in my ear. I assured her that I would be there before she came, and I meant every word of it.

Intending to make good on my promise, I raced the Maserati down the freeway reaching speeds of damn near 120 miles per hour. Having already drunk an ounce of syrup before leaving the house, I lit up a dutch of sour diesel to mellow it out. With Rick Ross's classic street banger, "Hustlin'," cranking out the stereo, I was in "G" mode.

That was until I looked in the rearview mirror and spotted a state trooper pulling out of his hiding place on the side of the road. Next came the sirens and that irritating-ass horn. Didn't this cocksucka know who ran these roads? Mashing down on the gas I decided to give him a run for his money. His 350 engine was no match for the Maserati's V6 horsepower. But once his backup arrived, shit got serious real quick. That's when I decided to stop playing games, and make the call to Officer Bob.

Seconds after contacting him and informing him that I was being pursued by a few state troopers inside my Maserati, the pursuit came to an end. From the rearview mirror I watched them cut their sirens off, slow down, and go on about their business. One of them pulled alongside of me farther down the highway. If facial expressions could talk his would say, "Who the fuck is this powerful nigga here?" I laughed in his face and blew weed smoke in the air before stepping on the gas.

When I walked inside Corrinne's apartment, I encountered the freak sitting asshole naked at her computer, talking on the telephone.

As I overheard her conversation, it became apparent that she was up to her old tricks. This specific scheme involved her printing up fictitious pregnancy test results that claimed a patient was in the early stages of pregnancy, and how much it will cost to terminate the fetus.

"You a scandalous-ass bitch!" I spat with disgust.

In return she put up her middle finger, and stuck her tongue out at me. When she saw me remove stacks of money from one of the duffle bags and place it on the dining room table, her eyes damn near popped out of her head. That got her immediate attention. She rushed off the phone and walked over to get a closer look.

"Oh my God, Boss!" she exclaimed before covering her hand over her mouth. "I'm in the wrong business. I need to be getting money with you."

"This a little something, but it ain't as much as it look. I do these types of numbers on my off day," I boasted Boss-fully. "You got a good hiding place around this motherfucka? We going to need a lot of space. I got this money, plus two more bags full of work."

"I got a perfect stash spot inside the kitchen pantry. Nobody will ever be able to find it," she responded convincingly. "But before we put the money up, can I see something real quick?"

"Of course. You know you're my number two bitch! You will never hear me tell you no or fuck you, unless it's in reference to that pretty thing between your legs," I reassured her while staring at her freshly shaved vagina.

With a seductive smile on her face, she bent down in front of me and started picking up stacks of money. Busting the rubber bands off of them, she began throwing the currency in the air. She continued this until every dollar of it was on the floor. Afterward she reached her hand out to me and invited me to her fantasy.

As I laid her down on top of the money my eyes remained fixed on the glistening jewel in the center of her thighs. The sight of it made my mouth water with anticipation. Instructing her to position her arms behind her calves, I was given full view and access to her VIP section. It smelled like roses, and looked mighty delicious.

Dropping my head to her midsection, I put my tongue on the very bottom of her vagina, and slowly licked it all the way to the top. I did this several times, before sticking the tip inside slowly. Her body began to jump and stutter, verifying that I was pleasing her in all the right places.

As her moans intensified, I realized that she was on the verge of having a massive orgasm. Intending to make it the best she'd ever had, I went ahead and readjusted positions. With her sitting on top of my face, I locked my lips around her swollen clit, sucking and slurping on it as if it were hot soup.

With no regards for my face nor my mouth, she grinded down on it while winding her hips from side to side. She was moving so fast that she had to grab hold of her titties to keep them from jumping out of her chest. Suddenly, she stared at the ceiling, then down at me. It was if she was trying to figure out who or what was satisfying her body on that level: me or God. Before long she gave up and released a waterfall of pleasure over the top of my face, and in my mouth.

For the next thirty minutes I dicked mommy down every which way possible. One thing I could say about her was she had remarkable stamina and the wettest pussy I'd ever had. As we lay there fighting to catch our breath, I happen to glance over at Corrinne, only to discover that there was big faces stuck all over her body. I never thought dirty, bloody drug money could look so good and make a person feel so great. *But then again, look at me.*

After gathering ourselves together, we put everything up inside the stash spot, and took a nice cool shower together. Once we retired to the bedroom I informed her that I was going to pay her twenty stacks a month on the strength that she was my bitch, and for allowing me to keep all of my contraband stashed at her apartment. When I suggested that she stop fucking with those petty schemes, she defended her hustle and explained how it worked.

She claimed that bitches all over the city were buying her forged, phony documents for one hundred dollars apiece. In turn, they would go out and present the papers to several men whom they were sexually involved with. Niggas was paying without question. Some bitches made thousands of dollars off of the scheme. Mainly because the papers were almost identical to those that came from Dr. Sam Shults's abortion clinic over on Thirty-eighth and Lancaster Avenue.

The mere mention of his name took my memory back to that night I went through the medicine cabinet and discovered those prescription bottles bearing the name. It so happened to be the same night Sophia revealed that she had a miscarriage. As much as I wanted to deny it, the facts were clear as day. The dirty bitch killed my unborn child!

How could she betray my love and trust? That bitch sat up there and cried with me, pretending as if she was so hurt, when all along she killed something that was part of both of us. How heartless! That made me question everything about her. Who was she really? And what else was she lying about? That night I strongly considered killing the bitch.

Chapter 42

During the three-hour visit with Victor, Sophia was overcome with a variety of mixed emotions. Love, hate, fear, and worry were on top of the list. The person who Victor had become was nothing like the man she fell in love with. It was as if the federal government had tampered with his dignity, pride, and swagger. His attitude, conversation, and intentions were twisted and far from his usual character.

The visit turned out to be the longest three hours of her life. Her prayers of time moving fast were denied. She was forced to sit there and listen to the selfish, self-centered bastard talk about how he was prepared to shit on anybody and everybody who had ever crossed him, as well as those who he thought might cross him in the future. His attitude was fuck the world. If she hadn't already heard enough bullshit as it was, he began asking her a lot of questions about Boss that made her feel uncomfortable. He seemed to think it was funny and all a big joke. When he saw the way she reacted to his questions, he began calling her bitch and whore. If that weren't embarrassing enough, he stood up and terminated the visit. But not before adding more insult to injury.

"Get the fuck out of here, bitch. I don't need your funky ass no more. You counted me out like the rest of them. But I got a surprise for all you motherfuckas. These walls can't hold me forever. I knew your scandalous ass was going to fall in love with that nigga!" he shouted. "CO! Cancel this bitch! Visit over!"

Feeling like a fool, Sophia left the federal detention center covered in shame and humiliation. After all the sacrifices and riding she did for Victor, he stood up there and gave her his ass to kiss. Here she had left a man back home who truly loved her and wanted to make her his wife, and she was all the way out L.A. visiting a nigga who wasn't worth the time of day.

The only thing she got out of the trip was closure. From that point forward she vowed to give Boss 100 percent loyalty and her all. He was far the best thing that ever happened to her. She did love him, and after today, she was truly ready to be his wife. No more lies. No more games.

Refusing to let the trip be a complete waste, she caught a cab down to Sunset Boulevard and had the best shopping experience of her life.

Chapter 43

When Sophia called the following morning and told me that her flight was scheduled to arrive in Philly early that afternoon, I started to tell her to go fuck herself, and that she wasn't invited back inside my house, nor my life. But I decided that when the time was right I would tell her about herself face to face. But for the time being I was more curious to learn who the bitch really was, and what angle she was on. If I found out that she was on some sneaky shit, she'd likely earn herself a bullet to the back of the head. For her to kill my unborn child was a deed that was unforgiveable. Therefore, things could never be right between us.

Because of her deceitful ways, everything she ever did or said was now in question. It made me start to wonder if her trip to L.A. was really to go see her sick grandfather. Since we'd been together she never even mentioned one word about him, but all of a sudden he gets sick, and she hops her ass on a plane to L.A.? One thing that I was for sure certain of was whatever she was doing in the dark would eventually come into the light.

That afternoon when I went to go pick up this deceitful-ass, ungrateful bitch of mines, I couldn't believe my eyes when I spotted her come walking out the airport, strutting like a model on the runway. The bitch carried so much luggage with her that it took two airport workers to assist her. One would have thought that she was traveling with two or three people. If she thought all that bullshit was going in my $100,000 car, she was sadly mistaken.

Unaware that I had switched cars up, she stood there looking around like a lost puppy. Making my presence known, I stepped out of the vehicle and snapped on her in front of dozens of people.

"Yo! What the fuck is all this shit? I thought you were going out L.A. to see your sick grandfather. How the fuck you have time to do all of this shopping?" I voiced suspiciously. "Ain't none of that shit going in my new car."

A look of embarrassment and surprise appeared on her face. Followed by sadness. That look might've worked on me in the past, but not today, and not ever again.

"If you coming, let's go! I got shit to do. You better get one of those taxicabs to take your shit over to the house, because it ain't going in my car. I mean that." I spoke harshly before turning back and returning to the car.

I watched from the driver seat as Sophia waved down a cab, and struggled to get all of her things inside the trunk and back seat of it. I offered not the slightest help. I was praying that she broke a nail or a heel in the process. I wanted her to hurt as I was, but more.

When she finally got in the car, she was sweating, out of breath, and pissed off. She had a nerve to slam my door, and turn my music off.

"What the fuck done got into you, Amin?" She snapped her neck as she spoke. "You never treated me with such disrespect. Whatever you're going through, you better put that shit in check with the motherfucka who did it, because I ain't done nothing to your evil ass."

The nerve of this bitch to sit here and continue putting on this façade as if she were so innocent and Ms. Do-right showed me just how crafty she really was. Or thought she was. It took me all the patience and restraint I possessed for me not to backhand smack her right in that lying-ass mouth of hers. On top of that I wanted to tell her so bad that I knew all about her trifling ass getting an abortion.

But instead I maintained my composure and bit my tongue.

"You're absolutely right. Don't mind me at all," I said apologetically. "Sorry! I'm just a little upset because I recently discovered that someone close to me did some snake shit behind my back thinking that I wasn't going to find out. It's cool though, because in due time they got theirs coming in the worse way possible," I mentioned while closely studying her reaction. There was so much guilt written over her face that she had to turn her head and look out the window to avoid looking into my eyes. That didn't stop me from playing a little mind game to see what else I could pick out of her.

"But anyway, fuck all that! How's your grandfather doing? With all of the shopping you been doing, I'm surprised you even had time to go and pay him a visit," I indicated sarcastically.

"Well actually he is doing a lot better. In fact, the only reason I returned so quick is because I told him that you just proposed to me, and he suggested that I return home to be with you. There's still plenty of family by his side, so he'll be just fine. Thanks for asking."

"That sounds like a hell of a guy. Won't you give me the information to the hospital and room number where he's being treated at? I'd like to send him a few get-well-soon cards and some balloons or something. I'm sure he can use all the support and best wishes he can get."

"Aw, baby! That would be so sweet of you. That will really make his day," she announced delightfully. "Here is the information right here."

To my surprise she produced a patient information form that included the hospital, name, age, and room where her grandfather was hospitalized at. I ain't going to lie, I was a tad bit relieved that she was able to provide the information without thought, hesitation, or delay. It came too natural to be a lie, so I eased up a bit on her. But that ain't mean I forgave her for killing my baby.

During the ride home, I happened to get a call from Gunner. The way he was running through the work, more than likely he was calling to re-up. Although I really didn't feel comfortable talking business in the presence of Sophia, my money came second to no one.

"Big fellow! Talk to me," I answered.

"You already know," he indicated in code. "I need you to get up with me ASAP. You know if motherfuckas don't see you at the door they going to assume it ain't no party, feel me?"

"I'm right on top of it. Give me a few hours and I'll be right down there. You know me, I'm never late for a party," I stated factually before disconnecting the call. At the mention of a party, I caught Sophia giving me that look as if she was waiting for me to invite her. The way I was feeling about her right now, I wouldn't take her to the cemetery to visit her dead parents' gravesite on their birthday! Let alone to a party! But I could show her better than tell her.

When I pulled into the driveway of the house, Sophia looked at me as if she was expecting me to go inside with her, or at least help with her luggage that the taxi drove to the house. I did neither. My facial expressions and posture must've said it all, because she got the point real quick.

"I guess I'll see you later on tonight when you get home from your little party," she insinuated sarcastically, before leaning over and attempting to kiss me on the mouth. With the reflex of a skilled boxer, I slightly turned my head and let the kiss land on my cheek.

If looks could kill I would've been dead! Her eyes seem to transform into a double-barrel shotgun and blasted me away with the look of death. Tears fell from her eyes before she stormed out of the car and stomped her Christian Louboutin shoes all the way up to the front door of the house. To say that she was on fire would be an understatement.

Love was a motherfucka. Even after the foul shit she did with the baby, I still loved the bitch. I wanted so desperately to go run after her, hold her in my arms, and confess how much I loved her. But that's what she wanted, and she damn sure ain't deserve it. In this instance, she needed to feel hurt and pain. After her heartless deed, misery and loneliness were the only things she had coming from me. With that in mind, I pulled off without the least acknowledgment toward her.

Chapter 44

Ever since being dropped off at the house, Sophia had been in a state of panic, worry, and fear. These reactions were a direct result of Boss's sudden change in the manner in which he treated and talked to her. The first thing that came to mind was that he had been in her truck and found the deceitful letters that Victor had written to her, as well as the ones she wrote to him but never got around to sending out.

If those letters were ever discovered by him, he would probably kill her, or be so hurt behind them that he might kill himself. At the least he wouldn't want nothing to do with her ever again. From there she'd be homeless, jobless, manless, and basically left to fend for herself.

A few minutes after Boss pulled off and left, she ran outside to her truck to see if he'd been inside there and found the letters. From the looks of it everything seemed to be just as she'd left it. Not one letter was out of place, or appeared to be tampered with. Relief set in immediately. The thought of losing him nearly broke her down. Although she wasn't completely out of hot water, she knew as long as it wasn't the letters, she could talk her way out of just about anything else. If that was even the case.

Maybe somebody close to him really did cross him and he was already mad before he came to pick me up. It probably sent him over the edge when he saw me coming out the airport with all of those damn bags. That was so stupid of me, she thought. *I see why he cussed my dumb ass out. I done put him through a lot of bullshit already but I'm going to make up for it,* she promised herself.

Chapter 45

My plans for the night was to briefly stop past Corrinne's crib, grab the work for Gunner, and go drop it off to him. Those plans went straight out the window the moment I stepped inside her apartment. She begged for me to put it in her mouth, and then fuck her with no mercy. Before it was all said and done, her back touched damn near every wall inside the apartment. After a workout like that, sleep was the only thing on my mind. Gunner would just have to wait.

By the time I finally got around to meeting up with the big fellow, it was damn near three in the morning. As soon as he sat down in the passenger seat I could tell that he had an attitude. It was all in his demeanor. The look that he gave me sent a chill up my spine, and for the first time ever, made me feel slightly uneasy with him in my company.

After a few moments of odd silence he finally decided to break the peace. "Listen, Boss, if you want me to continue running your operations, you have to give me your word that you will never me hanging like this after I done called you and told you that I need to re-up," he insisted with obvious frustration. "This shit ain't crack. When a dope-head need that fix, they got to have it right then and there. I don't like losing clientele or missing money. Understand that this my name and reputation on the line. I assure each and every last feind that the block going to be up and running unless police shut us down.

Even then, I'd just take over another block and we open right back up." He paused momentarily only to stare at the ground and shake his head, as if deep in thought.

"I couldn't have a customer come through and not get served because there's nothing available. The way those motherfuckas network, every feind in the neighborhood would've known that there wasn't no dope at the spot. That would have fucked up everything I worked and killed to build. I couldn't let that happen, so I start taking them inside the house, killing them, then throwing their bodies in the basement. I don't know how many I killed, but I know it's a lot of them. The spot already stink. But what else was I supposed to do?"

The sad thing was this crazy nigga thought that he had actually handled the situation in a logical sense. I realized that he was far beyond thrown off; the nigga was psychotic. At that point I told him whatever he wanted to hear just to get him away from me. Afterward, I gave him five of the remaining nine kilos of dope that I had left.

When I went to give him a handshake, he accepted my hand and gripped it tightly. Meanwhile, his other hand went under his shirt as if he was reaching for a gun. Even if I could've reached for my own gun, and pulled it out, it would've been too late. He already had the drop on me. The nigga I trusted the most was about to blow my head off and I couldn't do nothing but sit there and wait for it to happen. Damn! I never expected it to end like this.

Instead of a gun, he pulled out five large stacks of money and dropped them on my lap. With sweat covering my face, and fear in my eyes, Gunner knew he had me shook up. It was his way of sending me a message, and trying to put fear in my heart. I knew from that point on that our business partnership would be short-lived. But until that day came I was going to continue using him for everything he was worth. In all actuality, he wasn't shit but a yes man anyway. I made the nigga, and wouldn't hesitate to break him!

That night I decided to sleep over at Corrinne's place. There were several reasons why. When a man who had a house and a woman to go home to slept out on the streets all night long and didn't bother to call nor answer his phone, it meant one of three things: either he was dead, locked up, or with another bitch. Cheating was usually always the case.

I wanted her to know that the bed of my mistress meant more to me than being in the bed with her. I could imagine she had a sleepless night while envisioning me doing everything I did sexually to her to another woman. As well as another woman doing things to me that she never done. I wanted her to know that she was expendable and could be easily replaced. Maybe then she'd realize what she had, and get herself together. I had to worry about enough snakes on the streets. I'd be damned if I had to worry about one living under my roof.

When I returned home the following morning, I was expecting Sophia to come running up to me swinging a knife cutting, cussing, and fussing. But to my surprise she did the complete opposite. Instead she came downstairs, greeted me with a "good morning," and proceeded to the kitchen and began preparing to cook. She wore a pair of Seven jeans that were so tight they looked as if they were spray painted on her. Along with that, she wore a She by Sheree shirt that exposed so much cleavage she might as well just walked around with her titties out.

Like a hound dog in search of a runaway slave, she started sniffing all around the place.

"Is that you smelling like rotten fish?" she asked with a look of disgust. "You must have had a rough night. Go ahead upstairs and take a shower while I cook you some breakfast. Wherever you were at, it don't look like they fed you before you left, but I got you, boo," she remarked sarcastically.

"I thought that was you smelling like that," I replied on my way upstairs. "And for your information, there was plenty to eat where I just left from, but I ate it all last night," I confirmed before going into the bathroom.

Of course she had to have the last word. "I know how you do, boo. You eat anything and everything," she insinuated indirectly. "But anyway, after I cook your breakfast I have to go take care of some things. I'll be back as soon as I can. Love you, sweetie."

I knew the game she was playing all too well. I certainly wasn't going to feed into it. She was trying to be sarcastic and act as if she didn't care, but I read straight through it. On the inside she was crushed. When a beautiful, high-class bitch like Sophia started to feel unimportant, she would have no choice but to question and reevaluate herself as a woman. If she couldn't figure it out, she would likely lose confidence, self-esteem, and all respect for herself. After the foul shit she done pulled, I was starting to question if she had any in the first place. I was curious to see how and if she would bounce back from this point. Or would her pride cause her to walk away?

As I sat nude on the toilet contemplating these thoughts, the smell of burning food and smoke took over my senses getting my immediate attention.

"Sophia! Sophia! What the fuck is you doing down there, trying burn my motherfucking house down?" I hollered out. After getting no reply, I quickly wipe my ass, wrapped a towel around my waist, and ran out the bathroom to investigate. As soon as I stopped out in the hallway there was smoke everywhere. It was so thick that my eyes began to burn and water on contact. Once I made it downstairs, I spotted flames coming from the top of the stove. Realizing that it was too late to call up the fire department, I pulled the towel from around my waist and combated the fire myself. Asshole naked!

Fortunately, after five minutes or so I was able to put the fire out. However, my lungs had consumed so much smoke, it left me choking and hardly able to breathe. The bitch done finally crossed the line with this stunt. Not only did she almost burn down my house, but she could've killed me in the process. This meant war!

Chapter 46

As Sophia pulled out of the driveway, she was laughing so hard she damn near pissed her pants. From the dining room window, she'd just witnessed the entire incident with Boss unfold. The sight of him running around buck naked trying to put the fire out was one of the funniest things she'd ever seen in her life. Her only regret was that she didn't have a camcorder on hand to record it.

The fact that he'd stayed out all night was one thing, but his arrogant don't-give-a-fuck attitude and comments was another. They only added fuel to the fire that was already burning inside of her. In her mind she'd been burnt. Therefore it was only right that she show him how it felt. Eye for an eye. Fire for fire.

What she had in store for him next was sure to make him think twice before disrespecting her like that again. He'd most certainly underestimated her yet again. But he would soon learn.

Chapter 47

There was no way whatsoever I was leaving my house unattended with this pyromaniac bitch somewhere out there on the loose. Ain't no telling what a woman with unstable emotions would do when they reacted off them. With all of her clothes and other personal belongings still inside the house, I knew it was a matter of time before she showed back up. I couldn't wait to get my hands around her neck so I could squeeze the living life out of her.

One thing for sure, tonight all issues were being addressed and exposed. Fuck guessing and trying to figure them out. I needed to really know what was up with this crazy-ass bitch.

By midnight this trick still hadn't returned home yet, nor called. My patience was growing thin. By one o'clock a.m. I was on my feet pacing back and forth, staring out the window every few seconds. Still, there was not a sign of her. I was considering calling up the feds to see if they could tap into her GPS system and get her location. All types of thoughts were running through my head.

She had one more hour to bring her ass home before I made that call and put the *federales* on her trail. Meanwhile, to calm my nerves, I lit up a dutch of dro, and threw back a few ounces of syrup. As I sat there with my eyes closed in deep contemplation, my thoughts soon landed me into a light sleep.

The sounds of keys jiggling and locks unbolting bought me out of my resting almost instantly. Glancing at my

Breitling the time read 6:15 a.m. Even the sun had beaten her trifling ass home. Not wanting to startle her, I sat there in the shadows with my feet up on the table, and my arms crossed over my chest, concealing the gun that I held in my hand.

Before she walked through the door, I heard her laughing and telling whoever she was on the phone with, "Thanks for the good night," and she'd talk to him later. If that wasn't disrespectful enough, the bitch came walking through the door wearing different clothes from those she wore when she left, and her hair was all over the place.

The signs were all too clear. Unable to restrain myself, I jumped off the couch and ran up on her as if I possessed supernatural powers. Slapping her to the ground I stood over her and pointed the Glock in her face.

"Bitch! Is you out of your motherfucking mind? You feel safe disrespecting me like this? You don't know better? Look me in the eyes, bitch, so I can show you!" I shouted before grabbing her by the back of her head, and forcing her to face me. In the heat of the moment I spit in her face before pressing the gun against the side of her head. That's when she started laughing.

"Go ahead and kill me, you son of a bitch! Payback's a motherfucka ain't it? At least I'll go to my grave knowing that you see how it feels to be the bitch waiting at home scared, worried, and lonely while her man was running the streets doing God knows what," she indicated before the smiles and laughter turned into tears. "Pull the trigger, Amin! I don't even care no more."

"Stop it with all this fake shit, would you?" I spat harshly. "You think I don't know the shit that you did behind my back? Like killing my unborn baby? Huh? You ain't think I knew did you?"

As God as my witness, her heart was pounding so hard that it looked like it was ready to bust out her chest.

Her face was flushed of color and replaced with fear and surprise.

"Wait . . . Amin, wait a minute . . . please. Let me explain," she suggested nervously. "It's not what you think. Yes, I did terminate my pregnancy, but only because the fetus was stuck in my tubes and could've killed me," she claimed convincingly. "If you think I'm lying you can call the doctor up. The only reason that I didn't tell you was because I was ashamed and thought that you would look at me differently and not want me anymore because I failed to give you a child. I swear to God on my parents' graves," she professed.

After learning that my suspicions were wrong and it was actually Mother Nature that had prevented me from becoming a father, I put the gun down and helped her up off the floor. Embracing her into my arms, I held her tightly and rested her head on my chest.

"I'm sorry too, baby . . . I'm sorry for hurting you and lying to you . . . I . . . I love you, Amin," she cried.

Although she had my heart convinced, I couldn't help but to think of the deceitful actions that she'd displayed. That brought back to mind the fact that she'd been out all night, and the disrespectful manner in which she returned. My rage quickly returned, causing me to push her away. She knew exactly why and tried to clear it up immediately.

"Wait, Amin! I know what you're thinking but you're wrong. I was at the Ritz-Carlton hotel downtown by myself, eating chocolate and watching movies all night, crying my eyes out over you," she claimed persuasively. "You think I was just going to come walking in here talking to a nigga on the phone, knowing that your crazy ass was waiting for me to come through that door? I went to the window before I came in, and saw you sitting there on the couch and pretended to be on the phone, just to make you jealous. Here, see for yourself," she pleaded before passing me her cell phone.

When I searched through the call history, all the numbers in the incoming and outgoing log were mines. I admit, that made me feel a lot better, and made her story sound a lot more believable. Just as I went to pass her back her phone, it suddenly started to ring. Who would be calling at this hour of the morning from a blocked number? My rage and jealously had returned yet again.

"You almost had me convinced, bitch; this is probably the nigga you fucked all night calling you from a blocked number to make sure that you're still alive. You told the nigga to call and check on you didn't you?" I accused her.

Taking the phone from my hand, she answered it and put it on speaker phone. "You have a call from Victor. This is a prepaid call and you will not be charged for this call. To accept this call, press five. To block any future calls from this inmate, press seven now." It was an automated message recording.

"You know this nigga be calling me and you been knew the situation, so don't start no bullshit now."

"That was then, this is now. So either you tell that nigga it's over or tell me that it's over." I gave her an alternative.

"Fine!" she barked before accepting the call and taking it off of speaker phone.

"Hello. Victor, we need to talk . . . I'm sorry but this ain't going to work. Life goes on, and I deserve much better. It's over! What is it? Go ahead, you have one minute," she said, before allowing him to speak.

While she was hearing what the nigga had to say for himself, I walked behind her and started unfastening her pants. She knew better than to protest my advances. Instead she fully submitted and stepped one foot out of her pants and panties once I had them pulled down to her ankles. After sitting down on the La-Z-Boy, I guided her onto my hardness backward. As soon as I entered her, she began sucking on her teeth and breathing heavy. Still holding the phone to her ear, she bounced up and down on me slowly at first; then she went from zero to sixty faster than my Maserati. "Yes . . . I'm listening . . . I hear you," she talked slowly into the phone. "Umm. Ohh. He fucking me, Victor . . . He all up in this pussy and it feel so good . . . Damn! I'm about to cum on his dick right now. Ohhhhhhh! Ahhhhh! I'm cumming!"

The impact of the orgasm caused her grip on the phone to loosen, sending it crashing to the floor. Afterward, she began riding me with more intensity and purpose. She didn't stop until I was gripping the sides of her ass cheeks, and busting off deep inside of her. Damn! There was something about knowing that her ex was listening to us that made the sex so much better. On top of that he just happened to call after a heated confrontation had occurred. That meant he got to hear the makeup sex! Lucky him!

Now that all issues between me and Sophia were rectified, we were able to put the issues from the past behind and focus solely on our future. That gave me more time and energy to focus on wrapping up these last few business affairs. I had just enough dope left to supply Gunner one last time. After that, the only thing I could do was keep hitting him off with coke.

Finding a dope connection wasn't a common thing that could be easily done overnight. A nigga had to have major plugs to get a strong line that supplied killer dope. Shake was the only nigga I ever knew to have had that sort of arrangement established, and had the connections to make it possible. Well, used to have. Word on the streets was

Chapter 48

Sophia considered herself exceptionally smart, beautiful, and deserving of the very best that life had to offer. Being with Boss satisfied that expectation and some. At this point of the game there was nothing or no one whom she would allow to jeopardize her relationship or livelihood with the man who was in position to provide the things needed, wanted, and desired. That included Victor.

Yeah, he may have done this and that for her throughout their relationship, but he couldn't do shit from his cell but give her headaches, false hope, and stress. All of which she would do fine without. She could admit that the way everything went down was pretty foul, and should've been done in a more respectful manner, but the damage had already been done. Personally, she was happy that everything was bought into the open and addressed as it was. It gave her all the reason and courage she needed to end things with Victor once and for all. Boss only put the icing on the cake when he decided to sex her while he was on the phone.

If only he could've heard the threats that Victor promised to do to the both of them if and when he ever came home. Sophia had never seen or heard him cry, but before the cell phone dropped from out her hand, she was 100 percent certain that she heard him crying. She not only thanked God that he was in jail, but she also prayed that he stay there forever. That way he would never be able to hurt her, or destroy her relationship with Boss.

As she sat there deeply pondering her thoughts, the fact that Boss had yet to act on, mention, or bring up anything else about marriage since she came back from L.A. was driving her furious. After all she sacrificed, and the drama she went through, she felt as though she had invested enough in the relationship to be beyond the boyfriend-and-girlfriend status, and above the fiancée title. She needed that expensive diamond ring and for that paperwork to be in order. Only then would she be his official wife and entitled to half of everything he owned. Just then she got an idea that was sure to bring back his memory, and speed up the process along the way.

It'd been nearly four days since the last time I heard anything from Gunner, and that was highly unusual. Especially at the rate he was running through the work. When I drove past there earlier today, I saw his truck parked on the block, and business seem to be booming as always. I never been the type to be calling a nigga and monitoring his moves. It was too much like babysitting. I was sure when he was ready to come holla at me everything would be correct on his end. But even if it wasn't, it wouldn't hurt my pockets in the least. But for his sake, my money and dope better have been straight! Or else, no Vaseline for him!

Since I was already in North Philly neighborhood, I decided to slide by Master Street and cop me an eighth and an ounce. Usually a nigga will be traumatized while revisiting the place close to where he was shot and nearly murdered at, but not Boss. It actually had the reverse effect on me. I looked at it as a place where I discovered how truly invincible I really was.

As I drove through the streets, getting high and collecting my thoughts together, I got a call from Sophia. Upon answering it, I instantly detected excitement in her voice.

"Baby! Stop whatever you're doing and come home now. Please hurry up. It's very important," she announced before hanging up.

I was already on my way back home before she even called. But there was no way I could go the entire thirty-minute drive back home wondering what was so important that had her that excited. Curiosity and anticipation was a hell of a combination, especially when driving. I been done drove the Maserati into the back of a truck or something. I called her back, hoping that she'd at least give me a clue or explanation to what had happened since I left this morning.

"Hurry up home, Boss. Trust me you don't want to miss this," she suggested quickly and hung up before I got the chance to say anything. Fuck it! I just had to be patient and find out what this little surprise of hers was all about when I got there. Was she pregnant again? Did her grandfather die and leave her a few million? I wondered what it could possibly be.

Pushing the pedal to the metal, I decided to hell with patience. I needed to know what was up now, and right now!

Ten minutes later I was walking through the front door of the crib. The first thing I encountered was the pleasant, seductive voice of Johnny Gill singing "My, My, My." The music was crystal clear as if he were there in person with a live band, thanks to the state-of-the-art surround-sound system that I had installed throughout every room of the house. On the first floor I noticed that there was a path of rose petals leading the way upstairs.

So far I was mighty impressed. Although I had a clue where and who the path of roses would lead me to, I was anxious to discover what exactly baby girl had in store for me. Following the path of roses to my bedroom door, there was a heavy presence of sweet perfume awaiting me. Pushing the door open, I came upon Sophia and a beautiful Asian woman lying in the bed side by side, and completely nude.

Both of them appeared to be fresh out of the hair salon. Their makeup was perfect. Their pedicures and manicures were flawless. With the exception of the hair on their heads, there was not so much as a string of it anywhere else on their bodies. The Asian woman looked as if she could've been Sophia's sister or a close relative. There in front of the bed I stood mesmerized. Dick growing faster than weed in Jamaica.

"Since you're gonna stand there and watch, at least let me and Chyna Doll give you something exciting to see," Sophia suggested before spreading her legs open and pushing Chyna Doll's head down in between them.

As she drove Sophia crazy with her lips and tongue game, she arched her back up, giving me a full view and easy access to her ass and pussy. It was so wet that it glistened like a glazed strawberry. It was calling for me to come inside. Begging! She wanted this big black dick inside of her more than she wanted anything.

After stripping asshole naked, I walked behind her and drove it inside of her slowly. Any other time I was usually about eight and a half to nine inches, but at that moment my length had somehow expanded to the size of a ruler. I pushed it as far inside of her as it would go, before thrusting out backward, only to drive it forward with more speed, force, and power. Each stroke left her ass jiggling and pussy popping.

The cycle of satisfaction was soon established as we all played a significant role in providing enough pleasure that all three of us could enjoy. That night, and all night, there was double dick sucking, sixty-nines, pussy on pussy, one riding my face while the other rode my dick, and to end it off, they both allowed me to hit it in the ass. What a night! In fact, it was the best night of my life.

Although I remembered going to sleep with both of them lying across my chest, I woke up to Sophia sitting on top of me holding my own gun to my head. This bitch done changed up on me that fast. Just last night everything was all good. What the fuck went wrong?

"You was really enjoying yourself last night wasn't you?" she asked in state of jealously. "Good! Because from here on out the only time you ever get to fuck another bitch with my dick is when I say so or bring one home. Now that we cleared that up, do you remember the other day when you gave me an alternative? Well I'm giving you one. Either you marry me today or murder me right now! Because I refuse to live another day not being your wife."

With that said she lowered the gun, put it in my hand, and guided it into her mouth. The trigger on the Glock was so sensitive that if so much as a hair touched it, it would shoot. Yet she stood there with the barrel in her mouth while my finger and her thumb was around the trigger. I loved when she showed me her gangster side. So much so that I decided to marry her that morning.

Before heading down City Hall to the justice of the peace, we stopped at Jewelers Row downtown. The most expensive diamond ring they had in stock was a ten-carat VVS-cut stone that was composed of all diamonds. No band, no gold, no platinum. It cost me close to eighty grand, but who was looking at the price tag? My motto was if a nigga was worried about the cost of something, that meant he couldn't afford it. Certainly, I was far from that category.

Shortly afterward, we were pronounced husband and wife. When I slid the ring on baby girl's finger, she started jumping up and down like she had hit the lottery. In a sense, I guessed she did. It was every woman's dream to one day be married to a boss nigga. When they got that diamond ring put on their finger it was their trophy that represented how worthy of a woman they were. The more expensive and bigger the diamond reflected the value of the woman she was. Beyoncé said it best when she told niggas, "If you love it, then you need to put a ring on it!" That's every woman around the world's theme hit for a reason.

Today was a happy day for me as well. I had acquired yet another status that gave me lifetime rights to a beautiful woman's heart, love, and pussy. She was my prize, territory, priority, queen, whore, slut, and ride or die bitch forever! Clearly she was the other half that completed me as a man. That alone was more than enough reason to give her my last name and all that came along with it.

Chapter 49

After a few days of marriage, I discovered that Sophia made a better wife than she did a girlfriend. She made me feel like a king, and as if the world revolved around me. There was no more complaints, arguments, or shortcomings. Our relationship was so perfect that it scared me. Michelle and Barak ain't have nothing on us! My success, accomplishments, and achievements was at an all-time high. From here, there was no looking back. That meant it was time to liquidate and gather all assets, and move forward with the life that I built for me, my wife, and our future.

Just as I was striving to put my life in its proper perspective, I get a call from my past. Agent Sheen had contacted me, stating that he needed to meet up with me immediately concerning a few matters that had recently come up. It had been so long since I lined something up for them that I honestly forgot that by agreement and signature, they literally owned my soul forever. How foolish of me to forget that the devil never sleeps.

As I headed over to the designated location, I couldn't help but to wonder what exactly it was that these *federales* wanted from me. Hadn't I already done enough for these cocksuckers? What the fuck was they expecting, for me to do this shit forever? I was sure they had thousands of niggas around the city working for them already. With the benefits and money they were paying out, I wouldn't be surprised if the whole city was employed by the feds. So why did they still need me? I was anxious to find out.

When I arrived over at the federal building, I pulled into the garage and circled around until I spotted their Dodge Charger. Parking the Maserati alongside of them, I jumped out and got in the back seat of their car. No sooner did I sit down in the seat than Murphy started making his usual smart-ass remarks.

"That's a mighty fine car you got there, Boss man. Must've cost you at least a hundred grand. I can't even afford to drive nothing like that." He spoke with a heart full of envy. "You see how good we treat you?"

The fake smile he displayed after the comment he made only further revealed his obvious jealousy. I wanted to tell that cocksucker so bad that I'd been driving luxury cars since I was a teenager. Far before I was even thinking about having any dealing with them. But instead I humbled myself and let him have the glory of thinking and believing that they were the sole source of my success. If only they knew!

"Yeah, Murphy. We make a perfect team. If y'all ain't have my back I would have been lost in the sauce." I shot some bullshit right back at him. "But anyway! I know y'all ain't brought me all the way out here to tell me how nice my car look or how good y'all take care of me. So what's really good?"

"You're absolutely right, Boss. Let's move along here, shall we?" Sheen interjected. "Hopefully we won't be too long, but we really need your help. Our supervisor has been up our asses about these two ongoing investigations that the agency has been trying to gather enough concrete evidence to bring forward some indictments on. However, we haven't been able to get close enough to the subjects to get the evidence that we need."

"I guess that's where I come in, huh?"

"Well, with your experience and street creditability we believe that these matters will be a walk in the park for you." He attempted to stroke my ego. "The first subject is Lou's Pawn Shop on Sixty-ninth and Market Street. As you know, the business deals firearms legally, but we have reason to believe that they're also being sold illegally. In the past two years we've linked dozens of murders and other violent crimes to the guns that the owner has either sold to people using fictitious names, or reported that they'd been stolen from his store. All we need you to do is be a little creative and go in there and get him to sell you a gun. We'll take it from there."

"You can take care of that can't you, Boss man?" asked Murphy with that stupid look on his face.

Ignoring him and his stupid question, I replied directly to Sheen. "What about this other situation you were talking about? You don't think y'all asking for a whole lot out of me? I need a break from all of this shit. I just got y'all the biggest bust of y'all career, now this? That ain't playing fair at all," I complained.

"Okay. How does this sound, if you take care of these two matters for us, starting with Lou's Pawn Shop, we'll lose your number for the next few years and won't find it unless we really, really need you. Plus, you'll still get your yearly salary," he negotiated reasonably. "So, do we have a deal?"

"I'm on top of it first thing tomorrow morning," I agreed before returning to my car and leaving.

The very next day, here I was walking into Lou's Pawn Shop prepared to do the devil's dirty work. Dressed in all-black Dickie suit, tan Timberland boots, and a red Phillies fitted hat, I had the look of a typical neighborhood street thug. For extra emphasis I had two teardrop tattoos painted under my right eye. While browsing around viewing the hundreds of guns inside the display case, I happened to glance up and see Lou himself walking over to me with an insurance-man smile on his face. I recognized him immediately, thanks to the dozen or so photographs the agents had showed me moments before.

"Is there anything that I can help you with, homeboy?" he inquired with close eye contact. Although he was a white boy, he had the swagger and hustle of a common nigga.

"As a matter of fact you can. I'm trying to get my hands on something reliable and big. Preferably a MAC-10 or something."

"A MAC-10? Now what would a legitimate citizen such as yourself want with a dangerous weapon like that?" He was clearly testing the waters.

"Listen here, my man. If a motherfucka hit me again it's over! I just got hit five times a couple weeks ago, and I can't stand another shot to the body," I voiced before lifting up my shirt and showing him the aftermath of five shots to the chest. "Like I said, I need that MAC ASAP. These niggas out here ain't playing no games, so neither should I."

"Damn, li'l homie! Those bullet holes look like the work of a .45. Now I know that you're not bullshitting. I just needed to be certain. You understand right?"

"I respect that. Nowadays you can never be too sure of anybody. But I'm official in every sense of the word. My street creditability speaks for itself," I announced convincingly. After looking into my eyes for a few odd seconds, he bit the bait.

"Say that I was able to get you this MAC-10; how much money will you be willing to pay for it?"

I answered his question by pulling out a large wad of money. Approximately $3,500. Setting it on the counter before him, I advised him that if it wasn't enough, then there was plenty more where that came from. In turn he picked the money up and walked off to the back of the store.

A few minutes later he returned carrying a folded-up brown paper bag, similar to the one from a grocery store. Before passing it to me, he gave me a strong piece of advice.

"You ain't never seen me; I ain't never seen you. You be cool like you be cool, and always be safe, young fellow."

I acknowledged his statement with a nod of the head. After I received the bag, I unfolded it open and glanced inside. There sat a chrome MAC-10 with two extended clips and a box of shells. Showing my approval and satisfaction with the merchandise. I placed my thumb up and flashed him a smile before exiting the store. Little did he know that was the signal that let the agents who were watching know that I had made the purchase.

Before I could even make it up the street to meet back up with the agents and turn in the evidence, a taskforce of *federales* from the ATF were already raiding the store. The bust resulted in Lou and his employees being arrested and charged with dozens of firearm violations. The feds also confiscated hundreds of guns, including illegal assault rifles, fully loaded machine guns, and even a few silencers.

Something about this particular job had me feeling like a piece of shit on the inside. Here I done fucked a man over who was trying to do me a favor by giving me something that was supposed to protect my life. On top of that there was really no advantages in it. This was some real rat bastard shit that I done did. This wasn't what I signed up for. I play this shit for position, to manipulate, and get ahead. I couldn't see for the life of me how I'd be able to accomplish any of that by setting up a crooked firearms dealer.

If the next job was anything like the first one, I refused to be involved. Fuck that! They would just have to find one of their rats to do it. I was far beyond this kind of shit. When the agents tried to give me the praise and glory for helping them bring down Lou, I turned my back on them and walked away.

On my way home I got a call from Sheen. He questioned why I reacted the way I did. I told him I ain't feel good and wasn't up for celebrating another man's downfall. He seemed a little surprised by my response and suggested that I go home and get some rest. Before hanging up he scheduled another meeting for the following day at the same place as the previous one.

Desperately needing to get my mind off of the day's events, I decided to take Sophia's Escalade over to the Luxury Autos and trade it in for an upgrade. I didn't want her driving around in nothing that another nigga bought her. Let alone something that was made by the Americans.

Shortly after arriving on the lot, I came across the perfect car. Having remembered how fascinated she was by the BMW 750, I knew that she would really be impressed by the 650 convertible.

Sophia kept a bunch of pairs of shoes and other junk inside her truck that I refused to put in the convertible, or wait while they got all of that shit together. Instead I instructed the workers to package everything up for me, and I'd come back and pick it all up in a few days.

Before I even got the chance to deliver her surprise to her, baby girl was blowing my phone up like somebody done died. I didn't answer the first few times, but I assumed that something was really wrong, and so I answered the call.

"Yes, woman!" I shouted into the receiver. "You're a persistent little creature, ain't you?"

"No, nigga, I'm your wife and you better answer that damn phone when I call. It could be an emergency." She voiced her point. "Now where is my truck at, Negro?"

"I don't know where that ugly ol' thing at. Why you asking me?"

"Because your Maserati is parked in the driveway and you're nowhere around. Now bring me my truck, boy. I ain't playing with you. Saks is having a sale and you better not make me miss it!"

"Girl, you shop so much you smell like a fucking mall! Sit your ass down for a few minutes. I'm on my way."

When I pulled in the driveway, there she was sitting on the steps looking like somebody done stole her joy. Hoping to cheer up her mood, I jumped out the car with my hands in the air and yelled, "Surprise!"

Her reaction wasn't the one that I was expecting, but after it registered that I had gotten her a new whip, she showed some excitement while roaming over to the car and checking the insides out. The glove compartment and the trunk were the first places she looked. When she didn't find what she was looking for she snapped.

"Amin, baby, where is all my personal belongings at? Please don't tell me you threw them away or left them behind, did you?" she asked nervously.

"No, baby girl, I ain't do nothing with your shit. I had the workers pack it up for me. I'll go pick it up tomorrow for you," I reassured her. "Goddamn, girl! Do you like the car or what?"

"Yes, I love it. But I just wanted to make sure you didn't lose my personal belongings. As a matter of fact you can just give me the address to where they're at and I'll go pick them up myself first thing tomorrow. You done went out of your way enough for me, baby. I thank you so much, and you know that I love you," she declared. "Now, what's the first thing y'all niggas love to have a woman do when y'all get a convertible? You know . . . Well, I've always wanted to drive while getting my pussy ate. So are you up for it or what?" she proposed before seductively rubbing her hand over her crotch.

"You're crazy as hell, baby girl! You know I will never tell you no, but we both know that one taste of that sweet ol' pussy of yours will lead to us fucking for the next couple of hours. Unfortunately we both have some business to attend to. So I tell you what, how about you go handle what you need to handle, I'll go take care of my business, and tonight when we both get home, we can play a game of 'Sophia Says' inside your convertible," I suggested in my sexiest voice.

"Ummm! I can't wait. You know you're the best thing that has ever happened to me and I love you more than anything in this world right?"

"If I didn't you wouldn't be Mrs. Hussan now would you?" I responded while approaching her. Pressing my lips against hers I kissed her slow and passionately before professing my feelings. "Baby girl, I feel the same way about you. I ain't never loved a bitch the way I love you!"

"Boy, let me get out of here before my panties get wetter than they already are," she admitted before giving me one last kiss and getting inside her new car. "Thanks again for the new car, baby, I really appreciate it. But please don't forget to give me the address to the place so I can go pick up my things."

As she pulled off, I couldn't help but to wonder why she was so pressed about getting that junk that was in the truck. She must have reminded me ten times about the shit, even though I told her I would take care of it the first time she mentioned it. If I ain't know any better I would've thought that she was holding some top-secret confidential shit for the president or somebody. She seemed more concerned with the junk than she was about her new car. The average bitch would've sucked my nuts to my dick for a drop-top BMW.

The business that I claimed I had to take care of was actually a date with Corrinne. I'd been neglecting her ever since I been married, so I had to go and make up for my shortcomings. Our date consisted of two hours at the movies, a hour at the restaurant, ten minutes of head on the highway, and an hour of sex back at her place.

Afterward, I was out the door, only to return home and do the exact same thing with Sophia outside in the driveway, inside her new car. Thank God for purple haze and syrup for the stamina, and keeping me rock hard through it all.

Chapter 50

The next morning, the after effects of fucking and getting high all night had me grumpy and sore all over. Still I climbed out of the bed and went to go meet up with the agents. Once I arrived at the location and joined them in the back seat of their car, Sheen took one look at me and offered me his coffee and two Motrins.

"One of those nights, huh, Boss man?" Murphy remarked annoyingly.

"Listen, Murphy. I got a headache and I ain't for your shit. Let's just get this over and done with so I can take care of whatever I need to take care of, and move on with the things I need to handle in my personal life," I advised.

"Sure thing, Boss. Won't you go ahead and take a look at these?" requested Agent Sheen before passing me a large tan envelope.

As I began removing the contents inside I discovered that it was all pictures. When I viewed the first one, who and what it revealed nearly made me shit on myself. There before me was a photograph displaying me and Gunner inside the Clock Bar the night I took him out and made the proposal for him to run the business for me. The others showed Gunner sitting in a club with a few Spanish dudes. Based on their jewelry and appearance, they had kingpins, bosses, and shot callers written all over them.

I was confused. I couldn't even begin to figure out what all of this meant. One thing I couldn't dispute was the fact that they were still watching me. That was the only way they could've got that picture of me and Gunner. The questions now were how long had they been watching, and what all had they seen? My worst fear was that all my double dealings and double crossings had finally caught up with me. I just knew I was fucked!

Sheen must've have seen the distressful look on my face, because he wasted no time explaining the intricate situation at hand. "No, we're not following you around, Boss. You've never given us a reason to look any further then we already have. However, one of our informants who knows some things about your past saw you hanging out a little while back with another gentleman and snapped a few pictures in their camera phone. Of course they don't know that you work for us, so in their mind they thought that they had captured the infamous Boss himself on film with one of his associates.

"I know that you're always working on trying to reel someone in for us, so I paid the picture no mind. That is until one of our fellow agents saw the pictures from the club and noticed the same black guy from your picture sitting among some very powerful heavy hitters. The black guy is the kingpin you were going to meet when I got you out of the traffic stop a few weeks back right?" he asked leadingly.

"Ah . . . yeah, that was him. We met up a few times and discussed some prices and plans for the near future, but I never acted on them because I personally didn't trust him," I lied through my teeth, hoping that my story didn't contradict any of their information.

"I told you, Murphy," Sheen exclaimed before giving his partner a playful punch on his arm. "Anyhow, the two men he is sitting with inside the club are brothers Fred and Frankie Sanchez. The two are suspected of being two of the top heroin suppliers out of New York. After we took down the guy over in New Jersey, the heroin market over here experienced a grave recession. The Sanchez brothers caught wind of it and came here to flood the streets of Philly. They somehow linked up with the black guy, who runs a very prominent dope block down North Philly. Shortly afterward, they've been shooting, killing, and taking over the entire neighborhood block by block."

"What can you tell us about this friend of yours?" Murphy cut to the chase.

"His name is Rahim Dickson, aka Gunner." I snitched him out without second thought. "Just tell me what y'all want me to do and I'll do it."

"Well, there's a good chance that if we can get this Gunner guy into custody he may start cooperating and then turn over on the Sanchez brothers. So if you could get this guy to buy some drugs off of us, or sell us some, we'll set up a trap and bring him down."

"Done! I just need a day or two and I'll deliver him to y'all doorstep." With my word of assurance to handle the situation promptly, the meeting was concluded.

As soon as I got back in my car. I fired up the half of dutch that I had left in my ashtray the other night. Technically, I was still on federal property, but honestly I really didn't give a fuck. My nerves needed to be calmed down immediately, and weed was the only therapy I had on hand.

I couldn't believe the audacity of that shiesty, no-good nigga Gunner. Here I done put the nigga in the best position of his life, and had him making more money than he ever dreamed of, yet he done cross me out the picture and start doing business with the competition? Just like the typical South Philly nigga: limited by loyalty, and will cross their mother for the right numbers. No wonder why I hadn't heard from the nigga in over a week. With a major dope connect online, I was no longer of any use to him. How bold, yet disrespectful. There was no question that since he had moved on to bigger and better things, it was only a matter of time before I became the victim, and another notch under his belt. Too bad his plans had been exposed before he could carry them out. That put me back in the advantage. But for him, that meant no Vaseline and a thousand deaths, which I awarded to every coward who ever crossed me.

Ha! Ha! Ha! Once again I laughed in the face of death and its never-ending plots to return me to my Maker covered in shame and humiliation. *You missed again motherfucka!*

Later that night when I reached Gunner, he fronted as if he was excited and surprised to hear from me.

"What's the situation, my nigga? What you don't fuck with me no more or something? It seems like I only hear from you when it's strictly business." He talked assuasive. "I know it's been a minute since the last time I got at you, but something came up that I needed to take care of. But it's all gravy now, and I'm ready to come holla at you ASAP. Where you at?"

"We definitely need to get together so that we can sit down and discuss a few things. Go ahead and meet me at the Red Lobster off the boulevard. I'll be there in about an hour," I instructed before hanging up.

Clearly the nigga thought that he was still rocking me to sleep. That's exactly what I wanted him to think. That way, when I burned his ass, he would never know what hit him until he was sitting up in the federal building with a hundred-count indictment. But before I fed him to the sharks I needed every dollar he had. It was me that made him who he was, so it wouldn't be shit to break him and return to the condition of the dirty little purse-snatching thief he was before I met him.

"Who put this together? Me, that's who! Who do I trust? Me, that's who!" I imitated Tony Montana.

When I arrived at the Red Lobster an hour later, I spotted Gunner already seated at the table with a bottle of champagne and a few glasses. He was in the middle of a heated telephone conversation, but rushed off when he saw me approaching the table. As I sat before him, I noticed the drastic change in his appearance. It was the first time I'd ever seen him wear jewelry and name-brand designer clothes. The arrogance in his posture and demeanor seem extremely familiar. I'd be damned! The nigga tried to duplicate my whole style? He thought he was really me?

I wanted to bust out laughing in the clown's face, but instead I smiled and extended my hand. "Look at my nigga! And they say money can't buy happiness. Well, what the fuck they call this?" I shot a slick remark at him. My comment had him smiling from ear to ear. The fact that I had just played him obviously went over his head. His stupid ass took it as a compliment.

After placing our orders, we poured a few glasses of champagne and got down to business.

"Ay, G, check this out. What I'm about to tell you can never leave this table. I'm telling you because you're my right-hand man, and I trust you with my life." I had his acknowledgment and full attention, so I continued. "This morning me and the connect had a meeting. At which time, I informed him that I had reached all my goals and success that I intended on achieving when I decided to become a hustler, and I was calling it quits. Of course he wasn't happy with my decision, but he respected it. The only problem is that since I was basically the only nigga he supplied, he's going to be left with a large quantity of heroin and cocaine. So we both came to a respectful agreement. I give him one million dollars tomorrow night and he gives me the remainder of the work he has left. He assured me that what he has left is worth much more than a million dollars, but since I've always been good business that he'll consider it my farewell present. This man's word is priceless and I have no reason to doubt him." My story was so believable, it could have passed a lie detector test. As I talked, I could see the greed and interest building inside Gunner's eyes. Now it was time to go for the kill.

"You know the money ain't really a problem; however, most of mines is tied up in some other things at the moment, so I could only come up with probably half of it. Since you're going to benefit the most off the score, it's only right that you put up the other half. That sound respectable right?"

"Yeah . . . yeah . . . yeah! That's about right. But how soon do you need this money?" he asked as if he didn't have that type of money at his disposal. It made me want to question what he was doing with all this money he was supposed to be getting. Wasn't he fucking with the Sanchez brothers?

"Honestly, I was hoping to make that move by tomorrow night. You know I don't like to keep business on hold too long," I reminded him. "Why? You can't get your hands on that type of money by then?"

The question caused him to bust out laughing. I must've missed the joke. "Come on, Boss, you're insulting me. You really think that after fucking with you for all these years I don't know how to stack money? I was asking because I was going to put the whole million up. I love you like a brother, and I know how bad you want to get out of this lifestyle. The more you fuck with it, the deeper it's going to pull you back into it," he schooled me as if he'd been doing this before me. It sounded sincere, but it was all fake. "I'll have the whole million for you by tomorrow afternoon. That way you ain't got to tie your money up in this shit. Take that with you wherever and whenever you plan on leaving. Just make the transaction, and if you need me I'm here."

Okay, big baller! I thought. All that brother shit he was talking was in an attempt to further rock me to sleep. Too bad it was going to be him who got put to bed before it was all said and done. What made my plot so perfect was that he had willingly walked himself into it. On top of that, he'd volunteered to give me a million dollars plus help me put him in a trap? And they say there's no such thing as an easy free lunch? Shitttttttt!

Before we parted ways, he requested that I follow him back to his new apartment in the Northeast so that he could retrieve the money he owed to me, and put up the last few kilos of dope that I'd just given to him. I couldn't believe that this stupid nigga showed me where his stash house was. Didn't he listen to the Ten Crack Commandments rule numbers three and five? I guessed not. But after tomorrow night he was sure going to wish he had. . . .

Chapter 51

That night I ain't get a wink of sleep until I had my plan rehearsed and perfected from A to Z. First thing the following morning I contacted Sheen and made up some bullshit story that Gunner was currently in search of a new supplier, and was willing to spend $500,000 for wholesale of some good product. I told Sheen that I'd already assured Gunner that I could arrange for it to happen sometime this afternoon. Since I was the Boss, it was only right that I ran the show and strategized the entire operation.

I told Sheen to get a black Charger and place thirty bricks in the trunk. Afterward, I instructed him to park the car in West Philly across the street from Overbrook High School. I assured him that once he covered that end, I would personally deliver Gunner to him as I promised. Once that was in motion, it was only a matter of getting the call from Gunner and securing that million dollars in my possession.

Around eleven o'clock I got the call that I was expecting. The big fellow invited me over to the Northeast spot to pick up the money in full, so he claimed. Strapped with two Glocks, I headed over there, hoping for the best but prepared for the worst.

Shortly after leaving the crib, Sophia began blowing my phone up with the back-to-back calls. When I cut one off, she'd just call the others. That had to be the most irritating yet frustrating thing a woman could do. It was time for me to check her once and for all about her abusive calling.

"What the fuck is wrong with you, girl?" I answered, snapping at her. "Did it occur to you that I can't talk right now?

"Don't you dare holler at me like that! Who the fuck do you think you're talking to?" she snapped back. "I'm your wife. When I call, you better put off all business to see what's the matter with me. I come before all that other bullshit out there! Now where is the dealership at so I can go pick up my things?"

"What! Are you serious? This what you blowing my phone up about? I'm definitely going to pick it up now. Don't even worry about it." I ended the call and cut all of the phones off. Because she was acting so suspicious about her belongings, I was curious to learn what exactly was so special about it that she didn't want me to see it, and was so desperate to have it. I was making it my business to go pick it up myself as soon as I left from over Gunner's spot.

Upon my arrival at his pad, I must say that I was mighty impressed with how he had the place decked out. With the luxurious furniture and up-to-date electronics, the spot was plush and comfortable enough to suit a king.

"Make yourself at home, my nigga. I'm still trying to get an accurate count on this money. It shouldn't take no longer than twenty, maybe thirty minutes tops," he advised before walking to the back bedroom; and no sooner did the sound of money-counting machines come from the room in which he went.

BBBDDDRRRBBBBDDDDRRRBBBBDDRRR! I must admit that I was slightly envious that this nigga had what sounded like two money-counting machines, yet I had none. He really was trying to pass me up, huh? Unfortunately his career in the game was ready to end like two broken knees in the NBA. I smiled to myself before kicking my feet up and waiting for him to count my money up for me. I really couldn't wait to come back later on and see exactly how much money he was holding in that room. I was coming for every dollar of it, including those money-counting machines!

When he finally came from out of the room, he dragged a large garbage bag out with him. Placing it in front of me, he exhaled deeply and reminded me of one of the covenants he promised to uphold a little while back.

"Remember when I told you that as long as I'm the number two nigga, I will kill to keep you number one? I just want to let you know that I meant that shit, my nigga," he claimed with reassurance.

Fortunately, I knew better than to believe one word of it.

"That's the whole million right there. Don't forget that if you need me to come along with you, or for anything else, just hit me up, and I'm there."

"Since everything going to you anyway, I may need you to come pick it up. But I'll let you know," I mentioned before getting up and preparing to leave. He agreed without argument. While walking out of the door with the trash bag full of money over my shoulder, he said something that made my skin crawl.

"After we take care of business, Boss, I got a hell of a surprise for you. Think of it as a going-away present. It's going to fuck your head up."

Going-away present, huh? I bet he did have one in store for me. Too bad mine was coming first. I only wished that I could see the look on his face when he went to pick up the car full of work and got swarmed by a flock of federal agents. The nerve of him to think that I would let nigga beneath me outsmart me.

After leaving Gunner's apartment I drove straight over to Luxury Autos to collect Sophia's belongings. To my surprise one of the employees approached me and informed me that about twenty minutes ago a woman identifying herself as my wife had come in and picked the property up. In response, I gripped him up by his collar and unleashed a verbal attack that was sure to have him question his purpose in life and his status of employment. "Didn't I specifically tell your bitch ass that I would come back and pick up those possessions? I remember telling you to put everything together nice and neat, and I'll back for them. Didn't I?" I yelled in his face. Sprinkles of spit flew from my mouth as I spoke, landing all over his face. "Did you ever stop to think that the bitch was lying? What if those belongings were valuable? Could your broke ass replace them by working at the car lot? Fuck no, you couldn't! That's why niggas like you will always be workers, because you need another motherfucka to think for you! Stupid-ass nigga!"

After throwing him to the ground, I got back inside my car and peeled off. Sophia's actions had me burning up. Her snake-like ways were starting to seem more like an unbreakable habit. The fact that she had gone to great lengths to make sure that I never saw whatever it was she had confirmed to me that she was indeed hiding something.

I would deal with her later, but for now I had to focus my attention on these major moves still to come. First things first, I had to go drop this money off over at Corrinne's house. In fact, since I still had a little more time to kill I might drop something more than that! Like my pants to my ankles, and Corrrine down to her knees.

Because of the task I had ahead of me, I was a little nervous, stressed out, and worried. But after giving and receiving the business from Corrinne, I felt as if I could take on the world! Damn! Never again would I underestimate the power of a good dick suck and some wet pussy!

Once we recuperated from the mean fucking that just took place, I instructed Corrinne to go get us some latex gloves. Afterward, I had her help me remove five hundred grand from the bag and put it up in the stash. The other half was going straight to the agents. With Gunner's fingerprints all over the bag and money, it would be impossible for him to deny that it wasn't his. Before leaving to go meet up with Sheen I kissed Corrinne on her forehead and promised to return once I finished taking care of business. She knew that I was up to no good, but didn't try to slow up my progress. Her only words were, "Be careful!"

After meeting up with the agents and turning in the money, I assured them that Gunner would be coming to pick up the drugs within the hour. Before parting ways, they informed me that the keys would be on the top of the driver-side back tire. Now it was only a matter of Gunner taking the bait.

Upon arriving at his apartment complex, I searched the parking lot for his truck. There was no sign of it out front, nor in the back. Glancing up at his apartment window I noticed that there were no lights on, and appeared as if no one was home. That was all I needed to see.

Once I contacted him on the phone, I listened in closely to his background before speaking. I heard music, and somebody talking to some females. It sounded as if he was outside somewhere. "What's the situation, big fellow? Where you at?" I inquired curiously.

"Never mind that, my nigga. The question is, where do I need to be?" He answered a question with a question. Although he tried to conceal it, I could clearly hear the hunger and excitement in his voice. "Roll that other dutch up, li'l nigga, and stop fucking with those bitches!" I overheard him tell somebody before I could respond.

"Yo! Is you listening, nigga?" I checked to make sure I had his full attention.

"Yeah, I hear you, homie. Tell me what I need to do."

"As soon as you get there hit me back so I can let you know what to do from there."

"Give me ten minutes, and I'll be there," he reported before disconnecting.

During that ten-minute window, it took me sixty seconds of it to break into his apartment. Once inside I went straight into the bedroom. That's where I discovered so much dope and money lying around I figured it had to be fake. I'm talking about bags and bags of money, and bricks stacked on top of bricks. If I were to add up all of the money and work I seen throughout the course of my life it wouldn't equal up to half of what was in that room. I couldn't understand how this nigga was sitting so heavy.

Right then and there, I realized that there was a huge difference between a boss and a king. And it lay right there before me. Grabbing as many bags as I could, I began carrying them out to the trunk of my Maserati and stuffing them inside. On my second trip back up, Gunner called me back.

"I'm here. What's next?

"All right listen, look across the street and see if you can see an all-black Dodge Charger."

"Yeah, I see it. It's parked on the corner right?"

"That's the one," I confirmed. "Now check this out. On top of the back driver-side tire . . ." Just then a tinted-out Delta 88 pulled into the parking lot with a system so loud I could barely hear myself talk. Once he drove to the other side of the parking lot, he finally killed the music. "Hello! G, is you still here?"

"Yeah, I'm here . . . Finish telling me what you was saying."

"Right. As I was saying, on that back tire there's a key to the car. Go ahead and get the work up out of the trunk and hit me back once you got it in your possession." I quickly hung up before he could reply. That was the last time I probably would ever hear from him again. Nas said it best when he said, "A thug changes, and love changes, and best friends become strangers!"

Ten minutes after packing up the trunk and floors of the back seat, I finally decided to leave. But I damn sure planned on returning as soon as I dropped the money off. I was actually considering coming back with a U-Haul truck.

Just as I was turning out of the parking lot onto the street, I thought that I was seeing shit when I spotted Gunner's truck turning inside. There was no doubt that it was him because once our cars passed he stared me straight in the eyes. Suddenly his truck flipped a quick U-turn and initiated a dangerous chase.

How the fuck did he manage to slip out of the trap? I wondered as I push the pedal to the floor. In response, the Maserati shot from zero to sixty in the matter of a few seconds. The truck was no match for the Maserati's speed, but because we were on the small inner-city streets, he was able to keep up. When the fed line started ringing, I answered the call demanding answers. "What the fuck went wrong? How did he get away? I thought that you had this under control, Agent Sheen!" I barked on him.

"Yeah! Well if you would've sent us the right man, we would've had things under control. Instead of giving us Gunner, we got some young Spanish kid. He played us, Boss," he confessed. "Wait a minute! How did you find out that he got away?"

"How do I know? Because this crazy motherfucka is chasing me around the city trying to kill me as we speak. That's how I know!"

"Okay . . . stay calm. Remember we're on the same side," he claimed nervously. "What we're going to do now is tap into your phone's GPS system. That way we'll be able to pinpoint your location and catch up with you as fast as we can. Help is on the way. Try to keep a safe distance, but stay close enough to him to keep him chasing you. Don't let him get away!"

Besides the police, I'd never run from a nigga in my life. But since my hand called for it, I did what I needed to do. This nigga had me driving down one-way streets, head-on with oncoming traffic, and even sidewalks while desperately trying to keep him at bay, but away from crashing into my car. In the mix of the chaos two of my phones were ringing nonstop. Believing that I had picked up the "fed line" I answered in a state of panic. "Yo, Sheen, where the fuck is y'all at? I can't keep this shit up too much longer."

"Boss! What the fuck is up with you? You working for those people now, my nigga?" Gunner asked in disbelief. At that point it became apparent that I had answered the wrong phone. "You set me up, then tried to rob me? After all we been through, my nigga?" If I was hearing right, it sounded like he was crying. I done heard enough of the fake shit; it was time to put him on blast.

"Oh please! The jig's up, nigga, stop all of the fronting shit. I already know you cut me out and start fucking with the Sanchez brothers, G. You started this shit. I just finished it up," I explained to him. "And no, I don't work for those people, they work for me. In fact, they got your old job. But instead of killing niggas, they take them to a far worse place. Jail!"

"Hold the fuck up, dog! You think that I would've really crossed you for those fucking spics? Don't be stupid, nigga. If I wanted to cross you, I would've did that shit a long time ago. I gave you one hundred percent loyalty," he professed. "The only reason I fucked with those spics is because they were two stupid motherfuckas with so much money and dope they ain't know what to do with it. Robbery was my first and only intention for getting involved with them.

"Yesterday when you told me you needed that money, I went out and robbed and killed both of those niggas. You were in my apartment. You seen it with your own eyes. Didn't you?" he shouted with sheer anger. "That was my surprise for you. I was going to give you half of it and send you off to live happily ever after . . . but that was before I knew you was a rat. So take this instead."

In that instant a dozen of shots were fired upon the Maserati, sending glass flying, covering the car in bullet holes. I stayed low and kept my foot on the gas. This continued for several more blocks before I heard multiple sirens approaching from behind. When I glanced into the rearview mirror, there were several unmarked vehicles closing in on us from behind. About time! Now that the *federales* were involved Gunner didn't want to play anymore. He seemed to have forgotten all about trying to kill me, and was now just trying to get away. That was a major no-no. I couldn't afford to have a vicious killer like him on the loose. Especially after what I done did to him. In hopes of getting around me, he swerved his truck recklessly into the outside lane and drove at top speeds, desperately trying to escape. To stop his escape, I swerved over in front of him and hit the brakes. Subsequently his truck crashed into the back of the Maserati before flipping over on its side.

By the time I looked up again the agents had the truck surrounded and were pulling Gunner through the window. After they got him in handcuffs, they unleashed the traditional pre-arrest ass whooping. Based on the fact that the nigga just tried to kill me moments before, I felt as though I had rights to partake in demonstration just as much as they did.

Hoping to get a piece of the action, I jumped up out my bullet-riddled vehicle and walked over to where the thrashing was taking place. The agents who were present looked at me as if I was intruding into a personal affair. To my surprise, it was Murphy who ordered the agents to turn their heads for a few seconds, before giving me the green light to handle my business.

Refusing to waste one second of time, I stood over the washed-up hit-man-turned-drug-dealer, and open-hand smacked him in his mouth. As my hand swung through the air, I reversed it and landed a backhand smack to the other side of his mouth. The second hit was so hard it caused a teardrop to fall from the corner of his eye.

"Now look at you, nigga! You thought that you had all the brains, didn't you?" Smack! "You wasn't content in your own skin, so you tried to be me. You lame-ass nigga! You couldn't fill my shoes if you cut my feet off!" Smack! "Now get this bitch-ass nigga away from me before I kill him!" I ordered the agents as a HNIC (head nigga in charge) should.

Once they pulled him up on his feet, only then did he find the courage to speak.

"This ain't over you rat-ass nigga! I be home one day, and when I do I'm going to hunt you down and kill everything you love. I don't care how much time they give me, I'm going to stay healthy and nice and fit just to be in enough shape to rape your kids and your grandchildren before I kill them."

His threats were so sincere that I got goose bumps as a result of them.

"Everything with your blood in it is a possible rat that must be killed. Genocide, motherfucka!" He laughed wickedly before attempting to spit in my face.

Fortunately I had a fast dip game, or else he would've gotten me good. Instead, a few sprinkles landed on my arms and hands. That's when I lost it for real, for real. Charging him like a raging bull, I wrapped my hands around his neck and tried to choke him to death. It took the strength of all the agents to pull me up off him.

The aftereffects of the dramatic evening left my Maserati with severe rear-side damage, including broken windows and over a dozen bullet holes. Despite the damage my shit still drove, and I was extremely grateful for that. Had it not been operable the *federales* would have had it towed along with Gunner's truck. In that event they would've surely gotten a look at the contents inside my trunk and underneath the seat. How in the fuck would I explain that?

While the agents were clearing the scene, I noticed Agents Sheen and Murphy conversing back and forth with the local police. Whatever information was revealed to them, they gathered their fellow agents up and shared the news. Fortunately, I was close enough to them to hear the entire briefing.

"Gentlemen, there's been some shocking new developments with our investigation. About twenty minutes ago police responded to a report of a burglary. When they arrived, they noticed some damage to the locks and proceeded inside the apartment. After entering the bedroom they stumbled upon what they're calling a mother lode of drugs and money," he reported with satisfaction. "Neighbors reported that two Spanish men had moved in a few weeks ago. When they pointed out that a silver Mercedes parked out back belonged to the men, the police went to get a closer look. They discovered the remains of the Sanchez brothers. It appears that they had been dead for a day or two. I'm willing to bet my paycheck that we already have the one responsible for the burglary and killing in custody."

"That explains why Boss told us that the Gunner guy couldn't be trusted. Too bad the Sanchez brothers weren't listening," Murphy joked, causing laughter to erupt among the agents.

After personally hearing the agents basically confirm Gunner's story, I felt sick to my stomach. The big fellow was telling the truth all along. These *federales* had me so caught up that I had crossed every last person close to me. That was it for me. After tonight I swore to have no more dealings with the federal government.

Before leaving the scene, Sheen approached me and advised me that I needed to get out of the city as soon as possible. Having been exposed by Gunner, he was concerned that the word would be all over the streets within the next few days. He offered me immediate witness protection, which I kindly refused. I told him that all I wanted from them was to be free of all dealings.

His exact words in response were, "Go home and get some rest, Boss. You're talking crazy again. I'll have a nice check for you in the next day or so, and I'll be sure to throw in a little something extra to compensate you for the damage to your car. Meanwhile, stay low and think of a nice place you want to move to . . . Anywhere! I'll be in touch."

The nerve of this cocksucker! What the fuck did he mean go home and get some rest? Did he not hear what the fuck I was saying? I guessed I had to show him better than I ccould tell him.

Driving through the city in a crashed-up Maserati covered in bullet holes was one thing, but to be doing so with bags full of stolen blood money was another. I couldn't care less. Until I actually moved away, I still owned the key to the city and considered myself above the law.

When I walked through the door of Corrinne's apartment carrying several trash bags, she said something that put an instant smile on my face.

"Nigga, if that's what I think it is, we going to have to find a new stash spot because not so much as another penny will fit in there," she complained in search of a solution. "You need to be moving me to a safer location with me holding all of this shit up in here. If the police or the stick up boys run up in this bitch we going to have a problem."

"Never did I ever think I'd live to see that day where my biggest worries is needing another stash spot to put some money at." I voiced arrogantly. "Just put it up somewhere, girl. I'll have everything out of here in the next day or so. Now pick a bag."

"What do you mean pick a bag, boy?"

"This ain't nothing complicated, just pick one of these bags," I suggested while motioning to the biggest one. She eventually got the point, and chose wisely. "That's yours, mommy. You should be able to find you another spot, get a little business, and still have something nice left over."

To show her appreciation, the bitch actually ate my ass, among many other freaky things. After beating the pussy up for about a half hour straight, I called it a night and headed to the crib. Before I left Corrinne's little nasty ass tried to kiss me in the mouth. I ducked away from her lips faster than I did earlier that night when Gunner tried to spit in my face. Afterward, I hauled ass up out of there.

Before going in the house, I stopped at Pete's Pizza and ordered a cheese steak to go. When I walked into the crib, Sophia was sitting on the couch watching *Hip Hop Wives*. She had the nerve to ask me how my day was. I looked at her like she was crazy before stepping over her and sitting on the other end of the couch. Far away from her as possible.

Knowing how much she loved Philly cheese steaks, I ain't offer her so much as a bite. Instead, I ate with my mouth open, hoping to get under her skin. She did a good job ignoring me until Mandy from *Hip Hop Wives* bent over with some skin-tight pants on, showing the entire world how thick and banging her body was. I reacted how a married man wasn't supposed to.

"Damn, girl! I know that pussy is good! Umm umm umm!"

Snatching up the remote, she turned the TV off, then gave me the meanest look she could muster. "You being real disrespectful and rude. It's irking me, and you need to stop it right now!"

"Disrespectful? Rude? Irking?" I gave her the evil eye from head to toe. "Yeah, well that's how I treat sneaky-ass bitches who got shit to hide. Now cut my motherfuckin' TV back on before you make me miss them showing Mandy again."

"What!" she snapped before throwing the remote at the plasma. It was thrown so hard that it spider-webbed the entire screen. "Fuck you and that TV, nigga! I know exactly why you're acting like this. You're mad because I went and picked up my belongings, aren't you? That means you don't trust me right? Therefore, we don't need to be married. Take your fucking ring, Amin," she growled before removing the jewel from her finger and throwing it at me.

"Before I leave your stupid ass let me show you what I was hiding from you," she claimed before storming out of the house. From the living room I could hear her going through her trunk, and mumbling profanity underneath her breath. When she came back inside she carried several different bottles that appeared to be vitamins and medication. Before explaining what they were she threw them on top of my lap.

"Look, you self-centered asshole! In case you forgot, I just had a miscarriage by your stupid ass! When the baby died in my tubes, it caused damage to my uterus.

Therefore, I have to take these big annoying-ass pills three times a day in order to restore my uterus, and give you a healthy baby. But you don't deserve one, nor does he deserve to have you as a father," she insinuated before the tears began to fall.

"Some things a woman just has to keep to herself . . . especially something so personal . . . What man is going to want a woman . . . who can't make children? I can't do this no more. Good-bye, Amin."

With those last words, she turned and walked out the door. The way she broke it down to me, I could clearly see where she was coming from, and why she went out of her way to keep me from finding out. But I would've still loved her the same regardless. I couldn't believe that I had hurt this girl yet again. If I lost her because of my suspicions, I would never forgive myself.

Quickly racing outside, I caught her just as she was getting into her car. Approaching her from behind, I wrapped my arms tightly around her waist, and held on for dear life.

"I can't make it without you, Sop. If you leave me I'm nothing. All the money, this house, and these cars don't mean shit if I don't have you to share it with." I spoke straight from the heart. "I'm sorry, baby. I been under a lot of stress lately, but I assure you once we move away from all of this, there's going to be a lot of changes . . . A new start and new beginning. Just give me a chance to prove it to you, baby. All right?"

After a few seconds of odd silence, she finally responded. "I understand why you have the mindset you have. It's those streets, Amin. I know that when you're out there, you can't trust no one and you must always be on alert. But not with me! I'm your wife and I love you. Regardless of anything, I'm going to always have your

back. You have to trust and believe that. If not, it's not
going to work," she expressed wholeheartedly.

"So do you forgive me, baby?"

"I forgive you, Amin . . . But please . . . hurry up and get
us away from here," she pleaded.

Chapter 52

According to Shake's concept, to defeat your enemy you must first know them and understand them. This is where his closet associate, Mark Mitchell, came into play. With a past resume consisting of a police officer, federal agent, and private investigator, he retired from those professions years ago to work full time for Shake. Based on the experience and skills that he acquired from his prior occupations, he was able to keep close tabs on all of Shake's affiliates and associates, especially those whose integrity was in question or simply couldn't be trusted.

From Shake's perspective, having an ex-*federale* on his payroll was just as good as having an active one. The same practice and job description were applied, consisting of investigations, surveillance, wire taps, and documented profiles. Being as Mark had a brother who was a chairman over at the federal bureau, he was able to fish information out of him about anything big that was expected to take place in Philadelphia. This included indictments, busts, or major investigations. He'd usually learn about it a few days in advance, unless it was a spur-of-the-moment situation.

Ever since the doorman called upstairs and advised Shake that the visitor whom he was expecting had arrived, and was on his way up, he'd been anxiously pacing the floor waiting for the elevator to drop Mark off. It'd been nearly two hours since he got the call from Mark informing him that he'd discovered the source of all his problems.

He assured Shake that what he had to reveal was going to literally hurt his heart. The moment of truth had arrived the second Mark stepped off the elevator. The expression displayed in his face revealed absolute disappointment and pure anger.

"It's your kid, Shake. He's a fucking rat!" he declared undoubtedly. "Wait a minute, I take that back. He's a paid informant. From what I heard, he's the best they've had in a good long time. It's been confirmed that he's the one who made the call on Spanish Eddie. I've been watching him for a few days now, and I know where his stash house is. Just give me the word and I'll go take care of him once and for all."

"No! I'll take care of this matter personally. The last time I sent you to deal with this . . . this . . ."—he struggled to find the correct attribute—"this rat bastard, he was just a mouse. Now he's full grown. Had you dealt with this accordingly we wouldn't be having these motherfucking problems. Would we?" His anger had gotten the best of him. Before he literally killed Mark with his bare hands he walked over to the stocked bar and poured himself a drink.

Once he calmed himself down, he was able to decide the approach that would eliminate this problem once and for all. "Tomorrow I want you to take me over to the location where I can catch up with this little piece of shit. I got something real special in mind for him," he suggested with a devious smile.

Chapter 53

After last night's drama and all the other bullshit that'd been occurring in between, I took it as a sign that I needed to hurry up and pull away from this lifestyle before it all came tumbling down. My run was over, and unlike the majority of hustlers in this game, I'd come out on top. I had the woman of my dreams, the money of my visions, and everything in between. I came in this thing a winner and that's how I was leaving.

The very next morning me and baby girl was packing up the Gucci luggage like we were going on a world tour. Thanks to the money-counting machines, we were able to add the currency up much faster than we would've doing it manually. As much money that was lying around here, it would've probably taken us all night to get an accurate count. Once Sophia got the hang of it, I instructed her to wrap rubber bands around every $10,000 stack, before placing it neatly inside the luggage. I left her in charge while preparing to go to Philly to pick up the rest of my money, and try to off the remaining work for a wholesale price. I had just the nigga in mind who would take it off my hands for the low.

My little nigga Ceese was an up-and-coming hustler from out of West Philly. Shorty was indeed a paper chaser by all means. Whenever I would do a robbery that netted a lot of drugs, I'd sell them to him half price on the strength that he was my little homie. After contacting him and informing him that I had close to twenty pieces going for ten a whop, he hopped right on top of it. We arranged to meet up later that evening to make the transaction.

With that established I was convinced that the last few pieces of the puzzle had fallen into place, depending on this final move going smoothly. With me and Ceese's history, I had no reason to think otherwise. Now my only dilemma was to somehow talk Sophia into letting me use her Beemer. Of course she wanted some act right first. Afterward, she gave me her car keys, adjusted my collar, and checked the chamber on the Glock to make sure it had one in the head, before tucking it on my hip. Funny how the stroke game always brought out the best in baby girl.

Chapter 54

Having been released from federal custody earlier in the week on "conditional bail," Victor had no intention of sticking to the stipulations of his release until he rightfully claimed what was his. In order to accomplish that, he had to first go to Philadelphia. Knowing Sophia like he knew the back of his hand, he knew exactly where to find her.

After the first day of staking out the King of Prussia Mall, he observed Sophia going into the Neiman Marcus department store. An hour later he observed her come walking out with several shopping bags. At a close distance he watched her exit the mall and walk over to a cherry red drop-top BMW. After putting her bags into the trunk of the car, she went back inside the mall.

At that point Victor retrieved his rental car and parked close by her BMW. As he patiently waited for her to conclude her daily shopping expedition, he reflected on the relationship he once shared with the woman he loved more than anything in this world. The good times and bad times. He refused to accept the fact that she'd left him for dead to be with another nigga. To add insult to injury, she'd allowed him to sex her while he was on the phone. The thought alone brought tears to his eyes and murder to his intentions.

Once Sophia finally came out of the mall, she got in her car, put her glasses on, and pulled off as if she didn't have a care in the world. Boy was she wrong! Had she been on point she would've noticed that she was being followed by the man to whom she'd given broken promises, a broken heart, and her ass to kiss. Unfortunately she didn't, and consequently led him right to her front door.

Chapter 55

On my way down to the city I must've called Corrinne over a dozen times, only to keep getting her voicemail. I figured she was probably out blowing money on red bottoms and Gucci bags. It was definitely a newly innovated habit she'd picked up heavy ever since I came into the picture. I was hoping that she was in bed or the shower. Either way it was easy access for one final fucking before I left town.

Using my own set of keys to enter her apartment, I stepped inside and encountered a terrifying scene. There Corrinne lay face down on the floor in a puddle of blood. The apartment was ransacked, leading me to believe that it was the work of some ruthless robbers. Damn! It was too late in the game for this bullshit. *Damn, Corrinne . . .* These niggas done killed my little mommy.

As I stood there trying to figure out what to do next, my thoughts were interrupted when I felt cold steel being pressed against my temple. In the same motion my Glock was removed from my hip. Glancing out of the corner of my eyes I was shocked to see that it was my father holding a gun to my head. *What the fuck lead him to do all of this?* I wondered.

"A rat, Amin? A fucking rat? After all I taught you? What happen to the morals, the codes, and rules of the streets?"

"Shake . . . what is you talking about? I ain't no ra . . ." Before I could finish telling the lie, I was stopped in midsentence after Shake smacked me over the top of the head with his gun, sending me crashing to the floor in agonizing pain.

"You think I'm stupid, motherfucka? Don't nothing in this city transpire without my knowledge, nigga! What, you forgot?" he shouted over me. "Then you had the nerve to set up my connect and make it look like it was me?" he disclosed before kicking me on my side. "Here I was playing checkers, and your little rat ass was playing chess, using me as a fucking pawn. You're going to pay the ultimate price for that shit."

"Wait a minute, Shake, let me explain." I prepared to plead for my life. "I swear on everything, I never mentioned your name, pops. They caught me red-handed . . . I slipped up big time. But I can fix this. I got enough money back at the crib for us to move away and be comfortable forever. Even if I got to go to your connect's peoples and tell them that it was all my work and you ain't have nothing to do with it, I will."

"Listen to yourself! I can't believe this shit is coming out of your mouth. You can't fix this, you stupid motherfucka! The fact that my name has been associated behind some police shit has destroyed my reputation forever. You've disgraced me, nigga, and there's only one way to fix this," he declared before delivering another kick to my side.

"This is how we're going to do this. You're going to take me to where you live and give up all your fucking money and everything else you're holding of value. Afterward, I'm going to turn you over to those spics and see if you can talk your ass up out of that." He stated his intentions for me. "Now we're going to walk up out of here nice and easy. We're going to get inside the black Cadillac parked on the corner, and you're going to give us the directions to where the money at. One false move and I'll level you where you stand," he affirmed with great conviction.

The whole entire time I was thinking, *how the fuck am I going to get up out of this one?*

Chapter 56

Once Victor got himself a hold of a pistol he sought out to get retribution for all the disrespect, disappointment, and heartache he suffered by the actions of Sophia and her new boyfriend. The neighborhood in which the couple lived was too out in the open for him to be just parked up or posted on the street without drawing attention, so he watched their house from a vacant property directly across the street from where they lived.

When he observed a light-skinned nigga walk out and get into the BMW, he assumed that it was Sophia's new man. It surprised him that he didn't lock the door to the house, nor did he show the slightest bit of caution before getting inside the car and pulling off. No looking around. No circling the block. It puzzled him how he survived this long with his careless ways.

Despite his shortcomings with security measures, Victor couldn't help but to notice the immaculate swagger the nigga possessed. Everything from his house, cars, and appearance represented wealth to the fullest. With a woman like Sophia to go along with it, that equaled up to success. The thought alone left him fuming with hatred, envy, and profound jealousy. In his mind the nigga had stolen his entire life, and the time had come to get it back.

Emerging from the cut, he proceeded to the front door of the house and turned the knob. As expected it was unlocked. Upon stepping inside the first thing that caught his attention was the sound of running water, and Sophia's terrible singing. As bad as her voice sounded it was literally music to his ears. Especially since it pinpointed her exact location.

When he came upon the bathroom, he discovered that the door was wide open. From where he stood he could see Sophia's silhouette facing the opposite direction. It appeared as if she was washing her hair. The sight alone had awakened the raging beast from within. At that point his urges and desires became irresistible.

Quickly removing his clothes he slid the shower door open and stepped in behind her, slightly startling her as he entered.

"Baby! I thought you would be long gone by now. What, you came back to do a remix?" she asked excitingly before reaching backward and feeling Victor's hardness. "Well damn, boy! You definitely need another shot of this pussy. Ain't no way you leaving out of this house until I get that swelling down. Just give me a few seconds to rinse this shampoo out of my hair, and I got you, boo."

Clearly she was under the impression that she was speaking to her new boyfriend. To hear her speak those familiar words in reference to another man with happiness and ease put yet another knife into his heart. In retaliation he grabbed her by her hair and pushed her head into the wall before ramming inside her rectum with great force.

"Agggggwww! Ouccch! What the hell are you doing? Take it out please . . . you're hurting me," she pleaded with excruciating pain and discomfort.

Her pleading fell on deaf ears. Instead of complying, he went harder and deeper inside her. The only thing she had on her side was the fact that it was the first time he'd been with a woman since he been home. Therefore it only lasted a few seconds.

Almost immediately after satisfying his desires, he unleashed his grip and proceeded to wash himself off. No sooner did he let go did Sophia turn around with tears in her eyes, and an open hand preparing to smack him in his face. The sight of who stood behind her left her frozen with fear. It was as if she was staring at a ghost.

"Yeah, bitch! Daddy's home!" he celebrated. "Didn't I tell you I was coming home? Now hurry up and clean your ass and get your trifling ass up out the shower. You have a lot of explaining to do," he indicated before stepping out.

Chapter 57

"Listen, Mark, I'm on my way out now. I'm bringing some company down with me. We're going to take us a little ride over to the bank. If he tries anything slick be prepared to flee a murder scene," suggested Shake over his cell phone before leading me out of the apartment.

He made sure that he spoke loud enough for me to hear him. As mad as he was, I didn't doubt for a second that he wouldn't kill me without hesitation. As we walked out of the building, Shake stayed close to my side. With his suit jacket folded over his right hand, he concealed his weapon that was clearly aimed in my direction. The closer we got to the black Cadillac the more familiar it looked. Flashbacks of the day that I was nearly assassinated came rushing back to mind. I was 100 percent certain that it was the same car. At that moment it became apparent to me that it was Shake who tried to have me killed. The bastard was probably responsible for my other troubles as well. Let me find out this was rat-on-rat crime!

Before we could reach the Cadillac I noticed another familiar car; this one was pulling beside us. If I wasn't mistaken it was the same blue BMW X5 that was in the driveway of Shake's connection. Suddenly it was as if everything started transpiring in slow motion. First the back window to the BMW rolled down. Next, the long barrel of an assault rifle came out. Shake saw the hit coming and tried to run to the Cadillac while shooting recklessly over his shoulder. The Cadillac could have stayed long enough for him to jump inside, but didn't. The driver pulled off, leaving him for dead, as if he was in cahoots with the hit. Two shots from the assault rifle sounded off as result Shake's body was violently thrown to the ground.

That's when I took off running toward the apartment. Along the way several more gunshots erupted. Unsure if they were meant for me. I glanced backward to see. The shooter wasn't worried about me in the least; he was more concerned with making sure Shake was dead and received a closed-casket funeral. He stood over the man I once loved and considered a father and fired the fully loaded machine into his head and body. I continued running and didn't stop until I was back inside of Corrinne's apartment.

They say a cat has nine lives; I wondered how many a rat had because, once again, I somehow managed to escape death at least twice in the last fifteen minutes. However, something about this time was different from the others. Maybe it was because it had reached someone I truly loved behind my doings. It affected me worse than anything I'd ever been through in my life. When I turned Corrinne's body over I discovered that her throat had been slit from ear to ear. She had the most peaceful look on her face and appeared to have been sleeping. After kissing her on her forehead, I closed her eyelids and done something that I hadn't done in a long time. I cried . . . I cried, and I prayed for her soul and mine, begging the good Lord to deliver me from evil. Doing so actually made me feel at peace with myself and God.

While the police were still outside collecting any and all possible evidence from the murder scene, I was gathering up all the work and the rest of the money. It was nearly two and a half hours before the police had the scene cleared away, but they were still heavily patrolling the area. I decided to take my chances and hope no police nor stick up boys spotted me walking in the middle of Southwest Philly at ten o'clock at night with two large duffle bags. If I ain't make it back to the car I was sure to become a victim or an inmate.

The police would ask no questions. They would run straight down on me and violate every constitutional right I had just to get a look inside of these bags. While the robbers, on the other hand, would take one look at me and be able to smell money as a wolf can sense fear and weakness among an individual sheep in an entire flock. Sadly, in the event of a robbery, I couldn't even defend myself. Shake had died with my gun on his waist.

Fortunately I made it to the car without incident. All I had to do now was meet Ceese at the Sunoco gas station on Lancaster Avenue, make the transaction, and go home and pick up my wife. From there it was straight to the highway and getting as far away from Philly as possible.

Chapter 58

"Victor. Please forgive me, baby. I'm sorry," Sophia cried and pleaded. "I did everything you asked me to do. I swear to God I did! I told them about a shooting he did, and how he kept guns, and money, and drugs around the house, in his cars, and on him at all times. They could never get him. He was smarter, and always ten steps ahead of them," she explained from her perspective.

"They kept telling me that they would help you get out of jail in exchange for the information I gave to them. I waited and waited, and nothing happened. When I called them and asked them what was going on they told me that they would get back to me. After that they ignored my calls and I never heard from them again." She spoke the honest-to-God truth.

"You have no patience. I told you I was coming home, and to go ahead and do you until I got out, but your stupid ass went ahead and allowed your feelings to get caught up with the help. Bitch, you turned your back on me after all I done for your funky ass!" he snapped while choking her out.

Instead of trying to break free or defend herself, she took her punishment like a true solider. After he smacked her up, kicked her, and had his way with her, only then did she attempt to talk some sense into him.

"Okay now, Victor, that's enough. You done proved your point. I deserved that. Now are you ready to listen to what my plans were?" she implied with the hopes of getting back on his good side.

"What plans? You done already proved to me that you can't stick to no plan. I don't even know if I trust you anymore."

"Victor! Stop letting your emotions do the talking for you. Think like the old Victor would think. Do you know how much money is in this house, and how much he coming back home with?" At that point she'd clearly put the pants back on and given him the dress to wear, for she was in full control. "It's enough to keep us straight for the rest of our lives. Trust me, Victor, the only reason that I played along with this game was to get him for everything he had, just so I could get you a team of the best lawyers in the country. If you honestly thought that I would've left you for dead, then it's obvious you don't know the woman whom you claim to love so much." She professed her loyalty. "Now we don't have time to be sitting around bullshitting. He'll be back any minute now."

Chapter 59

While on my way to the gas station I got an unexpected call from Ceese. He informed me that he wasn't going to able to meet up with me tonight due to a family emergency. As if I was on his time and terms, he attempted to reschedule the arrangement for the first thing the following morning. Neither agreeing or disagreeing I responded, "Whatever!" before hanging up on him. Here I was trying to look for the li'l nigga, and he done left me hanging.

His claims of sudden family emergency was sounding real suspect. It sounded to me like he ain't have all the money right, and needed some time to get it together. All he had to do was keep it one hundred with me and I would've definitely worked something out with him. To get these motherfuckas off my hands I was willing to take basically anything as long as I got something for them. I'd fuck around and just bury those bitches somewhere in case of a rainy day.

In desperate need of escaping from the reality I was living, I took a quick shortcut down North Philly and stocked up on enough syrup and cush to get me through for the next couple of weeks. During the long ride home, I smoked and drank my pain away until my feelings were numb.

Once I arrived back home, I took the money out of the trunk, but left the drugs behind. Reason being, I wanted to get an official count on my paper. As far as the drugs, I vowed to never bring any back inside my home under no circumstance. Therefore, until I decided what to do with them, they was staying right where they were at.

As I approached the front door, I noticed the entire house was dark, with the exception of the bedroom. After all the counted and packing Sophia did I figured she was upstairs either resting or relaxing. Having been gone all day without calling and checking in, the poor girl was probably worried half to death up there. As soon as I stepped inside the house, baby girl was calling out for me.

"Amin! Come up here so I can cuss your black ass out for leaving me in this house all day without checking in," she complained. Although she was nagging, I could tell that she was really just happy that I'd made it back home still in one piece. But only if she knew the half of it!

"Oh shut your mouth, girl! You know daddy gots to get the cash," I boasted proudly. "You better have more than a cuss out up there waiting on me. And why in the hell is it so dark down here? What are you, a vamp—" My words were cut short by way of a metal object crashing into the back of my head. The last thing I seen before blacking out was the shadow of a man hovering over me, holding what looked like a baseball bat.

I didn't know how long I was out for, but when I finally came to, I had the worst headache imaginable. I'd taken two hard hits over the head within a few hours apart of each other. I wouldn't be surprised if I had brain damage. When I tried to move there was resistance. Only then did I realize that I was tied up to one of the chairs in the living room. What in the fuck was going on?

As if my thoughts were telepathically intercepted, here this high yellow-ass nigga come walking down the steps. Not only was he carrying the luggage that held my money, but the lame was also wearing my clothes and jewelry. I was thinking, *Where they do that at?*

"Well, well, well . . . We finally meet face to face. It's Boss, right?" He sought clarification.

"Fuck all the questions and talking. You got what you came for now get the fuck out of my house!" I demanded fearlessly. "And if you so much as put a finger on my wife, I will have you hunted down and murdered in the worst way possible. Now where is she?"

My statements and warning seemed to be a joke to him. He laughed in my face as if it was the funniest thing he ever heard. Once he gathered his composure, he filled me in on what all the laughter was about.

"Your wife, huh?" he questioned doubtfully. "Well, I put much more than a finger on her, so I guess I got it coming, huh? Let me share something with you, my friend. As a matter of fact I'm going to allow her to tell you. Sophia! Come down here and tell this husband of yours what's really good," he shouted up the steps.

My heart nearly bust out of my chest when Sophia came down the steps, carrying the remaining luggage. I noticed several passion marks on her neck and her hair was in disarray. On top of that she had that after-sex walk as if her pussy was sore and hurting. Something was indeed wrong with this picture. The more I tried to figure it out, the harder it was to understand. At the same time, I don't think I really wanted to figure it out or understand.

"Sophia, what the fuck is this nigga talking about? And who is this motherfucka?"

"Stop playing, Amin. You know exactly who this is. This is the sole owner of my mind, body, and heart," she admitted coldly. "When a woman loves a man like I do Victor, there is no limit to what she won't do to keep him protected, rich, and free. All that you were supposed to be was a replacement to get my baby home. The feds told me that if I gave them you, then they would give me my Victor back. I mean, you all right and everything, but you definitely ain't my Victor," she disclosed with a twisted smile on her face.

"Look at it on the bright side, boo. You got to hit this a couple of times, taste, and enjoy it. We left you some money upstairs to help you get back on your feet, but I must warn you that the feds is on your every move. Now that I got my baby back I really don't give a damn what happens to you, but the least I could do is put you up on game."

"You dirty, rotten bitch! It was you all along. I should've known better! Filthy whore!" I spat with sheer hatred and anger. "If it's the last thing I do in this lifetime, Sophia, I'm going to get you, bitch!"

"All right now! That's enough of all this soap opera shit. Baby, say good-bye to your little friend and go start the car up. I'll be right behind you," Victor cut in.

The bitch had a nerve to walk up on me and try to kiss me on my mouth. I turned my head as if her lips were poisonous. After removing her car keys from my pocket, she flashed me a smile and winked her eye at me. In response I spit in her face. That earned me a hard backhand smack to the mouth. Afterward, she turned her back and walked out of my life forever. Along with her she took my heart and the only reason for wanting to live. She was the last and only person I had left in this world and just like the others I loved, she'd turned her back and left me to fend for myself.

"It's always the ones closest to us ain't it? I know how you feel, but you should have listened to those old timers when they warned you that life was a bitch. Had you done so you would have never trusted one," he called himself schooling me before aiming his pistol at my head.

Before he squeezed the trigger Sophia walked back inside of the house. I just knew she was coming back for me. I could feel it. She didn't really mean any of those things that she said. All of that was a front to rock Victor to sleep. I knew deep in my heart that there was no way she would betray me for this lame-ass nigga. Or so I believed.

Boy was I wrong. The only reason her funky ass came back inside was to retrieve the duffle bags that I'd brought back from Corrinne's spot. The last and final time she walked good-bye. From there everything started to move in slow motion, just as it did in the earlier incident.

Suddenly a gunman burst inside the house, firing what appeared to be a MAC-11. Victor caught it first. His brains were ejected from the side of his skull, painting the ceiling and walls with blood and brain matter. I knew my turn was coming long before he aimed the MAC-11 at me and began shooting.

The bullets ripped into my body with such force that it threw me off of the chair and sent me crashing to the floor on my back. The burning sensation made my insides feel as if they were being consumed by flames. It wasn't long before I could taste the blood that was overflowing in my lungs. It was only a matter of time before it choked me to death. There was no way I was walking away from this one. Had the syrup not slowed down my heart rate and kept me calm, I would have gone into shock instantly.

I really didn't want to fight it, but when I looked out of the front door in the driveway, what I witnessed made me want to hold on a little longer. There I saw the gunman set the black Cadillac on fire before getting into the passenger side of the BMW. Afterward, the car took off in the direction of the highway. If I had anything to do with it, they weren't going to get far.

Triple-crossing bitch! Remembering my last promise I made to her, I intended to back every word of it up. Luckily for me, my iPhone was voice automated, so it didn't matter that I was tied up. All I had to do was call out a command.

"Call Bob . . . speaker phone . . ." Within seconds I heard his phone ringing. He answered on the third ring. Clearing my throat as best I could, I quickly stated my business.

"Bob, it's Boss . . . Listen up! There's a red convertible BMW 650 coming toward you . . . It's a female driving and a male passenger. They're super loaded with coke, guns, and money," I informed him. With each second that passed I felt myself getting weaker. That meant that death was getting impatient with me.

"Did you say a red BMW 650 convertible? Male passenger?"

"That . . . that's right, Bob."

"That's funny. They're a few cars in front of me. Hold on a second while I call in a road block," he mentioned before announcing some police codes into his scanner. At that point I blacked out and fell into a state of deep darkness. Somehow, I could still hear Bob talking. The last thing I heard him say before completely letting go was, "You have the right to remain silent. Anything you say can and will be used against you in a court of law. . . ."

Notes